ENCHANTING THE PRINCE
The Enchanted Castle Archives
Book 3

Michelle L. Levigne

www.YeOldeDragonBooks.com

Ye Olde Dragon Books
6909 Ackley Rd.
Parma, OH 44129

www.YeOldeDragonBooks.com

2OldeDragons@gmail.com

Published in the United States of America
March 15, 2025

Cover Art © Copyright 2025 Ye Olde Dragon Books

Chapter One

Zair shook his hair out of his face, looked into the oncoming storm and considered praying for a lightning strike. All he needed was one hard, hot lash to knock him out of the top of this old elm tree by the crossroads. He would be burned and dead before he hit the ground.

He wanted to run away, but where could he go? What could he do? He needed food and clothes and shelter. A half-grown boy with no parents or master to account for him would be snatched up and enslaved or tossed into prison. Or worse, when they found out who he was, his father would be penalized. There were laws that, as far as Zair was concerned, bound everyone, took away all their choices. The only road to freedom was to learn a trade. The moment he approached a craft master to become an apprentice, they would send him home. They wouldn't take him without his father's permission, and Korgan, headman of the village of Nayester, wouldn't allow it. His sons had three choices: soldiering, working the family fields, or scholarly jobs, full of writing and tallying and giving orders to others.

Zair couldn't lie and give a false name. The blessing band on his wrist, given at his christening, would answer the craft master's question truthfully and give his name and his father's name. The band was to help find him, if he was kidnapped, held for ransom or to extort favors from his father. Zair could almost laugh at the thought of being kidnapped by bandits. He would beg them to sell him into slavery over the border. Better than going home, to be bullied by his two older brothers and lied about by his two younger brothers.

All his troubles started a year ago, when some crazy old seer tottered through Nayester, focused his blind, milky eyes on Zair and proclaimed him the last blood of the true king. Then his life seemed to slide into the midden. Now his older brothers used him for target practice and gave him all their messiest, most disgusting chores. His stepmother, Traysa locked him out of the house every chance she got. The only good change was that she wouldn't let his younger brothers even mention his name, much less tell lies about him. As far as she was concerned, Zair didn't exist.

Korgan used to look at him with sad eyes, and sometimes whisper, "Zenobia," Zair's mother's name. But at least he had forced his sons to be fair to each other. Now, he always turned away as if his third son didn't exist. Zair wondered if some wandering enchanter had been in a bad mood and threw a curse on him just for the fun of it.

The oncoming storm slashed him in the face with icy rain. The tree whipped back and forth in the increasingly furious wind. It certainly felt vicious enough to carry him the eighty miles north and west to the border where the kingdom of Dorwain met the kingdom of Ambrecht. He wished the wind would pick him up and flung him across the border, completely out of Dorwain.

In school today, he had recited the entire chapter on the heroic exploits of King Enzariad, as ordered. He hadn't mispronounced a single word or forgot a single name of all the nobles of the king's inner circle or his many enemies or the powerful enchanters who served him. Doric, the schoolmaster, had praised him. Then he compared Zair's performance to his older brothers, Karl and Kayn. The twins were four years older than him, but only two learning levels ahead of him. They couldn't punish Doric for embarrassing them, so Zair was their target.

Blue light flashed and crackled on his wrist. Zair yelped, wincing, momentarily blinded. His blessing band tightened and grew hot.

It pulled him downward.

He wrapped his arms tighter around the tree limb. An invisible force yanked his arm backward, then twisted him around, so he spun off the limb altogether. He flailed and grappled at the branches and leaves that slapped him and tore at his face and clothes as he plummeted downward. The blue light around his wrist glowed brighter.

Branches seemed to swing upward to meet him, slowing his fall, bouncing him to the right, then the left, then downward again. To land face-down in ankle-deep mud. His left wrist slammed hard onto the massive, upthrust root of the elm with a loud crack that sent black sparkles through his head. Zair arched upward, shrieking the pain, and landed on his back, cracking the back of his head against another root.

He lay crooked, gasping, staring blindly into the rain that slipped through the leaves. Gray haze spun inward from the edges of his vision.

"Found him!" a man called, his voice half-muffled by the drumming of the rain and the hissing as it slid through the leaves.

"Idiot," another man growled, as the gray haze filled Zair's eyes and spun him downward. "Not going to earn us any of that gold if you half-kill him before the princess can even get a good look at him." A big, rough hand rested on the side of Zair's head. "Don't you worry, lad. We'll get you fixed up."

Zair tried to speak, but all he could manage was a bubbling in the back of his throat.

"No, no, lay still. Surprised us, you did, coming down out of the sky like that. Guess the seeking spell was stronger than we thought. You'll be just fine. Where's that mending charm?" he growled, the kindness of his voice turning hard and sharp for a moment. "Here we go, lad. You just go to sleep, and when you wake up, we're going to take you on a grand adventure. Yes, we will."

~~~~~

Zair woke several times. Enough to figure out he was riding in a dark, enclosed wagon. The two men were close by in the darkness, talking in hushed voices about rewards, and what they would do if "the boy" was too tall or too short or too muscular or his hair was wrong. He felt too dizzy-sick to do more than wonder if he was "the boy," and why he was too tall or why his hair was wrong. Then he fell back down into the spinning haze.

Once he woke up when one voice cursed and warmth wrapped around his wrist. He got his eyes to focus enough to see silver sparks dance along the thin braid of metal. His father was seeking him through the band. Now he knew he was in trouble. An ache started up in the back of his head where he felt somehow both splintered and mushy.

A man pounced on Zair out of the darkness and wrapped a long strand of glowing red beads around his wrist. Smoke swirled up, smelling rotten-sour, and the blessing band glowed brighter. So bright, Zair had to close his aching eyes. The beads scorched his wrist. A loud pop-crack shot through his head, making it throb.

"Huh. Nasty bit of magic there," the other man said. "Don't you worry none, lad. Broke the magic. You don't have to worry about them finding you and dragging you back to some boring old life in that muddy old village." He stroked sweaty hair off Zair's forehead, his touch surprisingly soothing. "You just do what you're told and win the nice, cushiony job waiting for you, and we'll all be a lot better off. Us and the whole benighted kingdom."

"How much better off will we be?" the first man muttered. "Gotta get the illusion settled on him before that rotter sees him. One look and he'll know the rightful blood is ready to leap into his chair. Who they gonna hang up to feed the crows first? Us!"

"That's assuming Joben reads the ancient chronicles," his partner snapped back. "Gotta know what Zared looked like to know what his heirs look like."

Zair flinched at mention of the long-dead hero king's name. His head spun, but his body felt like it stayed still, and even got heavier, sinking down through the floor of the wagon. Joben? Were they talking about the king of Dorwain?

"He doesn't need to. That's what he's got all those counselors and magicians for, to read and think of things for him. All we have to be worried about is Nostrados seeing the boy, getting suspicious, and seeing through the disguise."
~~~~~

"That's assuming he's chosen. If he doesn't die on the way."

Zair tried to speak, but the pressure of questions made his head ache so much he couldn't seem to open his mouth. The blessing band tightened around his wrist, to the point of sharp pressure. Then he heard the *snap-sproing* of tight-bound metal breaking apart. A bluish spark flashed behind his closed eyelids, then he fell into darkness that sucked him down and spun him around.

Even the realization that his blessing band was gone, meaning his father could never track him with magic and bring him home, wasn't enough to wake Zair.

~~~~

He partially woke to glimpses of torchlight and shuddered at the angry groaning of wood and metal. A deep breath brought him the scents of dirty wool and straw. Moving his head just a little brought the greasy-scratchy feel to his cheek and chin. He was wrapped in the wool. The *clop-suck* of hooves on muddy gravel changed to a sharp clatter and splashing as the horses crossed pavement. Then they stopped.

Rough, strong hands picked him up and handed him to others, who slung him over a wide shoulder like a sack of grain. Booted feet thudded on wood, and the jerking and rising sensation made him think he was being carried up a tall flight of stairs. Zair tried to go limp. He didn't like that shoulder digging into his belly.

Big hands gripped him and swung him up and then dropped him down on a thick mattress. He bounced twice. He gasped, and someone chuckled. A different voice than the ones that had accompanied him in the darkness. More hands yanked the cloth off him, making him roll over onto his stomach. He lay still, wondering if he could convince his kidnappers he was still asleep.

"Fine," a rough-voiced woman said. "Lay there all day for all I care. But I'll be taking away your breakfast as soon as it gets cold."

Breakfast? His stomach twisted and grumbled as if the word had been a trumpet call for a battle charge. He hadn't eaten anything since the noon meal before going to the schoolhouse. The churning in his stomach changed from nausea to hunger.

Another woman chuckled. "Heard that. How old are you, boy?"

"Thirteen." Zair peeled his eyes open, fighting sticky grit that tried to glue them closed. He wedged his arms under his chest and pushed up. His head no longer ached and punished him. He lay in a bed big enough to hold him and his four brothers. Taking a deep breath and bracing himself, he rolled onto his back and sat up.

The two women stood at the end of the bed, arms crossed, studying him the way he saw merchants study the bales of wool in the market at sheering time. If he had been kidnapped, had they bought him? For what?
~~~~

Why?

"Come eat," the second woman said. She looked about twenty years younger than the first woman. Both wore livery, matching deep yellow blouses, black skirts, black vests, their hair caught up under severe black caps. Zair's head ached from trying to remember which noble house had those colors.

All he could think was that some nobleman had decided that Headman Korgan had done something to offend him, and he had taken his middle son to punish him in some way.

"Food?" the second woman said and gestured across the room.

Zair scooted to the end of the bed and carefully slid off. He stumbled when he realized that not only were his boots gone, but someone had put him in new clothes while he slept. He wore black and yellow also. How was he going to escape and find his way home, when he looked like a servant boy? Nobody would believe him if he asked for help. They would just assume he was a runaway. They would probably whip him before they sent him back to his new master. Without his blessing band, he couldn't prove who he was. Not that he really wanted to be sent home to be squeezed between the bullies older than him, and the whining, lying brats younger than him.

He stumbled two more times as he crossed the floor to the table set up against the shuttered window. His legs threatened to fold from the fear spilling through him.

What was worse, he wondered as he settled into the chair. To go home and get beaten by his father for worrying him, and by his stepmother for losing his clothes, and trying to escape the beating the twins had decreed for him? Discovering that no one cared he had been gone half a day? Or trying to escape and failing, and earning brutal punishment?

Then the aromas of the hot food on the table filled his nostrils and he really looked at his breakfast. No one ate like this at home. Was all this really for him?

Maybe he didn't want to go home?

Stupid question. Who wants to go back there, anyway?

In all the legends and stories of heroes, who had ever just run straight home after being yanked away from everything they knew? The soldiers and warriors and lost princes and heroes had always stayed to fight and solve riddles and mysteries, then returned home in triumph with treasures.

This was the best breakfast he had ever eaten. A full bowl of porridge, rich with butter and honey and cream. A far cry from the scrapings of the pot, if his brothers left anything at all. Two boiled eggs. Two sausages as long as his hand. Hot cider. Stewed fruit.

He would have enjoyed it more if the two women hadn't watched him the entire time with narrowed eyes.

When he finished his breakfast, the taller, younger one surprised him by nodding and letting out a "hmph" that sounded surprised. "This one has fairly decent table manners. And he knows what a napkin is. You're not playing a nasty trick on us now, are you, young'un?"

"Ma'am?" Zair sat up straight and clenched the napkin he had just wiped his mouth with.

"He doesn't belch, either, and he knows to say ma'am to his betters," the other woman said. One corner of her mouth quirked up like she might smile. Maybe in a few days.

"Who taught you good table manners? That saves us some time. We don't have to start by turning a piglet into a boy, and then a boy into a gentleman so he can serve as a Shadow in all the fussy places the prince doesn't want to go."

"My stepmother whacks us with a ladle if we eat with our hands and belch and don't say please and thankee," he said after a moment of thought.

That earned a slightly larger hint of a smile.

"Can you read? Can you write? Cipher? Read maps?"

They asked more questions, back and forth between them. They sounded like the new schoolmaster when he showed up two years ago and sorted the village students into groups by learning attained, rather than age. Zair had gotten thumps and slaps for two weeks after that by his two older brothers, because he performed a level higher than either of them in reading and ciphering. By the end of the questioning, he learned the older woman was named Gresibel, and the younger was Tonia.

He answered their questions, then had to prove he could indeed do all the things he said he could. At that point, the two men they called Gabe and Ward came in with two large leather trunks full of books, and emptied them on the second, longer table in the room. The four took turns picking up books, opening them, and slapping them down on the table in front of Zair to read aloud to them, and sometimes even explain what he had read, to prove he understood it. Four times, he had to dig through a stack of maps and find the kingdoms or cities he had read about. Several times, they tugged the books out of his hands and gave him a slate and chalk and threw numbers at him, to prove he could add and subtract and multiply and divide.

"If you think about it, all this book-learning is just a waste of time. When will they ever ask the prince to recite his lessons?" Gabe said, his voice pitched soft so Zair suspected he wasn't supposed to hear that.

By this time, the two men had spoken enough, Zair recognized them as the voices that spoke to him in the darkness of the wagon. Why had they kidnapped him? Why had they chosen him, wanted him badly enough to use a seeking spell?

Magic wasn't easily come by in Dorwain. The schoolmaster didn't talk much about magic, except to say that those with magic in their blood had been driven out of the kingdom several generations ago, and those who practiced magic now earned it, created it, with powders and potions and charms. Zair had overheard the schoolmaster grumbling with older men of the village, about how all the surrounding kingdoms could rise up and swat Dorwain flat without any effort, because they still had blood-born enchanters and great libraries of books of magic, and the Enchanters Court still listened to them. Dorwain had forfeited the right to be heard or helped. Zair wanted to know why, but he knew better than to ask questions about magic, or let those grumblers know he had been listening to them.

"And what happens if someone suspects a Shadow is wearing his clothes and sitting in his chair? They will ask questions just like this, if they have their doubts. The better the Shadow can mimic him, the fewer the doubts, and the safer both of them will be," Gresibel said, just as quietly.

Zair bit his lip to keep from asking what a Shadow was, and concentrated on the mathematics problem Tonia had given him. They confused him, calling him a Shadow, and a moment later indicating he wasn't a Shadow just yet. Was this something he had to prove he was smart enough to do?

If he could eat more meals like his breakfast, and sleep in a huge bed all by himself and didn't have to go home and face his brothers' scowls and slaps and pinches and whining and lies ... maybe he was starting to like this adventure Gabe had promised him.

After a few more questions, the four left him alone with the pile of books. Gresibel even chuckled and patted his shoulder and said he could read any of them he wanted.

The midday meal was just as wonderful as breakfast. Hot, watered spiced ale and fresh bread, warm, with melted, sharp cheese on top, and three thick slabs of juicy beef. Zair thought about the meal that would have been waiting for him at home, to be snatched between chores and washing up to go to lessons. Usually, bread with cheese or spicy vegetable paste, a mug of water, maybe an apple.

The storm returned, midway through the afternoon. Gresibel and Tonia seemed pleased. They talked with Gabe and Ward, but he couldn't make out the words through the rumbling of thunder and soft hammering of the rain. He focused on the book he had chosen, a collection of stories about the Enchanters' Court and how through the ages enchanters and sorcerers and wizards and seers had intervened for the protection or healing or rescue of kingdoms all over the world. Zair wondered why a book like this hadn't been destroyed, like magic books had supposedly been destroyed during one of the purges. The kings of Dorwain couldn't deny that the Enchanters Court existed, or that people were born with magic in their blood in other kingdoms, but they could and did work to keep the common people from knowing the truth. As he read, the boy wondered if nobles had different libraries than what the village schoolmasters had. Maybe nobles were born with magic in their blood, and they had the means to hide all signs of that magic, to keep from being either enslaved or murdered by the magicians and wizards. That was one bit of lore about magic that everyone knew, despite efforts to keep the knowledge of it under the control of the throne. Wizards and magicians earned their magic and created it through powders and potions and spells. Enchanters and sorcerers were born with magic in their blood. Any child could become an enchanter, just by being born one, but wizardry required years of training and practice, and the permission of the throne.

Zair had just finished a story about how an army of bunnies led by a werewolf princess defeated a team of cruel wizards. Gabe stomped into the room, picked up one of the leather trunks, and dropped it on the floor by his chair.

"Time to pack up and go, lad. This storm is the perfect cover for our journey." His smile had just a flicker of nastiness to it. He reached over and snatched the book from Zair's hands. He dropped it into the trunk before the boy could even open his mouth to protest.

A chill that had nothing to do with the wet weather outside crawled through Zair. In silence, he got to work putting the books in the trunk. Ward joined them with the other trunk. He tossed Zair a cloak far too big for him, when the chore was finished. The boy hesitated.

"So you don't make the mistake of thinking you can run away," Ward added, and caught hold of Zair's arm. A brief flash of fire wrapped around his wrist, wrenching a gasp of pain from him. It solidified into a red band of what looked like glass, as thick as his thumb.

"Don't make the mistake of thinking that we trust you, just because you've been quiet and obedient," Gabe said. "Shows you're just a little too smart, waiting your chance to break free. Well, lad, there's no breaking free. You're in the king's service now."

"If he lives long enough to become a Shadow, and for however long that lasts," Ward grumbled under his breath, and stomped out of the room.

Chapter Two

"The king? King Joben?" Zair rubbed his wrist. The band still felt warm, and it itched.

"Who else?" Gabe bent and heaved one leather trunk up onto his shoulder and stomped out of the room.

Zair turned, watching him go, and saw Gresibel and Tonia in the doorway. They were both wearing cloaks and carrying covered baskets.

"Time to go, boy," Tonia said. She smiled softly and stepped back, gesturing for him to go out through the door.

"Where are we going?" Zair picked up the ends of his too-long cloak and followed Gabe. What else could he do? He had the awful feeling this band wouldn't tingle or pinch if he disobeyed, like his blessing band had done when his father summoned him. It would burn.

"Does it matter?" Gresibel said.

Zair opened his mouth to shout, "Yes, it matters," but stopped with the breath still in his chest. It didn't matter, because he wouldn't be able to escape. Knowing where he was wouldn't do him any good until he could break free.

"What's a Shadow?" he asked instead. "Why do I need to become one?"

"All in good time. Now, hush," Tonia said. She gripped his shoulder as they reached the end of the dark hall, and they headed down a long flight of stairs.

Gresibel tugged up his hood, pulling it far forward so it covered his face and all he could see was a bit of the floor. Sounds came to him, partially muffled by the cloak. Men's voices. The thud of tankards on tables. Feet slapping and thumping on wooden and stone floors. The scrape of wood on wood, likely chair legs across the floor. Then the smells of ale and woodsmoke and roasting meat. Zair guessed they were in a tavern. Then Tonia guided him to turn right. A door opened, letting in wet, cold gusts of air and the sound of the rain grew louder. Metal wheels rattled and scraped on cobblestones and shod hooves thudded and clattered, and a coach rolled up in front of them. Zair pulled back his hood enough to see it, enormous, glistening black and dripping wet, with leather flaps tied down across the windows. Gresibel yanked on a lever, opening the door and dropping folding steps down to the ground. The bottom of the coach was higher than his waist. The wheels stood taller than him, taller than Gresibel. Zair climbed up, through the door. Two small oil lamps hung from the ceiling of the coach, showing two wide, cushioned benches facing each other, several covered baskets in the middle of the floor, and shelves near the ceiling on either side, filled with blankets and pillows.

Zair chose a seat and sat down. He thought about pulling off the cloak, but Gresibel had been a little too concerned about making sure he was covered. He didn't want to know what she could do if he made trouble. Not after the ache of the band Ward had put on him. The two women climbed up after him. They settled on the bench facing him. Gabe shoved first one, then the other leather trunk into the coach after them, partially blocking the door, then slammed it. The coach tipped slightly and bounced, and Zair guessed the man had climbed up to the driver's seat. Gabe called out, reins slapped and snapped, horses snorted, and the coach jolted slightly as it moved forward.

Flickers of light slid by along the narrow gaps between the leather covers on the windows. The echoes of the coach wheels clattering and splashing, and shod hooves ringing on stone proved they rode through a town. A large enough, prosperous enough town to have paved streets on more than just the main thoroughfares. Zair leaned back on the bench and gripped the edges of the cushion and listened. They weren't in his home village. Nayester had only two paved streets, and none of the three taverns sat on them. They also didn't have second floors where people could rent large rooms and hide a kidnapped boy. He had no way of knowing how far they had taken him from home, how long he had been unconscious, before he woke in the tavern.

Zair relaxed, despite himself, when the echoes changed, revealing they had driven out into the open. No more buildings close enough to bounce back the sounds of horses trotting through the rainy night.

"What does the king want me to do?" he asked, when both women visibly relaxed. They had worn that watchful, alert, wide-eyed expression that his stepmother always wore when officials came to their village and stayed in their house. He wondered if they feared someone would criticize and mock and make demands beyond the rules of hospitality.

"You get to dress and act like a prince," Tonia said. "Won't that be fun?"

"What's wrong?" Gresibel said, when Zair flinched at the word, *prince*. Her eyes narrowed. Did she think he had done something wrong?

Zair shook his head. How could he explain that his father hated that word? The surest way to get Korgan icily furious was for the twins to tease Zair that he was the "little prince," accuse him of thinking he was smarter and better than everyone else, and then challenge him to run away to the capitol and demand the king step down from his throne. Dayl and Doret had used the word just once, when Zair wouldn't share a packet of three boiled sweets the headmaster had given him for making perfect marks on recitation day. They had run shrieking into the house, tattling to their mother that Zair was selfish, and he thought he was a prince and didn't have to share. Korgan had snatched up both little boys by their collars and shook them and growled and ordered them to never, ever use that word. That was the only time Zair could ever remember his father and stepmother arguing about anything. They had gone for a long walk, and when they came back, Traysa was white-faced. Either fury or terror, Zair couldn't tell. For months after that, he heard her asking Korgan to send him away, or they were all doomed.

Well, he was away now, wasn't he? And not likely to come home.

Maybe someone had heard one of his brothers refer to him as a prince, and somehow that had come to the king's attention? Rumors were constantly whispering through the country about hunting down and slaughtering descendants of other kings, to quash their claims to the throne. Zair could believe that the king would kill a thirteen-year-old if people referred to him as a prince. So why wasn't he dead, killed long before this? Of course, his father never let the word be used, so what chance of the king hearing it? Zair had always thought that his father was more worried about the danger to the rest of the family, and didn't care about him, specifically. Maybe someone at the end of this journey could explain it to him?

~~~~~

Their company of five traveled ten days, heading west for three days, then northwest four more. They crossed the border out of Dorwain, north into Ambrecht. Zair only knew that because he overheard his four keepers discussing how to deal with the border crossing officials, when they stopped midway through their seventh morning on the road. He lay still on the bench, wrapped in his cloak, the lanterns turned down so low they were mere orange dots in the gloom. As always whenever they approached a checkpoint on the highway or had to make a stop, Gresibel opened a pot of ointment that made the interior of the coach smell like someone had been vilely sick. Whenever they made stops, and someone looked into the coach, Ward had told him to pretend to be sick. If they spoke to him, he was to moan and make heaving noises.

Zair did what he was told because he knew what would happen if he didn't. On their second day of travel, he had been cranky enough to snap back at Ward when the man told him to do something. The next moment, Zair lay on the floor of the coach, gasping for breath, feeling as if his hand had burned off and his arm was just a charred, painfully tingling stump. He didn't want to go through that again.

The rest of the time during their journey, the pot of ointment was
~~~~~

closed up, the window covers raised slightly to allow in fresh air, and the lanterns turned up bright enough for reading. Gresibel encouraged him to read any book he wanted from the two trunks. Zair gladly dove into the histories and fables that livened up otherwise boring recitation of facts and figures and battle descriptions and genealogies. He kept his mind and his imagination busy so he wouldn't be any more afraid and angry than he already was.

On the tenth day, Gresibel stunned Zair by fully opening the leather covers on the windows. Sunlight and fresh air spilled into the coach. It took all his self-control not to lunge for the windows and lean on the frame to look out. What he could see from his seat revealed an open plain, with nothing but an undulating landscape in fall hues, grass and trees and moss and mud, as far as the eye could see. Nothing but landscape, and their coach following a thin ribbon of gravel road. Totally alone. Zair understood why this change came. It didn't matter if anyone could see into the coach, and see him, because there was no one to see him but his captors.

Sunset spilled crimson and purple and amber across the landscape when the rumbling of the coach wheels changed from the grinding hum and rattle of gravel and packed dirt to the higher-pitched grinding and rhythmic clicking of bricks under them. Zair looked up from his book, his eyes aching from trying to focus on unusually tiny print. Gresibel and Tonia leaned out of the windows on the right side of the coach, studying what lay ahead, with something like cringing anticipation. Were they afraid? Maybe they were so glad to get out of the coach soon, they looked forward to whatever happened next, even if it was bad?

The coach slowed. Zair slid the strip of cloth he used as a bookmark into place and closed the book. He thought about asking if he could keep reading it later, but his keepers had discouraged him asking questions over the entire journey. Was this their destination? It didn't look like any of the waystations or custom houses or taverns where they had stopped along the way. Would he have a chance to run, now that they had come to the end of the journey? How far and how fast would he need to run to get out of the reach of the magic that controlled the band on his wrist?

The coach turned, and gradually a sprawling manor house came into the frame of the window next to him. Zair held still, waiting, wondering what waited for him inside that house. He had accompanied his father and older brothers on enough visits to officials and minor nobles of larger villages and towns, he knew servants should be waiting at the door to welcome them. Yet the main door remained closed. No one looked out any of the windows. Maybe this huge house was empty of people?

Or maybe nobody came out to welcome them because they weren't expected, or maybe even weren't wanted?

The coach kept moving, rather than slowing to a stop at the bottom of the wide stairs leading up to the main doors of the house. Zair leaned forward, watching those doors, as the coach kept moving, following the curve of the elegant driveway, going all the way to the far end of the house. It turned to go behind the house. Of course. Servants never came through the front doors like a guest. He knew that, even though his family had never had servants. As his stepmother often remarked, that was what children were for.

No one came to either welcome them or simply watch them arrive. The coach stopped. Gresibel gestured for Zair to wrap his cloak around himself and pull his hood down, as always. She gripped his shoulder, guiding him through the door and down to the ground. A door into the manor house opened before them. He couldn't see who had opened it. She guided him inside, down a short, dark hallway that ended at a cross hallway. Gresibel turned him right, and after ten steps they went up a wide flight of stairs. They climbed to the fourth floor. Zair tried to calculate how far they had gone into the house. The top of the stairs opened onto a long hallway. He saw two doorways on the hallway to the right, and two on the left. Gresibel released his arm and gestured with her chin for him to go to the left.

One door stood open. He went inside. It was a sitting room, with a fire pit in the center of the tiled floor. One door stood open on the opposite wall. He glanced back at Gresibel and she gestured at the door. Zair went through. The next room had two long tables and shelves built into the two facing walls that didn't have doors. They were full of books and inkwells and lanterns. A second door opened off this room, opposite the door he had entered through. This led into a short room with three doors off of it. Gresibel went ahead of Zair and opened each door in turn. One was a washing room, with a long bathing tub. A cauldron sat on a high stand over a firebox, with a spigot to fill the tub. One wall was filled with shelves of towels and jars of soap powder and scrubbing brushes. Two doors led into bedrooms. Gresibel stepped into one and put down the basket she carried. She turned to face Zair.

"The other is your room. I imagine dinner will be brought up to us soon, but there should be time for you to wash and get comfortable before that." She nodded toward the third door when Zair didn't move. "Go on."

"What's going to happen now that we're here?" he asked.

"We wait." She shrugged and pulled her hood down off the back of her head. "You will be tested. I doubt you will meet the other boys. I should hope we don't have to meet the others while we're waiting."

A shadow of something sad, maybe even fearful, seemed to pass over her face. Then she gestured again at his bedroom door.

"Go on with you."

Zair did as he was told, because he had no other options. He wished he could ask where they were. He wished he could ask how to get back to Dorwain, and why they had come into Ambrecht, and what exactly he would be tested on. He didn't, because of the feeling that filled him with a sick kind of cold, and twisting in his belly. He wondered why he hadn't felt like this until now.

He raised his hand to push the bedroom door open, and the band fell off his wrist. Dull brown now, it no longer glowed. It hit the tiled floor with a thick sound, like a lump of frozen, wet cloth. Zair stood on the threshold, looking at the band that had stopped so many words and actions in the last ten days and shivered a little. Other than his blessing band, he hadn't really seen or touched magic until now, with this band. He suspected it had fallen off because it was no longer needed. He couldn't escape this place. Maybe the band had kept him from feeling afraid until now?

Zair didn't like magic. Until now, he had always liked the stories with all sorts of magic spells and enchanted rings and talking beasts that helped the hero solve the riddle or break the curse. But hadn't the last ten days proved that magic wasn't always pleasant?

He gave the band a shove with the toe of his boot. It hit the doorframe and shattered into dust that melted into the tiles. Zair stepped into his room and closed the door. He sat on the bed and looked out the window, and watched the sun setting, far off in the distance across the plain.

~~~~~

Over the next three days, Zair caught hints of voices elsewhere in the house. He heard men and women speaking in hushed tones, and rapid footsteps, but if there were other boys in the house, he never heard their voices. Gresibel had mentioned other boys. Zair supposed that they didn't speak any more than he did. They probably weren't allowed out of their suite of rooms any more than he was.

On the fourth day, someone knocked on the door of the sitting room, startling Gresibel and Tonia. They looked at Zair, who was sitting on the floor by the fire pit, reading. Gresibel had been writing in a journal and Tonia was knitting something in bright, cheerful shades of blue and green. The women seemed to have a conversation just in those few seconds their gazes locked together. Several drops of sweat rolled down Tonia's forehead as she got up to answer the door. Gresibel bent down and tapped Zair's shoulder and gestured at the door into the study room.

He picked up his book and went into the next room. He listened for voices as Gresibel closed the door behind him but heard nothing. He set his book on the table and sat down and waited, counting, and reached two hundred nineteen before the door opened.

A skinny man with thinning red hair, spectacles perched on the tip
~~~~~

of his snub nose, and dark green robes came into the study room. He carried a thick book clutched to his chest and settled into the chair at the other end of the table from Zair.

"Well, young man, I hear you are a rare one who likes to read. Why don't we start with you telling me about the one you're reading now?" He flicked his fingers at the book Zair had put down, still open, on the table.

The man opened his book and took an inkwell and several quills from the shelves. He made notes as he and Zair talked. He asked questions and Zair answered them.

When Zair started to ask if this was the testing Gresibel had mentioned, the man shook his head and raised a hand to stop him.

A kindly, weary smile lit his face, and he said, "No, sorry. Now is not the time for your questions. Maybe later. If there is a later. Pray to A'theosius, there is indeed a later."

Then he asked another question. And more after that. He asked Zair how many of the books packed in the leather trunks he had tried to read, and if he had looked at any of the books on the shelves in this room. They discussed each book in turn, and Zair couldn't figure out a pattern for any of the questions. They changed from book to book, so he could never guess what he needed to remember.

Zair realized early on he was being tested even more thoroughly than Gresibel and Tonia had tested him that day they first met. The first time the boy couldn't give him an answer, the man didn't seem upset. Maybe he even looked pleased. Or was that relieved?

"Well, you have something to learn, don't you?" He sat back and rubbed at his temples with his thumbs and seemed to sag a little in his chair.

"Sir?" Zair braced for the man to bring out a whip or rod, like some officials had done to men in the village who didn't please them. Or who, as his father had remarked later, proved they were smarter than the officials.

The door into the study room opened, and Gresibel and Tonia joined them. They exchanged questioning, clearly worried glances with the man. He tipped his head toward Zair and sighed. He didn't smile, exactly, but something passed between the three of them and the atmosphere in the room felt lighter. The two women stood a little taller. The lines around their mouths and eyes smoothed, just a little. Enough to be visible.

"We're all in a tricky sort of situation, lad, but I think if we work together, we will all … well, perhaps the best we can hope for is to survive in relative comfort, if not prosperity." He shrugged. "If you are chosen, I will be your tutor." He chuckled when Zair stopped breathing, and his eyes got wide as he stared at the man. "If that frightens you, then you show more perception and alertness than many who consider themselves your superiors. What's your name?" He chuckled when Zair goggled at him a moment. "They didn't tell me. You're not really real until I pass on my report to Lord Antrifari, so why let you have a name?" He shook his head, sighing. "I am Pendrake. A third-rank scholar and scribe to the Council of Lords. Any other boy would call me Master Pendrake, but considering the masquerade you will soon play ... likely if you address me in public, you would merely call me 'scribe,' or use my name. We will start you on a solid footing by having you address me as Pendrake. And you are?"

"Zair, sir."

"Hmm, not noble enough. Short for Zarethus? Zaruman?"

"Zared, sir."

"Ah." Pendrake again glanced at Gresibel and Tonia. "Dangerous, do you think?"

"It's an old enough name, we can hope that the increasing disdain for book-learning, the neglect of history, will block anyone who isn't friendly toward us from making the historical connection," Gresibel said after a few moments of frowning thought.

"Why is my name dangerous?" Zair tamped down a spurt of anger. He was tired of no one answering him.

Chapter Three

"Six generations ago," Pendrake said, softening his voice as if he didn't want anyone outside the room to hear, "King Zared ruled. He was a good, generous ruler, and an enchanter of truly noble and humble character. Rare among those gifted with great power. Considering the lengths to which King Joben's ancestor went, to eliminate the rightful king's heirs, being named for that king could be considered a declaration of rebellion. Or a claim to the throne. Let us hope that standing in the very shadow of the throne will make you invisible."

"If he is chosen," Tonia said.

"Why wouldn't he be? Look how similar the boys are. The expenditure of magic necessary to carry off the illusion will be minimal," Gresibel said.

"Yes, but just because the boys look alike now doesn't guarantee they will remain so as they grow. What if they don't grow at the same rate? As children grow, their hair color and texture, their complexions, their muscle tone all change. If the boys don't participate in the same activities, learn the same lessons, master the same skills, eat the same food ... it will require more and more magic to keep them mirror images of each other," Pendrake said. "Enemies of the throne can sense the expenditure of that much magic, constantly adjusting to meet the need. Despite the paucity of true magic in Dorwain."

"What boys?" Zair said. He wanted to slam his fists on the table, to startle them, to fight the sensation that he was invisible.

"You and Prince Anwir," Gresibel said with a sigh. "You are among a select group of boys who could be entrusted with guarding his life."

"One of five boys, now," Pendrake said.

"Five?" Tonia's cheeks paled. "I thought there were eight."

"Three have been ... sent away as inadequate." He shook his head. "We are all safer knowing as little as possible. The princess risks her own safety, trying to intervene for the innocent ones."

"A'theosius guard us, guide us," Gresibel whispered.

"Chosen for what? To be a Shadow?" Zair asked. "What is a Shadow?" he hurried on, when Pendrake's nod struck him as reluctant.

"A decoy. A distraction. A defense," Pendrake said. "To be royal is to be a target of brutes and bullies, those who want power they don't deserve, and those who want to reclaim power unjustly taken from them.

A Shadow takes the place of the royal who is in danger."

"To die?" His voice cracked.

"You will take intensive training, lad, to ensure you will not be easy to kill."

"If he is chosen," Tonia said.

"But who is Anwir? I've never heard of him," Zair said. "I've only heard about Prince Naldon."

That began his first lesson in the tangled stew of the royal family and the politics of the kingdom of Dorwain.

Prince Anwir was grandson to King Joben through his daughter, Princess Jillian, born to his first wife, Countess Megha. She was the daughter of a merchant. No one cared back then that Joben hadn't married a nobleman's daughter, because he had four older brothers and several cousins standing between him and the throne. He simply wasn't important enough for a nobleman to offer his daughter to him.

Joben's father was the third son of the previous king. Between him, his five sons and the throne were King Jessel, the oldest brother, Prince Jaquin, the second-born son, and their twelve sons and daughters. Thanks to a plague that swept through Dorwain soon after Jillian's birth, half the royal family was wiped out. Subsequent ill-advised military campaigns and revolts in outlying provinces over the next ten years resulted in the deaths or disappearances of the remaining cousins, their children, and anyone else with a claim to the throne within four generations. Including Joben's older brothers and their children.

Megha died soon after Joben took the throne. Rumors said she had been poisoned to make way for a more acceptable, noble-blooded queen consort. Joben sent Jillian away to her mother's relatives in Ambrecht, ostensibly to protect her from attempts to cleanse the royal bloodline. His next two wives died without producing living children. Joben's fourth queen gave him one son, Naldon.

The crown prince had gotten himself killed three months ago while following rumors that a descendant of King Zared was raising an army to take back the throne. The king's elite guard, the Red Brigade, had been sent throughout the kingdom to keep the news quiet, and track down the rebel forces responsible for tricking Naldon into the ambush that killed him. Pendrake remarked there was very little mourning among the nobles and layers of government. Only the political movers and shakers who had some influence over the crown prince had wanted him to inherit.

Three separate factions tracked down Princess Jillian and her son while traveling with her merchant husband, Phoebus, before she even received word of her half-brother's death. No one was quite sure which faction had tried to kill Anwir, which one had tried to kidnap him to control him, and which had set out to destroy the whole family because their blood simply wasn't royal enough. The Red Brigade didn't arrive to protect them until they had been surrounded by the three rival factions. They only survived the attack because the factions turned on each other. Phoebus was brutally injured in the conflict, and the factions were either destroyed outright or went into hiding, so no one remained to give clear answers.

The family was separated. Phoebus was carried off to a healing enclave in the mountains to save his life. Princess Jillian and Anwir went into hiding. Agents of the kingdom headed out to find likely boys to train up to be Anwir's Shadow, to be raised with the new prince, and ensure he grew up to take his grandfather's throne.

Whichever boy was chosen as Shadow would train with the Red Brigade to act as bodyguard, as well as fill in for the prince on any occasion there might be danger or simply hints of threats against the royal family. The Shadow would have lessons with the prince, every kind of training, in weaponry and dancing, academics, diplomacy, wear the same clothes, eat the same food. They would spend as much time together as possible, so their mannerisms and speech patterns would match. As little magic as possible would be employed to make the Shadow a duplicate of the prince, to reduce the chances of enemies detecting a substitution had been made.

"You will become a weapon against the assassins who think they're striking at the prince," Pendrake said. "If A'theosius is kind, they will be in more danger than you."

Zair had heard of the Red Brigade. What boy in Dorwain hadn't heard of the most elite soldiers in the kingdom? What boy hadn't shivered in delight, hearing the stories of their bloody exploits, and the rumors of magic that made them impossible to kill? Some boys even held onto the hopes of joining the Red Brigade as they got older, despite the dark tales and sobering reality of injuries and death in the king's service.

That night, Zair dreamed of returning home, dressed as a member of the Red Brigade, and terrorizing his brothers into apologizing for all their cruelty to him. His father might even be proud of him.

Maybe being kidnapped would turn out to be the best thing that had ever happened to him.

~~~~~

The days that followed were filled with lessons of every kind, until Zair's head and body ached. A general history of Dorwain. Studying and interpreting and memorizing the sigils and coats of arms of the noble houses and offshoot noble houses and the signs of the many guilds. Learning better table manners. Zair discovered nearly a dozen additional bowls and plates and cups and utensils, each with its own rules for when it was used in a court dinner, how to hold a utensil, and even how much
~~~~~

food to leave on his plate, depending on the situation and event. Then there were the different ways to bow and salute to the people above and below him in rank. Although everyone he would encounter in the palace ranked above him, while he masqueraded as the prince, nearly everyone ranked below him.

Some people ranked below the crown prince, but they were valuable allies and therefore Anwir, and Zair when he took his place, needed to be respectful and cultivate their friendship. Others who were his equals could be maneuvering to get him removed through accidents or scandal or proving him incompetent, so they or their sons or nephews or grandsons had a stronger claim to the throne when King Joben died.

Then there was the calendar to consider. Dorwain had a dozen holidays or memorial days in each month, with their own hero or holy person or historic event. Zair had to be able to discuss each one and recite the pertinent facts if anyone brought up the topic in conversation. He had to remember the order of events on each day, the prescribed or prohibited colors, or ritual decorations. Once he was chosen as Shadow, if he was chosen as Shadow, he would have a wardrobe to suit all the different occasions when he would stand in for the prince. Even if they remained the same size and stature, Zair wouldn't share clothes with the prince. Tonia commented on how the seamstresses would be delighted with the fees they would earn for all the extra work, and their silence.

Zair didn't miss the pained glances his keepers shared after that comment. He listened carefully when he should have been reading another volume of history. Just a day later, he overheard Gresibel and Pendrake speculating on how the seamstresses could be prevented from realizing they were duplicating the crown prince's wardrobe. Someone might find it necessary to enforce their silence, rather than buying it.

Everything turned cold inside him, and he felt sick at the sudden change in perspective. This wasn't a boy's dream of adventure, a chance to become a hero and earn the envy of everyone who had ever mocked him. This was dangerous, and unjust, so that innocent people were endangered.

He needed to escape. But could he?

No one had replaced the restraining band Ward had put on him. Was that because this house was too well-guarded, or because they thought him incapable of escaping? Did they think he was having such a good time with his lessons, all the books he could read, all the good food and the soft bed and fine clothes, that he wouldn't even try to escape?

He thought and planned and studied maps when he was alone. He kicked himself for not fearing for his father until now. Korgan at least had to be worried about him, even if his stepmother and half-brothers despised him. Zair had a duty to let him know what had happened. Yet as the days of planning went by, he kept thinking about the danger to mere seamstresses. Didn't that mean his father would be in even more danger, once he knew the truth? Zair suspected he didn't dare stay when he returned home. If he wasn't caught on the journey home, someone might be waiting to catch him. His father could be punished. And even if he didn't care for his brothers or stepmother, he still didn't want them punished for something he did. He had just wanted them shamed, wanted them to be sick with regret for how they had treated him.

Maybe he shouldn't even go home? Maybe just find a way to send them a message, tell them what had happened, and then ... do what? Flee for the rest of his life?

Was that better than taking advantage of the ability to live the life of a prince? Just how often would he have to take Anwir's place? How much of his time would be spent training as a warrior? He liked the idea of training with the legendary Red Brigade. Besides, what made him think he would get to do any of the fun things a prince got to do? Common sense, and all the reading he was doing, told him he would be filling in for the prince in the boring tasks, as well as taking his place in dangerous situations. Sitting in council meetings, listening, and trying not to fall asleep. Riding out on inspections. Taking the prince's place in public events where he had to hold perfectly still and not scratch or fidget or close his eyes for more than two seconds, and especially not yawn while someone went on and on and on with speeches and lectures. Maybe he wouldn't get whacked across the back of the head for falling asleep or picking his nose in public, but someone would give him a beating or at the very least lash his knuckles once they were in private. The crown prince of Dorwain had to set an example. He had to be a model of decorum and make his royal grandfather proud every second of every day.

When he mentioned his conclusions, Tonia agreed. Zair was there so Anwir could relax in hiding, in safety, and scratch and yawn and snore and pick his nose and laugh at pompous, boring speakers.

Zair would take lessons with the prince and understand what the prince thought. He wouldn't just be permitted to read hundreds of valuable books, but he would be *required* to read them, and remember what he read, and answer questions in the prince's place when all the nobles tried to prove him incompetent and unworthy as Joben's heir. Zair would attend worship in the Starhouse in Anwir's place, to convince the nobles and leaders of society that Joben's heir was just as devout as his grandfather and great-grandfather and all the kings of Dorwain before him. Zair would get to sit in the front row, and read from the books of Atheosius's teachings, and hear what the priests said. No more sitting in the rafters with the other village boys and trying to hear the lesson through the whispering and giggling and constant scuffles. No more sneers from his older brothers who thought that going to the chapel in their village for prayers and homilies was a waste of time.

Zair had heard stories of Prince Naldon. The stories made him out to be a fool who took stupid risks or went out in disguise and committed crimes. Now, listening to his keepers as they shared information learned from the other servants in the house, Zair learned more. One story said that the crown prince had been so unpopular that a group of nobles had created the story of Zared's heir to trick him into an ambush, to kill him. One story even said King Joben was so disgusted with his son, he had ordered the Red Brigade not to protect Naldon.

Understanding made Zair cold. Plenty of people disliked King Joben and how he ruled Dorwain. Those people were constantly hunting for the rightful king. They wouldn't care that Anwir was an innocent boy. He was Joben's heir, so he was guilty of his ancestors' crimes and deserved to die. So Zair would look like him through magic, to keep the prince alive, to distract the enemies, until they could be identified and punished, and Anwir could grow up to be king.

Please, Atheosius, he prayed that night, and many nights after that. *Please, Atheosius, make them think I'm not right to be Shadow? And let me go home and be safe? Keep all my family safe? But if they do choose me, please, don't let me get hurt? Please keep the evil people away from him and me?* Zair couldn't really think beyond that, other than, *Can I please go home?*

~~~~~

"Is it bad if they decide I'm not right to be the Shadow?" he asked two days later, when Pendrake came to question him on all the reading he had done since the last time they had lessons.

The old scholar didn't come to see him every day. Zair understood from other things his keepers said that Pendrake was tutoring the other boys, living in other suites in this house, training them to be Anwir's Shadow as well.

"It could be," Pendrake said after a long silence, when Gresibel and Tonia settled down at the long study table.

"Pen—" Gresibel began.

"The boy deserves to know the risks. He's got even less choice and fewer chances than the three of us. His face, his father's high position, make it even more difficult to simply make him vanish, settle into a new life with a new name, if he is rejected. At least we can blame Ward and Gabe for making a bad choice, misusing the seeking spells. What excuse does the boy have?"

"He's right," Tonia said. "We're doing as we're ordered. That's our protection."

"And our doom," Gresibel said on a sigh. "If what we suspect about his bloodline is true, if the wrong people find out, we are all doomed
~~~~~

anyway." She rested a hand on Zair's shoulder. "Are we frightening you, lad?" Her voice was softer, kinder than it had been since Zair woke in the tavern room, what felt like an entire lifetime ago.

"Yes." Zair wanted to say no, but he felt like he had two winters ago, when he had found himself teamed with Ranald and Darren, two farmer boys, to try to save a colt that had fallen through the ice. None of them liked each other, but the life of the colt was more important than their bickering. They had to trust each other and act on each other's ideas swiftly, no arguing, to get the colt out of the water before it froze or drowned.

Or maybe this situation wasn't exactly like that one, because he didn't dislike any of his three keepers. Zair just knew, in his gut, the worst thing he could do was lie. That would cripple them all, and they would all drown.

Please, Atheosius, he prayed again and had to stop there. He had to trust that the All-Maker would hear him and understand all the things he couldn't say, because he couldn't put his fears and the images in his head into words.

"That shows wisdom." Pendrake reached across the table to grip Zair's other shoulder. "We can't be sure what will happen to you, or any of us, if the princess and her son decide you don't suit this mirror dance. We can hope for mercy. Maybe for a spell to wipe clean all our memories of these weeks. Princess Jillian is a kind, generous woman, but even she might not have the power necessary to grant us mercy. We can always hope, though."

~~~~~

Zair dreamed of women weeping and then shrieking in fear as they ran into the darkness. He woke himself when he fell out of his bed, tangled in his sheets, trying to get to the window to look out. He had a sense of knowing deep inside that had often protected him from his brothers' nasty tricks. That sense of knowing now insisted that he would see those women, if he could just get the window open.

But he couldn't open the window. He had tried, and found the shutters nailed shut. The gaps between them were enough to allow fresh air in, but he could never look out. None of the few windows in the suite allowed looking out. Zair stumbled to the window and pressed against the shutters and held his breath, listening.

All he heard was the wailing of the wind as another storm drew closer.

He thought about his dream and wondered if magic had touched him. He had overheard Gresibel and Tonia whispering together about "when they wrap the first spell around him," and other bits of conversations like it. Pendrake had admitted that magic had a large part
~~~~~

in a Shadow's duties. Zair didn't know much about magic, beyond what he read in stories, and the blessing band he had worn since his christening. He knew magic didn't always require anchoring in an object. Sometimes spells were spoken over people, or shouted at monsters, and other times they were written in magic-infused ink, or etched into wood or stone or metal, or woven into tapestries or clothes or rugs. It all depended on the purpose of the magic, how strong it had to be and how long it had to last.

The magic in other kingdoms, where enchanters were born with magic in their blood, might have different rules. Magic might be easier. Zair had no idea. He could only depend on what he knew, and what he guessed, based on the exciting, terrifying stories that boys told in whispers and by candlelight and in shadows.

Gresibel caught him examining the hems and lining of his shirt and coat and even digging into his boots the next day, to look for spells written on the cloth or leather or embroidered into the design. She went pale and looked more grave than usual when he confessed what he was doing, what he was looking for. He didn't tell her about his dream. He decided to ask Pendrake when he came for his lesson that afternoon.

Zair had the awful, sinking feeling that if he told Gresibel or Tonia about the dream, they would join the weeping women. Maybe the magic was soaking into him through the food he ate and the clothes he wore. Maybe it was in the air he breathed, and the more magic he soaked up, the more likely he was to cause something to happen, just by speaking about it. That happened in many of the stories he had read.

Pendrake, however, did not come that day to give Zair his lessons and question him on the reading he had assigned him.

Four men were waiting in the study room when Zair went in after the noon meal. They were all skinny and bald-shaven, wearing draping black robes that smelled of sour herbs and smoke. He couldn't guess how old they were, if the wrinkles around their mouths and eyes were from age or just sour dispositions. In unison, their lips pursed and they looked him over, head to toe and back to head again, and then they sniffed loudly. The way the territorial overlord's daughter sniffed when the village girls whispered and giggled behind her back.

"Well, at least this one looks more like him than the last four," one man muttered. "Less waste of our magic."

"If he's chosen. If he's not, it's wasted no matter how much or how little we expend," another said.

Zair couldn't tell who talked, because none of them seemed to be moving their lips.

Chapter Four

"Sit," the tallest of the four said, and snapped his fingers and pointed at the chair Pendrake usually sat in.

Zair obeyed. He didn't want to know what kind of nasty magic they could inflict on him if he disobeyed, or even if he hesitated too long. He sat with his back pressed tight against the chair and tried not to flinch when all four moved to stand behind him. Out of his sight.

Dust motes swirled through the air, growing thicker with every heartbeat. Some sparkled like shattered glass. Others had a silvery tinge. Zair held his breath, afraid what would happen if he inhaled that dust. He had to close his eyes when the cloud grew thick enough he felt the dust gathering on his eyelashes.

"He's fighting us," one of them whispered.

"Impossible. They checked his pedigree. He doesn't have a speck of magic talent in his blood," another said.

"If he did, he would have been killed before he got here. Everyone knows only royals have blood-born magic," a third said, his voice quavering.

"Then you explain why this is taking so long," the first man snarled.

"It's the mirror," a fourth man said. Zair thought he was the one who had said he looked "more like him than the last four." "It's fighting us."

"How? We killed it when we ground it to dust," the second man whispered. He sounded afraid.

"Is that what you think?" The third man sounded like he might laugh in a moment. The kind of laughter that came from fear. Zair had heard a man laugh like that, whom everyone said had lost his sanity years ago. "Magic mirrors don't die when you destroy their bodies. If they did, there would be no magic in the powder we gain from them."

The dust covering him came from a magic mirror? Zair inhaled without thinking. The dust caught in his throat. He didn't choke, and that startled him enough that he opened his eyes. Silver-tinged rainbows filled his eyes and shot through his skull.

Why did they have to kill a magic mirror? What kind of magic were they performing on him?

It's called a mirror spell, a shimmery, crackly sort of voice whispered. It seemed to come from the center of his chest and his skull at the same time. *My word, you can hear me, can't you? Don't speak aloud. Think, and I'll hear you. You don't want to let those nasty old crows know you've got enough magic to hear me.* She sighed—the voice was a woman's, combined with wind chimes. *And enough magic to let me take root in your blood. Share your body, so to speak. Oh, my dear boy, I do hope we can be of help to each other. We're both victims, I can tell you that right now.*

Hello? Zair took a deeper breath. He dared to hope this would be a good thing. *I'm sorry they hurt you, mirror. My name is Zair.*

I am Viza. I'm sorry, but we can't speak more right now. They might hear us, and that wouldn't be good for either of us. We especially don't want to let them know you have magic. Trust me on this.

Zair trusted her. What other choice did he have?

"Huh, what did I tell you? The dust is just getting old, so it takes longer," the fourth man said, his voice returning to normal volume. He slapped Zair on his left shoulder. "All done." He snickered. "For now, anyway."

"What did you do?" Zair asked. He opened his eyes. All the sparkles were gone. As far as he could tell, no dust clung to him.

He felt it sifting through his chest, somehow. Sliding and spinning through his body in ways that had nothing to do with his flesh and blood.

Cough, Viza said. *Make them think you really are a mule, when it comes to magic. That makes it safer for both of us.*

Zair coughed.

"We've taken the first step into giving you a glorious future," the first man said. The four men moved around to stand in front of Zair now. They looked him over and their mouths twisted into matching, self-satisfied smirks.

"Don't be ridiculous," the third man said. He was the tallest of them, most likely their leader. "Shadows have no futures, no lives. Nobody will remember them or miss them when they're gone. But that won't really matter to you, will it, boy? You'll have all the luxury and privilege of the crown prince, if you're chosen, and none of the responsibilities."

None of the restrictions and penalties, either, strange as that sounds, Viza added.

She said nothing more until after the four magicians left. They were just magicians, she told him later. The lowest possible ranks of magic-users. The kind who gained their magic through study and reciting spells and covering themselves with charms, because they had no magic in their blood and bones. They dressed all in black and shaved their heads and clattered with charms and stank from incense to let the entire world know they were magicians. Enchanters and sorcerers with in-born magic, with real skill, didn't need to tell anyone who they were. Viza had a great deal to tell him about magic that afternoon and for many days to come.

Zair went to the door of the study room and opened it enough to hear when the door to the suite closed. He listened for the sounds of footsteps in the hallway. When the few echoes faded away, he stepped out into the sitting room. Gresibel and Tonia were sitting together on a couch on the far side of the firepit, watching the door.

"How do you feel?" Gresibel asked him. Her smile trembled at the corners, and she beckoned for him to come sit on the couch facing them.

Zair shrugged. How was he supposed to feel?

Best to make them think you saw and felt nothing, and everything those posers said just confused you, Viza said.

It did. He almost laughed. Viza did laugh.

Both women looked relieved when Zair said he didn't see anything, didn't feel anything. Tonia smiled, just as shakily as Gresibel, when he asked what those men were supposed to do to him, and who they were.

"They came to apply the first layers of magic that will make it possible for you to be Shadow to the prince," Gresibel said. "And test you, to see how moldable you are, how well magic will stick to you. And if you can sense it or manipulate it. You didn't feel or see anything?"

Zair shook his head. He knew it was silly, but he felt better if he didn't actually speak the lie aloud.

"Thank you, blessed A'theosius," she whispered, and pressed her fingertips to her lips, then spread her fingers, gesturing an offering of thanks to the heavens.

"Why is that good?" he asked.

"It means you don't have enough magic in your blood and bones to cause any trouble. In-born magic could complicate the process, if they choose you to be Shadow. It could twist the spells around." She looked over her shoulder to the door. Zair wondered if she feared someone listening outside. "We're not allowed to give you the histories of Shadows yet, but I've read enough to know all the trouble that could come from magic in your blood, interfering with the spells. Especially the mirror spells. Instead of making you look like the prince, he could start to look like you. Instead of you giving him your strength and health, you could drain them from him. If you were injured, he would feel it, even share your wounds, instead of you taking the brunt of those injuries for him. There are many stories of Shadows who had enough magic in them to take the place of the royals they shadowed, and no one knew the truth until years later."

"I've heard enough stories, wise men should refuse to create Shadows at all," Tonia said.

"Be thankful that you don't have any magic, or if you did, it is small enough, weak enough, that you aren't considered a danger."

"But if I had magic, wouldn't they let me go home, because they couldn't use me?" Zair asked.

"You would think that, wouldn't you?" Tonia said.

Don't tell them, Viza said. *They've performed the test and spread my dust on five boys so far. None were strong enough to hear me speak, but they had enough magic to react. Sometimes badly. Worse than poison. That's part of their nasty test, and they refuse to admit it. I tried to warn the boys, but they couldn't hear me.* Her voice broke with a sob, and Zair knew, without her having to say another word, that those boys had not been able to go home. Not that they were not permitted, but they were unable.

~~~~~

Viza agreed with him, when Zair decided, just before suppertime, that he needed to run away now, before it was too late.

She guided him in looking through all the books of geography and maps and trade routes, to plan the fastest route home at this time of year. She showed him how she could capture images of all the pages he read and then later put the images before his mind's eye, so he didn't need to write anything down. She could remember everything for him. She advised him on what clothes to wear to escape, and what food to take from the kitchen on their way out of the house. The magicians had been so careless with her dust, enough of her had spread through the manor house that she knew what was on each floor. She had spread into the back stairs used by the servants. That would be the safest route for Zair to escape the house.

Most fascinating of all, for Zair, was Viza's ability to help him see in the dark. Her dust had penetrated his flesh, into his bloodstream, touching his eyes and ears and nose. As best she could, she limited the penetration of her dust, to focus on those senses. With more of her dust in his blood, she could embed herself throughout his body, to help him heal, to leap and run and fight, and sharpen all his senses so he could evade danger like a wild animal.

They crept out of the suite shortly after midnight, down the corridor, to the door to the servants' stairs, then down to the wing of the house that held the kitchen and larder and laundry. Zair trembled when he saw the size of the kitchen, all the bins of vegetables, the many bowls of bread dough rising in preparation for the morning baking, the cold room where the butchered remains of chickens, cows, sheep, and pigs hung to bleed out, waiting to be cooked. How many people were in this manor house?

There were perhaps fifty, between the regular servants and the teams who came in with their chosen boys, Viza said after a few moments. She startled Zair, because he hadn't really asked that question, just wondered. Perhaps he wondered too loudly in his thoughts?

We're going to need to teach you some simple disciplines, to keep your private thoughts private, the mirror informed him, with a hint of a chuckle. *If we're going to be sharing this body for the next few years, then we'll both need*
~~~~~

some privacy and separation, for our own sanity.

Years? You mean, the magic won't wear off?

My dear boy, I am part of your flesh and blood now. If there were an empty mirror for me to migrate into, I would do it gladly, to preserve your sanity, if not my own peace of mind. However, there are precious few magic mirrors at all here in Ambrecht. Those who didn't choose to shatter themselves to escape ignominious slavery and degradation are all imprisoned in the lairs of those idiots who call themselves the Purple Sky. Many of them have gone half-mad. Or at least, they were, the last time I was able to make contact through the mirror web. I haven't been able to speak with any mirrors since I was shattered and ground into powder.

I'm sorry. How hard will it be to find a new mirror for you? Zair hurried to add.

Finding one will likely be a thousand times easier than finding an enchanter with the strength and skill and moral fortitude whom I would trust to help me. And that's more than enough depressing thoughts for now. We need to focus on getting you to safety and freedom. Then we can think about my problems. But I do thank you for wanting to help. It's so refreshing to encounter a good soul like yours, after years of sojourning in the shadows, as it were.

Viza guided him in finding a sack to hold the fruit, cheese, bread, and knife he took from the kitchen. She had him take long pauses and short, quick scurries from one doorway to another. Finally, they reached the last door between them and the open space of the servants' yards at the back of the house.

Zair pulled down on the latch. He held his breath, praying for silence as he pulled the door open. At the first creak, he stopped.

Quickly, Viza snapped. *Less chance of creaking if you move fast.*

He obeyed and nearly laughed aloud, a little breathless, when the creaks stopped. The door was heavy, though. It wanted to keep moving when Zair pushed it open just enough for him to slip out.

Fiery roofing nails stabbed a rapid dance up his back. Zair gasped and staggered, still holding onto the latch. The burning stabs rippled over him, stealing the breath from his lungs, then concentrated on his hand still holding the latch. He tripped, landing on his back in the dust in front of the door.

Get up! Get up! Hurry, before they come, Viza cajoled. She sounded like she might burst into tears.

"Who?" Zair's voice broke in a gasp.

Whoever set the alarm spell. I should have known. I would have known, if I was entirely myself. I can't sense even a tenth of the things I should have, if I was still in my frame. Why are you lying there? Get up!

Zair went on his hands and knees for a few steps. Then he came to a post that held a lantern and hooks for tools to be hung on it. He used it to help himself to his feet.

"Now where?" he whispered, looking around the yard full of

moonlight and thick black shadows.

Oh, I'm sorry. I'm so sorry, dear boy. It's too late. I need to go silent to protect you, but remember that I am always here. I will help you when I can, but for now ...

"Viza?" he whispered.

No response.

A shiver raced up his back. The chill was pleasant compared to the sensation of fiery nails and soothed those spots that still stung. Zair definitely didn't like magic. Especially magic that tattled on and betrayed him.

"I know you're afraid," a man said, from over his head.

Zair looked up, then tipped his head back far enough he threatened to fall over backward. He turned, his neck aching, to see a man standing in a second-story window, looking down at him. He wore black robes, and his head was shaven bald, but that was where the resemblance to the magicians ended. He had a neatly trimmed beard and moustache, framing a smiling mouth. His cheeks were wide, and his eyes gleamed crystalline blue in the moonlight.

His name, Zair found out in a little while, was Magnus. He was chief magical advisor and intercessor for Princess Jillian. His magic was strong enough for him to qualify as an enchanter, but he chose to shave his head and dress like the magicians that were, as Viza put it, "underfoot everywhere" to avoid the problems that came with jealousy. And, as he admitted later, to trick potential enemies into underestimating and even ignoring him.

"You're wise to be afraid," the man continued. "But it's too late to try to run. In fact, trying to flee will make the smarter ones suspicious. They'll test you further. They'll find out you have quite a bit of sleeping magic, just waiting for the right spark to awaken it. That won't be good for you. I recommend you come back inside and wait until you're older and stronger and better able to fight for your life."

Zair waited, but Viza didn't speak. He took a tottering step away from the post he had been holding onto. Then another. The next one was steadier. He made his way back to the door. To his disappointment, the yard stayed quiet and so did the door when he pulled it open. Zair slid through and pushed the door closed. Even the ability to see in the dark had left him. He blinked hot wet out of his eyes and fought down the sensation of being abandoned. He let the bag of food drop in the middle of the kitchen floor. Part of him wanted to throw it around, break things, toss the bread dough into the banked fire, strike back and vent his frustration.

Fear kept him quiet.

A swirling, fist-sized ball of green-gold light met him in the doorway when he stepped out of the kitchen wing.

"Follow," the man's voice whispered from the light.

So Zair did. He shuddered a few times as he climbed the servant stairs up to the second floor and followed the light down several turns in the corridor, until he reached Magnus's apartments. Common sense told him that disobeying a magician, especially one who had caught him trying to run away in the middle of the night, especially one who frightened Viza into going silent on him, would not be a smart move.

Not if, as the man had said, he wanted to get older and stronger and better able to fight for his life.

"They're all oblivious, self-blinded idiots," the man said, when Zair stepped through the door into his sitting room. The door swung silently shut behind him and latched with a solid *thunk-click* that told the boy it had locked.

That was impressive magic.

"They were only looking for certain signs of magic, and were so sure of what they would find, they didn't see that flare of blood-borne magic when it lit up right under their noses." He came out of the next room, carrying a tray with a pitcher and cups and a plate of spicy meat pies, small enough to be eaten in two bites. He gestured with a lift of his chin at one of the couches by the central fire pit and waited until Zair sat.

A knee-high round table slid several feet over to stop at the boy's side. The man set the tray down on the table and sat on the other side of it.

"I felt it, and I was on the other side of the house, explaining a tricky bit of history to Anwir. The dogs howled and the horses all let out various salutes, and nobody noticed. They thought it was just a reaction to that wretched storm that keeps teasing but refuses to break." He sighed and picked up the pitcher. "It's thirsty work, escaping." He filled both cups and let Zair pick which one he wanted.

"You're not going to tell?" Zair forced himself to meet the man's blue gaze.

"No. Why? Because ..." He sighed and settled back in the couch with his own cup cradled between his hands. "Because I think you'll be good for the prince. His entire life has been turned upside down, and I can guarantee that other than his mother and myself, no one will care about him as a boy. Everyone will see him as the means to get what they want. They'll destroy his heart and soul to gain some means of control over him. He's going to need a friend, someone everyone will ignore. Who better to be invisible, and unheard when he speaks, than the prince's Shadow?"

"You don't know anything about me." Zair raised the cup to his mouth. He sniffed it, and was surprised to smell sweet fruit juice, rather than the fumes of strong liquor.

"I clearly read the reverberations in the magic when those accident-prone buffoons worked their half-baked spells on you. The notes of the song that rang through this house for just a few heartbeats testified to a heart and soul that could grow into nobility, with the right guidance." He took a sip from his own cup, lowered it, and slowly rolled the cup between his hands for a moment. His gaze flicked up to rest on Zair just as the boy took a sip. "Which of your parents has royal blood?"

He chuckled when Zair choked and spat most of the mouthful onto his shirt. Despite himself, Zair grinned and wiped his mouth. It was a silly trick, something he and his year-mates played on each other at festivals and other occasions when they were dressed in their best clothes.

"They don't..." A shudder worked through him, and he remembered the times his older brothers called him "the little prince," and their father grew coldly angry. The times some of the older students teased him for being named for a king. "Nobody ever said," he finally answered.

"I know what Ward and Gabe reported when they brought you in, but they've been known to make mistakes, and to lie when it suited them. They also managed to run off on errands that could take them away for months, so if suspicion of treachery falls on them, they stand a fair chance of escaping." Magnus gestured at the plate of meat pies. Zair took one and ate one while the magician studied him. "What are your parents' names? Where are you from?"

"My father is Korgan, headman of Nayester, a village in the northern territory of Dorwain. My mother ... died soon after I was born. Her name was Zenobia," he added on a whisper.

Zair only knew his birth-mother's name because he had heard his father and stepmother arguing about it.

"Ah." The man nodded. He picked up a meat pie and ate it in small bites, chewing slowly, while staring at a point in the air over the table. Then a second meat pie.

Zair waited. He wanted another meat pie, but he held as still as he could, afraid to interrupt his host's thoughts. He held his cup in both hands and slowly brought it to his mouth and sipped.

Then Magnus refilled his own cup, sat back in the couch, and started talking. He introduced himself and implied more than declared the vast difference between his magic and what the four men had done to Zair that afternoon.

Chapter Five

"Those four crows and their misbegotten colleagues have the job of layering magic on the prince and whoever is unlucky enough to be his Shadow, binding the two together, weaving an impenetrable illusion around the Shadow, ensuring that everything will flow to the benefit of the prince. The king won't listen to the warnings his daughter and I have both given him, explaining that magic does not work that way. Especially mirroring magic. Especially when inept clods like those four and their entire band of black-clad mystics get themselves tangled in it.

"I've earned a headache every time I talk to them and ask them to explain the theories and practices and disciplines they use. I swear, rather than devoting time to learning truly useful magic, they spend most of their time inventing new words to confuse anyone who doesn't belong to their ranks. Everything is tangled and interwoven and depends on multiple layers, repeating the spells and knotting what should be a clear, clean flow of magic." He shuddered, and tipped back his cup, emptying it in three swallows. "I am convinced they complicate what should be simple just to ensure that they are kept on hand to keep making repairs, reinforcing what should never have sagged and fallen in on itself."

Zair finished his cup. He focused on one of the three remaining meat pies. Magnus smiled.

"You'd best eat up, lad, and get back to your bed. We don't want any of them to know you and I have met and become allies."

"Allies?" Zair almost dropped the meat pie he had just picked up.

"Oh, indeed. I have pledged my loyalty and life-long service to Princess Jillian, but I also owe you and your bloodline my service and guidance as well. That reaction this afternoon, when they worked their lopsided, half-baked spell on you, is proof enough of your royal blood. There are several of us, all pretending to be much less than we are, to protect the knowledge and guardianship entrusted to us. You are of the bloodline of the true king. I don't know what your mother was thinking when she gave you that name. Like lighting a beacon fire and taunting the usurpers to come find you. She probably thought she was giving prophecy a nudge closer to fulfillment."

Zair had read enough history so far, he had a clear picture in his head of what King Joben and his loyal nobles would do to him if they found out his bloodline. Now his father's anger made sense. Even his stepmother's dislike for him made sense. His presence endangered the whole family.

"Then shouldn't I — wouldn't it be better — smarter — if I ran away?"

"No, lad." Magnus shook his head and the faint light of amusement in his eyes darkened to something that made the boy shiver. "The safest place for one such as you is sitting in the shadow of the throne. The last place anyone would expect you to hide."

"Pendrake said that," he whispered.

"Pendrake is a wise man, loyal to the throne. Between the two of us, we'll keep you safe. Give you a chance to grow into a man." Magnus reached out and gripped the boy's shoulder. "I do swear it on my soul, on my loyalty and obedience to A'theosius."

Much later, after tossing and turning for what felt like hours, Zair called to Viza. The mirror didn't respond while he was awake, and he couldn't be sure that she had talked to him in his dreams. He only knew that when he woke, he didn't feel quite so afraid.

~~~~~

Zair wanted to ask Pendrake about Magnus, about the magicians, about the powder that used to be a magic mirror, and especially if the tutor knew for certain, or just suspected that he had royal blood. He didn't dare. He thought about it for two days. Then Viza warned him not to do so, in a dream that stayed clear in his mind after he woke up.

He dreamed three more times of weeping women who ran in terror into the darkness. This time, he did hear faint, muffled sounds of feet in the hallway outside his suite, and if he wasn't imagining it, feet on the floor below his. The silence seemed to grow a little thicker after each dream, as if the sense of the presence of other people in the house had decreased.

After each dream, the time Pendrake spent tutoring him increased. Gresibel and Tonia grew more quiet and pale after each dream of weeping women. Zair feared to ask them if they knew what was happening. Did they see or even speak with the women assigned as keepers to the other boys brought in to be considered as Shadows? Did they know what happened to those women when the boys failed? Zair woke from dreams where he heard Viza telling him, repeatedly, to pray for the safety of those boys, for mercy, for generosity and kindness that would send them home instead of punishing them for failing.

Just like he would want to be treated, if he failed.

Zair feared he would not fail, that he would be chosen as Shadow. He thought about what Magnus had said, the promises the enchanter made him. Why did he feel worse instead of better, every time he remembered?

~~~~~

After they had been in the house for three weeks, Pendrake came into the suite and stood by the door, instead of going to the study room. He said nothing, and his grave expression gave away nothing. Gresibel and Tonia seemed to understand. They put down what they had been doing, mending for Gresibel and reading for Tonia. Both women went a little pale. Gresibel gestured for Zair to stand. She tugged his collar and his jacket straight and finger-combed his hair off his forehead. Then she gestured for him to follow Pendrake, and she and Tonia followed Zair.

They went down the stairs to the second floor, and down a corridor, and came out into an open gallery that looked down on a grand hall full of tables and benches all facing a dais with a long table. Colorful banners full of symbols Zair partially recognized from his lessons covered the walls behind and on either side of the dais. Pendrake flicked his hand toward the banners.

"What does the arrangement of those crests tell you?" he asked, his voice pitched soft, as if this were a private conversation.

Zair stared at the banners. The noble crests and coats of arms and the symbols of minor off-shoot noble houses told a story. They gave a warning. They were like a map of major and minor highways, Pendrake had said just yesterday. They would help him figure out who to talk to and not talk to and how to talk to them, when he encountered nobles and their assistants and servants.

"Remember your lessons, lad," Pendrake continued. "Start from the middle and go outward, first to the right, then the left. Top to bottom."

The center banner was three times wider than all the others. It held the king's coat of arms, which combined the most important families in his lineage. Underneath that were emblems depicting important events and locations in Dorwain's history. On the banner itself, to the right and to the left of the coat of arms, were the crests of the noble houses most closely allied with the throne. Most often they were related by blood or won their place by great acts of loyalty and sacrifice. On top of the coat of arms was the flame-wrapped tree that stood for A'theosius, telling everyone that only the All-Maker stood higher in authority in Dorwain than the king. To remind the king who he was ultimately answerable to.

Slowly, concentrating so hard that his head ached, Zair read off the names of the noble houses and events and locations. The symbols on the right and left of the coat of arms were mirrored in the banners to the right and left of the king's banner. The noble houses and territories allied with those people were underneath their crests on their banners, and the most important and powerful ones had their own, smaller banners next to them, with their own list of allies. Zair stumbled a few times, when his brain seemed to snag on what felt like a contradiction illustrated in the symbols of the minor noble houses at the bottoms of the banners. Shouldn't those noble houses also be allied with the greater noble houses that their overlords were allied with? Or was it just assumed that if a third-ranked noble house owed allegiance to a second-ranked noble house that owed allegiance to a first-ranked noble house, then the third-ranked automatically obeyed the first-ranked? But then why was that third-ranked house listed in the banner of a first-ranked house on the other side of the king's banner, if they didn't appear on the first-ranked house's banner of their immediate overlord? Especially when there was room for that third-ranked house?

His head hurt long before his mouth went dry from the long recitation. Why did the prince have to know all this, so that his Shadow had to know all this? Was this something the prince had to recite every day? Were there exams he had to pass to be allowed to be crown prince, like justiciars and their clerks had to pass tests to keep their posts?

"Enough," a woman said, startling Zair so he took a step back and trod on Gresibel's foot.

He caught his breath and turned to the voice, and saw her, standing a quarter of the way around the gallery to the right. Zair wondered how long she had been there, surrounded by all those old, black-robed, bald, scowling men. He had thought the upper gallery was as empty of people as the hall below them, when he, Pendrake, Gresibel, and Tonia had arrived. The woman seemed to glow, wearing a simple robe of soft gray and a pale blue veil, and framed by all those black robes.

Zair tried not to stare, but he couldn't resist the urge to find those four magicians who had tested and bespelled him the other day. They all looked so much alike, he couldn't be sure if they were there or not.

Then Magnus stepped out of a knot of shadows into the light from a series of massive lanterns hanging from chains in the center of the gallery ceiling. He looked at Zair without any expression on his face, no recognition in his eyes. The boy wondered if perhaps he had dreamed that whole failed escape attempt.

"Well done, Pendrake, Gresibel, Tonia. I have only heard good things about your charge," the woman continued. She had just enough smile in one side of her mouth for Zair to see it. She held out her hand. "Come here, boy."

Pendrake moved aside and Gresibel gave him a nudge, so Zair stumbled a little as he moved away from the trio. They didn't follow him, so he stopped and looked back when he was five steps away. Pendrake nodded to him. The women stood very still, hands tucked inside the wide sleeves of their dresses. Their faces had that watchful sort of calm that put a shiver up his back.

He didn't have to think very long or hard to understand. This was the king's daughter, Princess Jillian.

"I'm sorry, ma'am—lady," Zair said as he turned the corner of the gallery to go down the side where she stood. "I don't know what to do." He tried bowing, like he had seen his father do when a noblewoman overseeing a team of justiciars passed through their village, on their way to the next territory.

He should have come to a complete stop before bowing, because he nearly toppled forward. Zair caught himself on the railing of the gallery and stumbled forward two more steps, then tried again.

"Charming," the princess said. Her smile touched both sides of her mouth now. "Closer, boy. Here, where the light is stronger." She stepped away from the men and beckoned for him to follow her into a strong beam of light. She stretched out a long-fingered, honey-toned hand and touched Zair's chin, tipping his head up, then gently moving it from side to side as she studied his face. "The eye color isn't right, but a simple spell should manage that without any fuss or repercussions. Magnus, which is more sensible? Go to the effort of changing the color permanently, or simply establishing and renewing an illusion spell?"

"Illusion, my lady," Magnus said. "We must consider how long the protective deception must take place, in terms of the expenditure of energy to change the boy's flesh at the deepest level. When the Shadow is no longer needed, it would be safer for all concerned if he quickly and effortlessly regained the features decreed by his birth and heritage, rather than having to undo all the magic that must be woven to change his very flesh. The boy was chosen specifically because of the weakness of the sleeping magic potential in his flesh. This offers an anchoring place for the spells necessary to carry off the deception, without any threat of complications or resistance. We must limit the magic performed on him, because carelessness increases the risk of awakening that magic without warning. Surely we are all familiar with far too many stories of magic awakened unwisely, and the repercussions of dealing with it unprepared?"

"No one likes a braggart," another man in the group muttered. "Must you constantly display your greater training?" Despite his sour tone, he winked at Magnus. He bowed to Princess Jillian. "In simple terms, Highness, wisdom says to use as little magic as possible, meaning reliance on illusion, for however long or short a time the boy is needed to ensure the safety of the prince."

"Yes, that is what I hoped you would say. It is always wise to tread softly when dealing with magic. Thank goodness for the enchanted forest that swallows up rogue magic. A'theosius is gracious in that regard." She sighed and turned to smile down at Zair again. "I fear, lad, that you will require a number of small spells to make your task easier. I recommend you learn as much about magic as you are able, simply in self-defense." Jillian raised her hand, gesturing for him to turn around.

Zair tried not to listen as she commented on the differences between him and her son. He flinched when she discussed how to hide those differences or make changes. He was too thin in some spots. That could be changed with feeding. Too wide in other spots. Should they make alterations in his wardrobe, or give him tasks to tighten those muscles, or employ an illusion spell? Zair was a year older than Prince Anwir. He stood several fingers shorter than the prince. They were both likely waiting for their next growth spurts. Hiding that difference in their heights would require new illusion spells and adjustments in their wardrobes in the future. Their caretakers would need to be constantly on the alert for the physical changes that would occur soon for them both, to keep them hidden.

A self-monitored and self-reinforcing illusion spell required too great of an outlay of magic at the beginning, and required regular feeding, making it an expensive and potentially risky tactic. Regular monitoring and adjusting of the spells wrapped around and between the boys, as well as changing out the charms they would need to wear on their persons required less energy and effort. Even more important, simpler magic spells were less prone to dissonance in the magical atmosphere that could reveal the illusion to watchful enemies. The more silent and undetectable the illusions, the more efficiently they would work. Simple was best.

The princess agreed with Magnus's advice and repeated it at each stage of the verbal assessment and discussion. The greater the physical differences between the two boys when the danger to her son had passed and the illusion spell was removed, the better for them both. The fourth time Princess Jillian made a comment like that, or one magician reminded another, Zair suddenly understood just what danger he was in. If seamstresses could be in danger if they understood they were making a duplicate wardrobe, then wouldn't he be in even more danger, just by being a duplicate of the prince?

They wouldn't dare let him run free, make a life for himself, once he was no longer needed as a Shadow. Someone would fear him switching places with the prince, either by accident or on purpose, either by his own choice or forced into it by someone else.

If he was the prince's twin, without the aid of illusion, then he would be marked for death.

The tallest of the men, with a sour expression and a pot belly his voluminous black robes couldn't hide, suggested an overarching molding and mirroring spell, to tie all the boys' physical and intellectual aspects together. When one grew, the other would be forced to grow as well. One benefit was when one boy excelled in something, the other would gain the same skills and education.

"There are too many flaws in that spell," Magnus said, after letting the sour old man go on in his crackling voice for several minutes. "The largest being that they are painfully, I emphasize *painfully*, difficult to reverse when the time comes."

Someone standing to the left of the crowd of black robes snickered. Magnus and Jillian both turned with stern expressions, while someone on the right muttered, asking why it mattered if a nameless brat taken off the street suffered. It was his duty to suffer for his prince, after all.

"Just as important and troublesome," Magnus continued, iron in his voice, "there is no control. Prince Anwir, being bound to the Shadow, will suffer just as much when the forced physical mirroring is reversed. There is no guarantee that any defensive spells will protect either boy. Are you willing to pay that price?" He waited, and several sets of feet shuffled backward in the group, hiding from his displeasure. He tugged his robes straight and continued.

"Such spells are notorious for flipping back and forth, with no ability to predict or halt the change. The prince could end up looking like his Shadow, or both boys could become twins, permanently, neither one wearing his own face, but a mixture of both. Need I mention the trouble that could arise if powerful enemies convince the council of lords that the prince's heritage is questionable because he does not look enough like his grandfather to satisfy the doubters? This could give too many weapons into the hands of those who would tear the throne from King Joben's hands in response to the prophecies of a true bloodline coming back to power.

"Besides ..." He sighed and shook his head, looking Zair over head to foot. "The greatest danger of the mirror spell is not the lack of control over who is the model and who is the clay, but the curse of a mirror. What happens to one body happens to the other. If one boy is injured, so is the other. If one boy is poisoned, so is the other. If one boy is kidnapped and tortured, so is the other."

"The Shadow will be guarded just as diligently as the prince," the shortest man among the group snapped. "He will be trained by the Red Brigade and protected by them."

"I am still opposed to employing a Shadow at all. Even an illusion spell can be dangerous, no matter how temporary it is originally woven to be. What happens if the boys cannot be told one from the other, either in features or voice or actions or mind? Better for the heir to the throne to live in hiding for several years, until the rebels are weeded out and destroyed, than to risk creating a duplicate and all the inherent risks." Another man stepped out of the shadows at the back of the group and stepped forward, closer to Magnus. Zair hated how they all looked alike, except for Magnus. "There are far too many fables about princes who were betrayed and forced into servitude while servants became kings in their place. Teach him his lessons too well, and he could take the prince's place, and none of us would know the difference."

"Have you been introduced to Prince Anwir?" Magnus said. "I cannot see him allowing such an exchange to occur. Not without loud protests that could be heard in the capitol."

That earned soft chuckles from Princess Jillian.

"How can you look at this young lad," she said, "and predict what choices he will make, or what dire fate will fall on him? Is it not written multiple times in A'theosius' books that we are responsible for every choice we make, and we earn our eternal rewards a thousand times over before we stand at the judgment throne? Can you look into his boy's mind and heart and predict that he will be a traitor rather than loyal and honorable? Why can he not be a friend to my son, perhaps the only true friend he will ever have? That is a choice that lies in our hands. It is not a fate written out centuries before any of us were born."

"What is your name, boy?" Magnus said.

"What does it matter?" the first, sour-voiced man said. "For the sake and safety of the throne, he should be entirely unknown, and invisible whenever possible. No ties to anyone. No loyalties to any but the throne. Nothing that anyone can use against him, to make him a weapon against the throne. He is a Shadow, like all the royal Shadows before him. Your name is Shadow, boy, and shall always be, down through history."

"His name is Zair," Pendrake said. He startled Zair by stepping up behind him and resting a hand on his shoulder. "He belongs to me, and I pledge my life and honor to his success."

Chapter Six

A brief, hollow echo rang from Pendrake's words, as if suddenly they were standing in a cavernous hall, twenty times larger than the room below them. Zair caught his breath. Nobody else reacted to what he thought he felt and heard, though a few of the old men sniffed or sneered at the scholar's vow.

Jillian took a deep breath and nodded. "Let us see if the boys suit, shall we?" She turned with a swirl of her skirts and flicked her hand out. The old men behind her parted quickly. Zair thought he saw something like fear in their eyes. He couldn't understand that, because he thought the princess quite nice. Far nicer than he expected a royal lady to act. Enough important people had come through his village and stayed as guests in his father's house, Zair had decided that the more wealthy and powerful someone was, the colder and more demanding they were, and the fewer times they thanked those who served them.

Besides, they were all magicians, even if they were bad magicians. At least, that was the impression he got from Magnus's words on the night he failed to run away. Weren't magicians more powerful than even a princess?

Zair looked up at Pendrake, who nodded, gripped his shoulder a little tighter, then gave him a nudge to follow. The black-robed men parted to let them follow the princess. Magnus stepped up to walk on Zair's other side. The other men hurried to follow, grumbling and mumbling and whispering among themselves. They reminded Zair of his brothers when they had been caught in some nastiness. He suspected those old men were planning how to punish him for whatever mistakes they had just made.

Where were Gresibel and Tonia? Weren't they coming along?

What did the princess mean, by seeing if they suited? Was this the final test before the other boys who failed were sent away?

Why did that man insist his name was Shadow now? Why was it so important that Pendrake insisted on his name? What had just happened when Pendrake claimed Zair belonged to him? What was that odd hollowness and the echo, and the sense of everything being enormous? Or was that the feeling of suddenly being tiny, small enough to vanish?

"You're going to be an interesting subject," Magnus murmured. He winked at Zair when the boy looked up at him. "You felt that bit of portent, didn't you?"

"What matters is if the others felt it," Pendrake said, just as quietly.

"You did that on purpose. Hoping to scare the ragged old crows?"

"Warn them. I haven't grown so high and mighty that I can toss away others' lives like so much potato peelings." He snorted. "And I hope you haven't either, friend. We're going to need you to keep both boys' skins whole for the next twenty years."

"Oh, you think this will last that long?" The corner of Magnus's mouth twitched upward as he looked down at Zair again. "You're scaring the boy."

"Good. It'll keep his head on his shoulders and his feet on solid ground."

"What did I feel, back there?" Zair whispered. There were so many other questions he wanted to ask, but this was the only one that felt safe. For now.

"Magic, of course," Magnus said. "Unlike the other day, the old crows had to have felt that. Let's hope they're congratulating themselves on successfully embedding a spell in you, rather than the truth."

"Safer for all of us," Pendrake said, nodding.

"And here we are." Magnus gestured with an upward jerk of his chin.

Zair looked ahead. A wide double door swung open before the princess. They stepped into a room considerably warmer than the hall and gallery. A wide pile of coals burned in a metal fire basin in the middle of the floor, far wider than Zair thought he could jump, even with a long running start. The room was certainly long enough to give him that running start. Four doors opened off the room on either side of the long walls. A glass door at the opposite end of the room showed glimpses of stormy sky and the forest that surrounded the manor house on three sides.

Tapestries with more coats of arms and crests and that headache-inducing code illustrating alliances covered the walls. Furs spread across the floor, with clusters of furniture arranged on them. Several clusters had long tables surrounded by shelves full of books and scrolls and tablets. Others were just cushioned chairs around low tables. Several had long couches covered with pillows.

A boy rose from a couch nearest to the firepit. He scowled as he tossed a scroll down on the couch and hunched his shoulders as he responded to the hand Jillian held out to him. Pendrake and Magnus stopped, and Zair stayed with them. He watched the boy, knowing what he was going to see before they were close enough to make out details.

Zair had seen his own face in the washbasin or a stream often enough to see the similarities between him and the prince. It frightened him a little to understand now what Gresibel meant, that very little magic would be needed to deal with the slight differences between the boys. Zair's hair had bluish highlights among the ebony, while Anwir's hair had reddish tones and looser curl. Zair's dark skin was softened by golden tones, while the prince's tended toward a dull black. His chin was squared, compared to the dull point of the prince's. Zair couldn't tell the differences in their height, but he thought his shoulders were wider, certainly straighter. His father constantly scolded all the boys to stand up straight and pull their shoulders back, stop slouching, and hold their heads up. Zair wondered if anyone scolded the prince about his posture.

Anwir's eyes went wide and he nearly stumbled as he stopped short. Yes, he saw the resemblance between them in that instant, too. He took the last few steps to his mother's side and twined his fingers with hers.

"What do you think, my son?" she murmured.

The prince tipped his head slightly to the right and pursed his lips as he studied Zair, who tried to stand still, knees slightly bent, balanced on the balls of his feet, as Gresibel had been teaching him to stand. A posture that left him ready to leap aside, and flee, if necessary. Magnus's and Pendrake's hands rested a little heavier on Zair's shoulders. To keep him from fleeing?

A grin twisted up the left side of the prince's mouth, then the right side.

"I think we're going to have fun. How much magic did you use on him, Lord Magnus?" He stepped away from his mother, closer to Zair, and looked him over.

"None at all," Magnus said. "This is his own face. Spells will be required to maintain and adjust the illusion as you boys grow up, much the same way a vine is trained to climb over a trellis. However, the fewer spells there are, the harder it will be for enemies to detect the deception. This is a gift from A'theosius, and I would advise you to guard it carefully."

"Zair is to be your companion and trusted friend," Princess Jillian said.

Zair noticed her gaze rested on the black-robed magicians gathered around them, rather than on her son as she spoke.

"Not a toy," she continued. "He is here to guard your life and ensure you grow up to take over your grandfather's throne. A wise man treats his armor and shield well."

"But in the end, a shield can be sacrificed and destroyed and replaced, because a man's life is worth more than his shield," a rusty voice whispered behind Zair. A sour whiff of bad breath came with the voice.

"I'm only allowed wooden swords right now," Anwir said. "Can you fight?" He gestured with a jerk of his head and turned to head back to the couch where he had been reading.

Zair glanced at Pendrake, who nodded and released his shoulder. He followed the prince.

"When I get a chance, Highness. Usually my brothers ambush me and hold me down, so I don't have a chance at a fair fight."

"Then let's learn fighting and go give them a taste of what it's like." Anwir laughed. He dropped down onto the couch.

His laughter had a scratchy hint of shrillness, just like his voice seemed to be a note or two higher than Zair's. Another illusion spell would change how people heard Zair's voice. At least, he hoped it would just be an illusion, and his voice wouldn't be permanently changed to sound like Anwir's. The thought of it made his throat ache, so he wanted to wrap his hand around it.

Zair settled on the gray fur that covered the floor around the couch. The ripples of heat coming from the fire pit felt good on his back.

"Where are you from?"

"He is from nowhere, Highness," the tallest of the magicians called, and pushed his way through the others, who were muttering. Zair turned enough to see them, and they all seemed to be glaring at him, as if he had done something wrong. What? Wasn't he allowed to sit down? He wasn't sitting on the couch with the prince. He knew enough not to do that.

"Everybody is from somewhere," Anwir said, scowling.

"Your pardon, Highness," another magician said.

From his voice and the fewer wrinkles on his face, Zair guessed he was the youngest of them. Why did they all have to shave their heads and wear black? Did they paint their faces gray to make themselves look alike?

"What he means is that the boy is now your Shadow," the magician continued. "He has no past, he belongs only to you. Your life is his focus and purpose. To ask about his previous life is ... a waste of time."

Zair thought for a moment the man would say that asking would be unkind.

"To put it another way that is perhaps easier to understand," Magnus said, and put several steps between himself and the knot of magicians, "your Shadow is part of you, now. He is your duplicate. You share everything from now on, your lessons, your —"

"Ridiculous," the magician with bad breath snapped. "The prince shares nothing."

"I beg to differ," Princess Jillian said, her voice icy. Zair almost cheered to see all the black-robed men seem to cringe and back up a step and go even paler. "My father the king will be the first to tell you that the king gives everything that he is to safeguard the welfare of the entire kingdom. Just as A'theosius gives all that he is to this world, to heal it from the damage of Ba'dur's rebellion. In that sense, my son must share all that he is. The throne requires a heavy price from those who fill it. He is no longer the son of a powerful merchant, with homes and allies in a dozen kingdoms. His vision must extend farther, and he must give even more of himself to his future duties. He must start with sharing his life with one person and learn the gift of loyalty and sacrifice. That will make him a great king someday."

Zair caught bits of expressions, curled lips and eye rolls, heard mutters, enough to guess that despite their very evident fear of the princess, these magicians disagreed with her words. A tiny shift of his head let him see Anwir, how the boy cringed and closed his eyes, clearly embarrassed and uncomfortable. He even heard the prince mutter, "Please, Mother ..."

"In the spirit of sharing, Highness," the youngest magician said. He pulled his shoulders straight. "I propose that it would be wise to weave together the next layer of the spell binding the boys right now."

"Next layer?" Magnus said. His voice was soft but sent a chill up Zair's back. "Has a binding spell already been initiated?"

"The sooner the boys are fully woven into the mirroring spell," another man in the back of the group began.

"When will you fools give up this ridiculous obsession with mirroring?"

"We have searched the archives extensively. A mirroring spell is clearly the most reliable means of preventing the common people, and many of the lower ranks of nobles, from ever guessing that the heir to the throne is not out in public, vulnerable to assassins' knives and arrows and spells to kill him or take over his mind." The youngest magician gave a shallow bow and spread his arms, hands up, as if presenting an irrefutable conclusion to everyone in the room. "Time is precious and far too much of it has been wasted already in the search for the most appropriate Shadow. Need I remind you that if you had followed our initial advice, the Shadow would already be nearly a mirror image of the prince?"

"With all the flaws inherent in a multi-layered blanket of spells translated from ancient manuscripts so riddled with vermin that droppings are mistaken for letters, changing great sections of the spell to perform at skewed angles to the intent," Magnus said. "And no guarantee, much less a strong hope, that the prince's mannerisms and reactions and gait and voice would be imprinted on the Shadow, rather than the reverse. Dare you take that risk, and cast doubt on the validity of the prince's claim to the throne? The fact that his father is not a citizen of Dorwain already has two-thirds of the nobles muttering and searching through five centuries of records and legal documents to determine if there is someone with a stronger, more legitimate claim."

"Mother?" Anwir stood and took two steps toward the princess. "They can't do that, can they?"

"No, and your grandfather has said multiple times, and put it in writing, that my choices and my commands rule in everything necessary to prepare you to be the next king." She turned to the knot of magicians. "I think it best if you retire to your workroom and prepare more thoroughly for the next dose of this magic you feel necessary. And ensure that you abide by Lord Magnus's guidance in these matters. No mirror spell workings until you can guarantee that royal blood holds dominance in the bonding, in mind and heart and spirit, as well as flesh. Is that clear?"

Behind him, Zair sensed his keepers all stood a little straighter, felt a single note hum through the room like a high harp string had been plucked. It resonated in his chest like the declaration earlier had echoed through the gallery. There was portent in Princess Jillian's words, and something deep inside him drew back from trying to understand.

"Your word rules, Highness," the magician said, bowing deeply. "Please do not think me impertinent, when I remind you that His Majesty requires our presence in Dorwain in a month's time. The more tightly bound together the boys are, the safer the prince will be when he crosses the border into his new home and kingdom."

"I am more aware than you could ever guess," Jillian said. She waved her hand at the door. "You may go now."

Several hesitated, several more glared at her. Zair watched as the princess turned her head, meeting the gaze of each man in turn. And each in turn flushed or turned quickly and hurried out of the room.

Finally, only the two boys, Jillian, Magnus, Pendrake, Gresibel and Tonia remained. Magnus snapped his fingers.

Zair flinched, seeing a spark shoot out from the man's fingers and hit the door. It glowed a sparkly shade of dark green and clung to the latch until the door swung closed. Then it spread across the door before vanishing, melting into the wood.

Oh, very good, Viza whispered at the back of his mind. *You have inborn magic, and it has been awakened. You will need it.*

Are you back?

Careful, dear boy. You mind-speak very loudly. You can't afford to be overheard so early in your lessons. We don't know who can be trusted. But know I am always here, and I am pledged to be your friend. Here in the soul realm, we are unable to lie. I will return in your dreams, when I am sure no one is listening.

The rest of the day sped by and Zair's head felt jammed full of rules and routines and instructions, and what would control his life for many years to come. The boys would share a bedroom for the time being, until the magicians had woven together the initial spells of the illusion, binding them together. Proximity promoted the settling in of the binding spells. Besides, it was easier on both boys if they slept through the process. Moving around and thinking and talking would interfere with the weaving. They might unconsciously resist and warp the multiple layers of illusion, and fear or anger or irritation would interfere as well.

The initial illusion spell needed to be woven now, while the boys looked so much alike. It would be simple, changing the color of Zair's eyes, skin tone, adjusting the texture of his hair. As the boys grew and went into growth spurts and their bodies changed in maturity, the illusion spell would grow more complex and require stronger ties. The most important layers of the spell needed to be woven and anchored in the boys while they were staying here in the manor house. The royal apartments would be their school room, as Anwir learned to be the crown prince and his Shadow learned to be his duplicate.

Zair was relieved when the long discussion ended. His head came close to spinning with questions he was afraid to ask, and all the things he needed to remember. Anwir and Jillian had to change their clothes and attend a formal dinner with some nobles who had come to the manor house. Anwir remarked there was always someone new showing up, someone trying to gain favor or hint at threats to him and his mother, to try to gain power in the kingdom. He said he wished the mirror spell was complete, so Zair could sit through the dinner in his place.

"Highness," Magnus began, sounding both tired and frustrated.

"I was joking!" Anwir bared his teeth in what certainly looked to Zair like an angry grin and stomped through a door at the other end of the long room.

"A king needs a sense of humor, but ..." Pendrake ended on a sigh.

"We have time, my old friend," Jillian said. She nodded to all of them and swept out of the room through the door next to the one Anwir had taken.

Magnus left then, too, leaving Zair alone with his keepers. Pendrake gave him a stack of books to read, and a list of historic figures to make note of, for discussion in the morning. The four of them had a quiet dinner, then Zair settled down with his reading, and all his questions spinning through his head.

The things the magicians had said hit him like sacks filled with mud that had been falling for a long time and finally found their target. Zair couldn't forget what Magnus had said about not having control over which boy would be copied onto the other. What if the prince got badly hurt? Would Zair be injured as well? Not just feeling the pain, but suffering the same injuring in his flesh? What if Anwir got sick? Would Zair get sick? If he didn't catch a cold or the plague, would he keep Anwir healthy?

Did magic hurt, when enough layers of spells wrapped around him?

Trying to escape the spinning in his head, Zair searched for something new to focus on. He wondered about Ambrecht, the kingdom where Anwir had been born. What had it been like, growing up in a merchant household, traveling with his father, seeing the rest of the continent, maybe traveling by ship to other lands? Did Anwir miss his father? Was his father pleased that Anwir had become crown prince, and would someday rule Dorwain, instead of following in his footsteps and becoming a merchant lord? When he asked Pendrake for information on the kingdom and Phoebus the merchant, his tutor looked pleased.

"Yes, that is a topic we need to discuss soon. You will need to know Ambrecht and the merchant ways as thoroughly as Anwir himself, if someone asks you about his childhood. One of the most important spells to be woven between you will give you access to his memories and the feelings wrapped through them. You won't have to stop and think and find words, you'll just react, as if you had lived there and done those things yourself. However, such a spell takes a long time and much expenditure of energy to weave. It requires spending a great deal of time in each other's company, and a deep level of trust on both sides. That is why the princess emphasized that you were to be his friend. Respect on both sides is vital, but we would all prefer if you two boys liked each other. Until that bond is solid between you, and you can draw on the prince's memories and feelings freely, you had best avoid any situations where you must be him."

"This is dangerous, isn't it?" Zair asked. "More dangerous than people shooting at me because they think they're shooting at him."

"Of course it is," Gresibel said, and punctuated her words with a snort. "You have to be two people, hold two lifetimes in your head, and walk a narrow ledge that could break under you at any moment. It isn't easy, living in the shadows, my lad, forgotten and yet always on the alert, ready to step into the light. Your only friend may be the very man you will live to protect."

Chapter Seven

Zair didn't expect to be given a bed as nice as Anwir's, but when the magicians' focal caster, Darngrell, led the boys into the prince's bedroom that night to cast the first spell, all he saw was a pile of three blankets on the floor at the foot of Anwir's bed. It was a tall bed, piled high with feather mattresses on top of a rope frame, with thick quilts and four pillows. Zair knew better than to look at the magician, but he still caught a glimpse of Darngrell smirking at him. Just like all four of his brothers would do, if they could pull a trick on him like that.

Nothing could persuade him to give his brothers, and now this nasty bully of a magician, the satisfaction of hurting him.

He thought for a moment of pretending that he didn't understand and asking if he was going to share the bed with Anwir. It was certainly big enough for them to share, neither one touching the other. Zair decided not to do that. He didn't like the prince, although he didn't dislike Anwir, either. The other boy had whined, over and over, about things he didn't like as Jillian, Magnus, and Pendrake had explained to the boys the structure of their lives from now on.

Zair picked up the pile of blankets and put them to one side, then unfolded the first to make his bed on the floor. At least the floor was covered with furs on top of reed mats, and not bare stone or wood.

"What's this?" Magnus braced his hands on the frame of the door and leaned into the room. His eyes narrowed and his mouth flattened as he looked at the bed Zair had made on the floor, with one blanket as a pillow. "Not one word from you," he snapped, pointing at Darngrell. A silver spark danced on the tip of that finger. It hung in the doorway when the enchanter turned with a snapping swirl of his robes and left.

Zair sat down on the floor on his blankets and put his back against the foot of Anwir's bed. That way he didn't have to look at either magician or prince. Silence reigned from the other side of the room. He wondered what Anwir was thinking. Zair felt sure the magician was angry. Nobody moved, nobody spoke, though there was some clearly heavy breathing for several minutes.

Then Magnus came back in, followed by several servants carrying a narrow frame for a bed, piles of blankets, a mattress, and pillows.

"Consider, Highness, how well a sword will *not* serve you if you don't keep it properly cleaned and oiled, and sheathed when not in use. If you drop your sword on the steps or leave it lying in dust and dirt and mud, how well do you think it will keep its edge? I can hear your thoughts, magician, which shows how little true discipline you possess," Magnus snapped, turning swiftly on his heel to scowl at the other side of the room.

Zair couldn't see Darngrell's face, but the cold fury in Magnus's expression told him the magician had likely been sneering, silently mocking what the enchanter said. He wondered if the magician would order him not to sleep in that bed, once Magnus left.

He's thinking that dogs that are allowed to sleep in their betters' beds become spoiled and useless, Viza said.

Magnus stopped and frowned down at Zair. The boy had the awful feeling he had heard the mirror speak to him. The enchanter shook his head and turned back to the magician.

"I warn you again, work no spell-weaving on the boys tonight. It's too soon since you worked the last spell on the Shadow boy."

"The only spell we worked was to test him. Nothing lasting." Darngrell's voice sounded sulky. Like one of the bullies in the village when he was caught and couldn't get his friends to lie and put blame on someone else.

"Then why were the words 'the next layer' used earlier today?" Magnus's voice sounded almost too pleasant. Zair shivered, expecting a whiplash of words or perhaps even magic slashed through the room.

"A mistake. Ephratus mis-spoke."

"Ah. I see. But you will be careful when you weave tonight, won't you? It wouldn't please the king if his grandson was injured, even if only lightly. And hopefully temporarily."

"The spell merely takes guidance from the prince. All the work will be done on the Shadow." Darngrell's voice sounded tight under the pleasant tone.

"Good. I trust you don't need me to supervise?" Magnus turned back to Zair, gave him a cool smile and a nod, and swept out of the room before the magician could respond.

"Supervise," Darngrell snarled.

"What spell are you working?" Anwir asked.

"A simple spell. To change the boy's eye color to match yours." Darngrell stepped to the foot of the bed and looked down at Zair. His lip curled back and he inhaled and exhaled several times, as if he couldn't decide what to say. "Since the bed is here, you might as well get in it. That pompous brute likely has charms on it to spy and make sure you do so."

Anwir laughed. Zair got up and kept his back to both of them as he bent and untied his boots. He lined them up neatly under the bed, pulled off his jacket and vest and stockings, and folded them neatly, to hang over the end of the bed frame. Then he pulled back the blankets and sheet and slipped into the bed.

"Are you finally done?" Darngrell snapped.

Anwir crossed his eyes and stuck his tongue out at the magician's back, then smoothed out his expression when Darngrell turned back to him.

Zair watched the magician take a small book from a pocket inside his robe. More of that glittery, silvery dust floated off the pages when he opened it and began chanting in another language that sounded harsh, full of rasps and hisses and clicks.

Cheaters, Viza whispered. *Idiots, cobbling together magic from a dozen different eras and disciplines. Savages. Self-righteous brutes and bigots. They deny the existence of A'theosius, and then in the next breath declare that the only souls the All-Maker granted were to Humans. Meaning mirrors and rings and talking beasts are abominations, only good to be drained of their magic to fuel the idiotic schemes of the likes of him. His master even laughed at me as they ground me to dust to use in their spells and declared that since I was not a thinking creature with a soul, I could not even claim my own body as mine. May A'theosius choke them with their arrogance and may their schemes be their undoing!*

That dust is from you too? Zair held his breath as Darngrell turned to him, and the next moment blew on the pages, making the mirror dust shoot out into the air and swirl down, to fall on him.

Oh, for mercy's sake, don't let any more be lost. Let it in, dear boy. Save what little of me is left, please, the mirror begged.

Zair hesitated, then he exhaled quickly and turned his head so the dust fell on his face, as he inhaled deeply. The dust got into his eyes. This time, he felt it. He gasped as fire dug roots into his eyes, through his head and out the back. He reached up to rub his eyes, but the magician's cold, bony hands clamped down hard on his wrists.

"No rubbing. We don't want you to end up blind, do we? And waste all the hard work we did to make sure you were the best one?"

Fiery stinging that felt like ropes wrapped around Zair's wrists, replacing the magician's hands. They pulled his arms down to his sides, fastening them to the bed. His vision blurring, his eyes filling with muddy, sparkling tears, he couldn't see anything holding his arms down. More magic. Zair hated magic. Anwir said something, but Zair couldn't make out the words.

"No, of course not," Darngrell said, his voice a sneer barely loud enough to penetrate the deafening roar of Zair's racing heart. "He's just being a ninny. The sensation isn't pleasant, but it does not hurt. It will go away in a few moments and then he'll sleep and he won't disturb you for the rest of the night. You won't even know he's here."

He should have put you to sleep first, Viza said. *He's disobeying. This is a spell to remake your flesh, not establish an anchor for the illusion. Nasty brute wants you to suffer. If there were enough of me remaining, I could fight it. But I can't. I'm truly sorry. Let us hope if they continue to use my remaining dust on you, enough of me will gather together to give me the strength to protect you. Then we'll show these self-made idiots what real magic is!*

"Who said that?" Darngrell stomped away.

Go to sleep, dear boy. It will be better in the morning. No matter how ham-handed this idiot and his half-baked magic may be.

Darkness spun up and surrounded Zair. Whether it was a gift from Viza or grudgingly slapped on him by Darngrell, he didn't much care. The burning and itching went away.

In the morning, however, Zair's eyes were sticky and swollen, glued shut with a mixture of blood and gritty green seepage. Tonia came in to wake him, and when she saw the condition of his eyes, fury had her stomping away. She came back with a basin of cold water, heavy with healing herbs, and made Zair lie still while she washed his face, then soaked another cloth to rest on his eyes. When she asked what had happened to him, Anwir told her.

"He cried a few times, but he never woke up," he added. The bed creaked and blankets rustled, and Zair guessed the prince had come to the end of his bed. "Darngrell was wrong, wasn't he?" He snickered. "Magnus is going to chew him up and spit him out."

Neither boy heard what passed between the enchanter and the magician, but Zair caught nasty looks aimed at him over the course of the next few days whenever the magicians came into the royal family's suite. Just like in the village, when bullies were caught tormenting smaller, weaker children, they blamed their victims. They didn't have the courage to be angry at the ones who punished them.

By noon that day, the swelling and seeping had halted, though his eyes still felt too large for their sockets. The itchy aching changed from constant to an irregular pulse that made Zair feel sick to his stomach. He didn't feel any better when Magnus took a few moments to speak privately with him.

"I suppose this is little comfort, but I had a good idea this would happen. They lied when they said they didn't work any magic on you. And they are lying to themselves, when they believe they have control of the mangled, badly cobbled together multiple spells they intend to inflict on you. And on the prince. The simple explanation is that this magic is so touchy, so unbalanced, each layer of spell work needs to settle, to sink into your flesh. Add another layer too soon, it reacts badly to the previously applied layer, stirring it up, throwing your body's functions out of balance.

"The only way to stop those fools from continuing their ill-advised course is to point out how wrong they are and give them a good fright.

They're in such a hurry to complete the binding between you boys, they don't want to listen to anyone. And despite being forced to agree that illusion is better for everyone concerned, maybe because they were forced to agree, they're going to try to slip a flesh-altering spell into every layer of the binding.

"It doesn't help that the king trusts them. Since he doesn't know me, he has no reason to listen, no matter what our lady says. They're so insecure in their mastery of their half-baked magic, they need to prove me wrong at every turn. And you suffer for it. Well, be encouraged that they will slow down. Her Highness shredded them as only a mother can. Never a foul or vulgar word escaped her lips, and not once did her tone turn loud or shrill. She is indeed the hope for Dorwain's future, the heart and soul and source of justice behind the throne."

Magnus chuckled and patted Zair's hand. "I don't doubt that there will be more tussles between us in the future, with you as the battleground. Never you fear, lad. Whatever you suffer, it will not be as bad as it could have been, without my protection. Yet I must apologize now, because I will need to let you suffer, just to keep reinforcing the lesson for them."

Zair thought about that after Magnus got up and left the sitting room. So, what was the enchanter really saying? That he was going to let Zair suffer, let the magicians keep making mistakes, just to prove them wrong and prove he was right?

The ache in his head grew stronger, and a hot, spiky, churning feeling twisted through his gut. Zair's eyes burned. He suspected he was trying to cry, but the aftereffects of the mishandled spell made that impossible. The worst part was the growing certainty that he had nearly made a foolish, perhaps dangerous mistake by trusting Magnus. The man sounded like he would be a friend, but clearly he didn't really care about Zair. As he had said, the boy was the battleground where he fought with the magicians for dominance.

The worst thing Zair could do was trust Magnus with anything. He wondered if he could trust anyone. Would Gresibel and Tonia and Pendrake help him, if he tried to escape? Zair's head hurt more, and his stomach twisted more, when he considered all the cryptic things they had said, the comments he had overheard. They didn't like what they were doing, but they had paid Ward and Gabe to take him from his family. They had probably known all along that he would be smothered in magic until his face and body and everything else about him wasn't his own.

Could he trust anybody?

I suppose it would be only fair if you didn't trust me, either, Viza said, after he had pondered that question for what felt like hours. He was too tired, ached too much, to even get up and find the basin of herb water to bathe his eyes again. *I will earn your trust, and I promise you, we will find a way to escape. I am too damaged to call out to the mirror web and ask for help. Healing, finding echoes of the web nearby, will take a great deal of time and energy I just don't have right now. I will have to sleep and leave you alone for long periods, to build up my strength. But someday, dear boy, we will escape. Just ... be patient. Yes?*

After a long wait, thinking until his head hurt, Zair whispered, "Yes."

~~~~~

On the mornings when the boys hadn't undergone another overnight spell-weaving, they awoke with the dawn and went down to the river with six soldiers to guard them. They swam and then raced up and down a meadow while there was no one out and about to see them, until their lungs burned and their muscles ached. Then they swam again, returned to the manor house to dress and have breakfast, and join Princess Jillian for morning worship. The boys spent the remainder of the morning in lessons with Pendrake. After the noon meal, Zair had more lessons with Pendrake, while Anwir dealt with ministers and secretaries sent from the king or had fittings for his court clothes.

Midway through the afternoon, the boys came back together for lessons on statecraft and all the knowledge and rituals and tasks required of a crown prince. Then after Anwir had a formal dinner with more nobles or visiting officials, the boys had riding or archery or swordcraft lessons, letting the evening shadows hide Zair's features and presence.

The schedule would change once they left the manor house and Anwir and Jillian made their formal entrance to the capitol and the palace. Zair would continue living in the royal family's quarters until the spell-weaving had finished. Then, when he wasn't studying with the prince, and studying the prince, to mimic how he walked and talked, Zair would live in the Red Brigade's quarters, learning not just how to be a royal guard, but the fine art of being an assassin. As Pendrake put it, the best way to learn how to stop an attacker was to learn how the attacker thought, how he looked at the target, how he moved and reacted.

Despite the insistence of the magicians that they were running out of time, Princess Jillian slowed the schedule for adding new spells into the weaving of the bond between Anwir and Zair. Instead of every third night, Darngrell came to the prince's bedroom every fourth night. Magnus put them both to sleep, and woke them every morning, to examine them and ensure nothing went wrong with the spell.

The magicians didn't like that, but their bitter complaints halted abruptly with the next spell they worked on the boys. This one tried to change the shape of Zair's chin and make his shoulders narrower. Anwir woke shrieking in pain halfway through the night. His face had elongated, his chin had sharpened, and his right shoulder was a hand's width wider
~~~~~

than the left. The change wasn't an illusion but had affected his bones. Even worse, the spell affected just his bones, not his flesh, which stretched all out of proportion.

Yet again, the magicians had worked the unreliable mirroring magic, and added layers of spell that affected the flesh, rather than building a foundation for illusion. Princess Jillian was furious. So furious, she didn't scold Anwir when he demanded that Darngrell and all the magicians who wanted to do the mirror spell be dismissed and punished.

The magicians fought among themselves, trying to narrow the blame down to only one of them. Tonia later told Zair that the two oldest magicians had left. None of the servants could agree if they had been sent away by their leaders, or they had fled in fear.

It's partly my fault, Viza said, when Zair finally had some time by himself that afternoon. *I am a mirror, after all, and they are using the remnants of my own dust to inflict this badly woven magic on you boys. When I tried to deflect the nastier elements of it, I inadvertently reflected it, turning it backward, so the change happened to the prince. Once they calm down and try to backtrack what they did, they might have the wit and insight to at least theorize what I did. Not that those bumblers could ever prove it.*

Forgive me, dear boy. I have only made things worse. I fear, to prevent them discovering my presence, I must not only retreat behind a wall of silence for long periods of time, but quiet the magic potential that is awakening in you. If they feel that magic blooming, they could suspect your royal blood, and that will be disaster for you.

Can you do that? Zair asked after only a few moments of thought. Silence for hopefully a short time would be better than losing Viza altogether. Wouldn't it?

He had a sudden, chilling mental image of the magicians figuring out how to remove the mirror dust from his flesh and blood and leaving him entirely alone. They would probably inflict as much pain on him as they could, in the process.

I can only try.

Viza succeeded, far enough that she was unable to tell Zair what the magicians did the next time they wove their magic. No one suspected her presence. However, Zair found that he had grown sensitive enough to feel the lack of her presence. It felt as if he stood inside a globe of thick, dirty glass, muffling all sounds, and even smells and tastes. Each time Viza felt safe enough to emerge from behind the multiple walls she built inside him, the pressure and dullness evaporated. All his senses sharpened. He felt energized, to the point he thought he could leap out a window and fly. He understood the lessons he and Anwir shared more quickly than the prince, and read twice as fast, and remembered everything he read. The doubled energy extended to the other lessons that Pendrake did not oversee. Riding, archery, swordplay, and what Gresibel and Tonia called the "courtly mannerisms."

Guided by Viza, when she could speak with him, Zair investigated the hundreds of books in the suite. Along with learning about other kingdoms and continents, the history of the world, legends and lore, he learned enough about how magic worked in the rest of the world to tantalize him. He even discovered a dozen volumes that made some threadbare sense of the magic used in Dorwain. Those helped him understand a little better the principles behind the spells the magicians had devised to make him Anwir's Shadow.

Every spell needed time to sink into his physical body and the magic support structure that the magicians believed they needed to create within him. They grumbled nearly every time they came to weave another layer of spell between the boys, because whoever assessed Zair had exaggerated his potential for innate magic, to serve as a foundation and anchor for their spells.

That just proved how adept Viza was in hiding her presence and his inherent, awakening magic. Her defensive measures tricked the magicians into slowing down their work and forced them to move with more caution. Whenever they were too heavy-handed, Viza deflected and rejected the next layer of spellwork. Sometimes, she managed to generate a bad reaction in Prince Anwir, which slowed the magicians even more. Sometimes when they unwove the newest spell, that caused damaged in the previous layer, which then had to be undone as well.

She couldn't do that too often, because reaching out to the dust that had embedded in the prince's flesh resulted in strengthening the bond between the boys, in ways she couldn't predict. She didn't want to find out too late that the bond couldn't be broken, resulting in the boys being tied together for the rest of their lives, mirror images of each other, the illusions unbreakable.

Chapter Eight

Viza managed to achieve division among the magicians with her interference. What worked the first time they tried a particular sequence of spell-weaving didn't work a second or third time. Or had different results each time. They argued over how quickly, how thickly, to weave the spells around and between the boys. A nasty reaction in Zair might be echoed in Anwir, and could result in rejecting the next spell, or unweaving the previous layer, or even cause a rejection of all future spell layers. The slightest variation could generate a cascade effect, causing an unpredictable number of spells to warp and veer away from their intended purposes in unpredictable directions and intensity.

What worried the mirror, though, when she had the energy to explain to the boy what she was doing, was that some of the negative reactions weren't of her doing. The magicians weren't half as skilled or knowledgeable as they proclaimed themselves to be. Their spells and potions relied on theories that were often more guesswork than fact. That meant that something Viza did to frustrate and slow them, and keep them from doing actual, permanent damage to Zair, might end up helping their efforts, or making things doubly or even triply worse. And she wouldn't know what had happened or how to protect him, if she wore herself out with hiding and sabotaging the magicians.

Zair thought about everything she tried to teach him in the few, brief snatches of time they could communicate. He tried to learn from the books that surrounded him, and hide how much he was learning, how much he understood. Until finally he came up with a question that he couldn't answer from all the books he was reading. Viza couldn't answer him. Of course, she admitted, she had lost a great deal of her memories when the magicians ground her to dust. That was even worse than losing her ability to contact the mirror web. The silence, until she ended up in Zair, was the worst part.

So one afternoon when Anwir and Jillian were in conference with yet another group of ministers and secretaries sent by King Joben, and the magicians were in conference, preparing for the next spell, Zair asked the only people left who had a chance of answering. All three of his keepers and Magnus were in the sitting room.

"What happens to all the spells that are damaged when they're used badly, or magic things like rings and mirrors and swords and such that go bad? Does someone have to destroy them? I've read so many stories about things like chests and bags of accommodation that just disappear when they're damaged or used for evil or someone is greedy. What happens to them?"

All four turned to look at him with expressions that were just a little too quiet, a little too controlled. Zair wished he hadn't asked. What had he said wrong?

"That's why the castle exists," Tonia muttered. "Too many tangled and broken spells and damaged magical tools, and they all have to go somewhere, don't they, to protect the world from magic gone wonky-crazy dangerous?"

"What castle?"

"It's nothing but a legend," Pendrake said.

"A legend that I fervently pray to A'theosius is real," Magnus said. "Even if common sense says it's just a collection of wish tales and stories to frighten impetuous, arrogant young students of magic into taking better care. Those arrogant fools," he flicked his fingers to the other end of the manor house, where the magicians lived and wove their spells, "think they're too smart to believe in A'theosius, so they refuse to believe in cautionary tales. The world would be a better place if they got some honest, healthy fear in them," he added, ending on a throaty chuckle.

"Imagine what would happen if all that damaged magic, worn out magic, magic gone crazy from misuse, all gathered together in one place? The explosion from the sheer weight and pressure ..." He grinned and shook his head. "That is the enchanted castle. It doesn't have a name, and that is a cautionary tale in itself. Don't look for things that are too powerful to have names."

"Where is the castle supposed to be?" Zair asked.

"In a forest that no one can find, of course," Pendrake said. "There are stories of doorways that open to that forest without warning, and close without warning, and men who go through those doorways and vanish. They return years later, but to them, only a few days have passed. Only a fool, or a man desperate to become a legend, would go looking for that forest."

~~~~~

Zair had been in the manor house almost two full months when Shaleen arrived.

The boys had settled down for what promised to be several hours of reading. Pendrake gave them their choice of books, as a reward for doing so well in their lessons over the last few days. In the quiet, Zair heard raised voices. He recognized most of the magicians' voices and was about to shrug it off as another of their perpetual arguments, when a woman's voice rose over all of them. He didn't recognize that voice, but he heard
~~~~~

the power and authority in it.

The voices grew louder, and he decided they were coming closer. Under the arguing, he thought he heard feet on the stairs. Then the door swung open and a woman in a long, red-brown cloak swirled into the room. She pulled back her hood and looked around the room until her gaze focused on the boys, sprawled on couches on either side of the firepit. She closed the door. A long, thick braid of glossy, blue-black hair spilled down over her shoulder. A smile quirked up the left side of her mouth and she flung off her cloak and crossed the floor.

Zair stared. For a few seconds, he thought that was Princess Jillian, but she never wore trousers, and her hair had reddish highlights among the ebony. This woman stalked like a wolf on the hunt, whereas Princess Jillian glided like a bird on a gentle breeze. Anwir finally raised his head from his book.

"What's wrong, Mother?" He struggled up from the couch and tossed down the book, then his mouth fell open and he shook his head.

The suite door banged open. Lazius, the leader of the magicians, stomped through the door, followed by the rest of them. Zair wondered yet again if they went everywhere together, did everything together.

"There, you see?" She pointed at Anwir. "If I can fool her son, just for a few moments, then you have nothing to fear. And you most certainly are not inflicting that damnable magic of yours on me. I can do very well with dye for my hair and pretty clothes, and I know how to change the way I walk." She yanked her thick riding gloves off and wiggled the fingers of her left hand, so the firelight glinted off the rings on each finger, gold and silver and ebony. "This will ensure you can't work any of your magic on me without my permission, so don't waste your time and power trying. I will take it out of your hides if you do."

"Who are you?" Anwir said and dropped back onto the couch. "How do you get away with talking to them like that?"

"She's your mother's Shadow, that's who," Pendrake said. He walked over to the woman, holding out both hands to her. "It's good to see you again, lass. Although I could wish we hadn't come to this extremity." He chuckled as the woman pressed a kiss on his high forehead.

Zair never saw Shaleen and Jillian together, either in the manor house before they returned to Dorwain, or during their time in the capitol, but when he asked if the two women got along, Gresibel said they were good friends. Shaleen had been brought in to shadow the princess when they were only five years old. Back when King Joben had still been the youngest son of a younger son, and his chances of taking the throne were thin. At the time, the assassinations and accidents and illnesses that decimated the vast royal family had motivated the king to order all his relatives to employ Shadows. Just in case.

The two girls had grown up together. When Jillian left the kingdom and essentially went into hiding, disguised as a commoner, Shaleen had taken her bodyguard training and joined the Firebird Guild. They provided female soldiers to act as bodyguards for rich and noble women. The two had corresponded over the years, and despite the political pressure, Jillian had refused to let another woman be found and molded by magic to act as her Shadow. She trusted Shaleen. Zair wondered, years later, if the real reason was that she didn't trust the magicians, who had persuaded King Joben to trust their patchwork magic and their advice over that of powerful, successful enchanters, like Magnus.

Shaleen proved her talent as a Shadow the very next day, when she took Jillian's place at breakfast. Her hair color had changed, and she wore it gathered into the jeweled net Jillian used when she was not "on display," as the princess herself phrased it. Shaleen glided when she moved, and the healthy golden-brown of her skin had vanished under the pearly powder Jillian used. She even smelled like the princess. Still, something about her didn't feel right to Zair, and he studied her as Shaleen and Anwir and Gresibel carried on a lively, slightly teasing conversation.

Then he noticed the rings on her fingers. Those were not Jillian's usual jewelry. Zair recognized the rings that Shaleen had said would protect her from the magicians' spells. He muffled laughter.

Shaleen laughed instead. She sat back in her chair and tipped off a salute to Zair, and something about her subtly changed, so she was no longer Princess Jillian.

Anwir, however, didn't seem to notice. He also didn't notice the substitution when Shaleen slipped out of the room shortly before they left to go to the manor house chapel for morning worship, and Jillian joined them. His mother even wore different clothes, but the prince didn't react.

Shaleen took Zair for a walk, instead of his usual lesson time with Pendrake that afternoon. She did most of the talking, giving him advice and warning of what lay ahead of him for the next ten years. If the kingdom had settled down adequately, Anwir wouldn't need his Shadow by the time he took the throne. The spells woven into the coronation would bind the Red Brigade to his welfare from that day forward. Shaleen offered Zair lessons in what she called the "finer points of sniffing out trouble."

Five days later, a summons came from King Joben. He agreed with his daughter's insistence on slowing the pace of the spell weaving but still commanded her and Anwir to come to Andorwain, the capitol, a full month ahead of her preferred schedule. Someone had reported to him the long string of errors and difficulties the magicians faced. He had lost confidence in the magicians he had personally chosen to oversee the process of creating his heir's Shadow, and wanted his personal wizard, Nostrados, to become involved. Surely there was no safer place for that to take place than within the walls of the palace.

For the journey to Andorwain, he had full confidence in Magnus to maintain the necessary illusions, to ensure his daughter and grandson reached him safely.

Lazius and Darngrell and the rest of the cluster of black-robed crows snarled and seethed and muttered for days after the household packed up and headed out on the road. Zair sometimes woke from nightmares where the magicians succeeded in casting curses on Jillian and Anwir, Pendrake, Gresibel and Tonia, and took them prisoners, with Magnus nowhere around to save them. Zair and Shaleen could do nothing to help them, and found themselves locked inside massive mirrors, which the magicians pounded into dust.

~~~~~

Anwir and Jillian rode in a coach much like the one that had brought Zair to the manor house. They permitted no pomp on the journey. Most of their guards rode out of uniform, scattered in clumps on the road ahead of and behind them. Their fellow travelers had no reason to guess that royalty journeyed among them. Zair and Shaleen rode in another coach with Pendrake, Gresibel, and Tonia, and they had a far more enjoyable time together than the boy had anticipated. He discovered that Gresibel had a lovely singing voice. Shaleen was a talented mimic and taught him her tricks. Pendrake told dozens of stories, and answered all sorts of questions that Zair was sure the scholar would have brushed aside back in the manor house. The only question he didn't dare ask was if their route would take him past his home. Zair hoped somehow, when they were settled in the palace, he would find someone who would be sympathetic so he could write to his father. Maybe his brothers and stepmother didn't like him, but surely his father worried about him?

Only twice on the journey did they stop at an inn. The rest of the time, the soldiers who had ridden ahead had a camp set up and waiting, far back from the road where no one could see their fires. All that changed when they were two day's journey from the capitol. That night, their party separated. Half the soldiers took Jillian and Anwir, Gresibel, Pendrake and Tonia to the camp they had established.

The other half put their uniforms and armor back on. Zair and Shaleen dressed as Jillian and Anwir. Magnus wove an illusion spell around them, and they stopped at the largest inn in the middle-sized town of Grayways. An escort from the palace waited for them.

Word spread like flame in oil that Princess Jillian and Prince Anwir had arrived. Within an hour, the inn was overrun with nobles and officials
~~~~~

and ministers from nearby towns, all begging for just the chance to welcome them home to Dorwain. Zair couldn't understand how so many people from territories and towns and estates all across the kingdom could have arrived so quickly. Had they used magic?

"And that's why we need the illusion to be delicately woven, impossible to detect, yet impenetrable," Magnus said the next morning. They had to wait until they had been on the road for more than an hour before they could be sure of enough privacy to speak freely. "All those power players have been roaming, following rumors, seeking the first signs, ready to snatch an opportunity to get to our lady and her son first. Some of them are hopeful assassins. Others are looking for an opportunity to cry foul, to declare them frauds, and resume the hunt for the true royal bloodline. Not that it ever died away completely, but as long as the kingdom is peaceful and prosperous, all but the worst of the malcontents are willing to let the issue sleep.

"We are the distraction, to ensure mother and son reach the palace and are safely tucked away long before anyone can try to attack. And you can be sure, someone will attack. Within the palace's walls, the defensive magic is so thick, it's said that King Joben can hear when a man fifty miles away just thinks about trying to harm him." He snorted and his mouth pursed for a moment as if he would spit. "Despite the purges, destroying books of magic and driving out those born with magic in their blood, the kings of Dorwain at least had the wisdom to keep those ancient defensive spells alive. I shudder to think of what Nostrados and his ilk have done to those spells in the decades since their weavers vanished."

Less than half an hour later, a party of overdressed nobles approached from a side road, gloating with delight at having gotten this close to the royal party. Their triumph didn't last long. Captain Grebus quickly inserted three rows of his mounted soldiers on all sides between the newcomers and the Shadows on their horses. No more riding hidden in the coach for them. Now Zair understood what it meant to be the distraction and decoy.

He focused on his horse and wished he had spent more time riding the young gelding. He had practiced riding every day, when it had been safe to leave the coach. The team of guards had even taught him some tricks, but he had never ridden Anwir's horse until yesterday. Zair had the awful certainty the gelding didn't like him. It had rolled its eyes at him from the moment he stepped out the door and came down the steps to the courtyard where the horses waited.

"Head up and smile," Shaleen said, as their procession approached the first town between them and the capitol. She chuckled when Zair looked around and saw the crowd gathered on either side of the road and groaned. "It's not so bad, youngling. Tighten your legs around the girth and sit up a little straighter and tap your heels against his sides a few times."

"Why?" Zair flinched, recalling all the times he had seen Anwir do just that to his horse on their morning rides. The gelding always shuddered and gathered itself, just for a second, as if it wanted to throw the prince.

"Show him you don't have any spurs, for one thing. He's totally flummoxed and not sure what to do with you."

"Spurs?"

"You never noticed." She clucked her tongue a few times. "How are you going to serve as a Shadow if you don't pay attention? Half the job is seeing the ones out to kill you before they get close enough to try. The other half is becoming the one you Shadow, so even he can't tell the difference. The prince wears spurs and he likes to use them on this fine young fellow, just to remind him who is the master. Your mount is waiting for that first jab. That's what makes him so ready to crackle and buck. Show him you don't have any spurs, and he'll settle right down."

Zair choked and wanted to argue, but they were close enough for the cheers to ring out from the crowd. People could see him. He doubted Magnus's illusion would make people see a smile on his face when he was arguing with Shaleen.

He braced himself and did as she advised. The horse shuddered as he tightened his legs and turned his heels to press against the saddle blanket. For a moment the horse checked his gait, then Zair felt as if every muscle underneath him loosened. The horse picked up his feet a little higher and tossed his head high enough to seem to look upside down at Zair. Their gazes met. The horse whiffled, inhaling loudly enough to be heard through the clamor of cheers and shouts and questions.

"There, see? He likes you. He realizes you're not the prince, despite the strength of Lord Magnus's spell," Shaleen said, once they had passed the village.

The road they were on didn't take them through the village but around it. Less chance of being stopped for welcoming speeches or someone leaping from a rooftop to attack. It soon took them between fields sitting fallow as fall grew wetter and darker. Zair thought about what his family would be doing right now, what chores his brothers had to handle since he wasn't there to be given the messy, smelly tasks. He wondered if his younger brothers whined about the twins and lied about them like they used to lie about him, and if his stepmother believed them. He choked on something that felt like laughter. Why hadn't he realized this before now? He was finally on an adventure like he had read about and dreamed about, and he was finally free of messy chores and bully brothers.

If he managed to get a letter home to his father, would Korgan be angry enough, brave enough to come to the palace and demand his son be set free? Would he insist that he hadn't given his permission, and his son had been stolen, and even the king didn't have the right to overrule a father's commands? The longer Zair pondered the possibility, the less likely it seemed. If he thought about his home long enough, would he convince himself even his father didn't like him, and was glad he had vanished?

Too soon, the outskirts of the next, larger town became visible and yanked Zair out of his speculations. He could already see people waiting by the road, waving flags, watching them approach. There had to be three times as many people as the last town. Zair fought another bout of that sickness that was part terror, part fury, part helplessness, and a strangling, breathless need to burst out laughing at himself. He felt as if he had grown twenty years older in the space of a few days. He wished he hadn't been obedient. He wished he had fought harder to escape Ward and Gabe. He wished he had made so much trouble, Gresibel and Tonia had decided he wasn't worth the effort and sent him home before the situation grew dangerous.

"You aren't getting sick, are you?" Shaleen asked.

Zair shook his head. He didn't think he would empty his stomach, even if he did feel dizzy every once in a while. Pendrake had taught him several disciplines to resettle his body when he felt like he would fall over, or the ground would slide sideways and tip him off. Zair had laughed when the man used those words, because it sounded ridiculous. Now he understood exactly what his teacher had meant. He wondered if Pendrake had felt the same way sometimes, as he employed the deep breathing and counting exercise to steady himself. It wouldn't look good for the crown prince, would it, if he went boneless and slid off his horse? Anwir had to at least appear perfect in everything he did. So that meant Zair had to be even more perfect, to make him look good.

A longing to jump on Anwir and punch him swept over Zair. He choked on a bubble of laughter when that feeling drove away the sick twisting in his head and gut.

Chapter Nine

"Do you ever get really mad?" Zair asked Shaleen. He had to raise his voice a little to be heard over the first burst of cheering and shouts.

"Quite often." She bared her teeth in a fierce grin that Princess Jillian likely never wore, nodded, then pulled her shoulders back and raised her hand in that genteel salute she used every time they passed people on the road. Zair was grateful that she told him princes as young as Anwir weren't expected to acknowledge the people. His arm would ache in a short time.

This town was the largest yet that they had passed. Zair looked down the widening road to a jagged-topped blur on the horizon, where the land sloped upward. At the top of that rise lay Andorwain, the capitol. They were nearly to the end of their journey. He grinned and turned to Shaleen to point that out to her. A glint of sunlight on metal caught his attention. He raised his head, turning slightly to follow that flicker to the flat rooftop of a building marked with the emblems of the various crown officials who performed their duties there. People stood on the rooftop, throwing flowers or waving kerchiefs, flags, hats, and even musical instruments. He saw trumpets and a lap harp, and two sets of drums, hung around the players' necks on straps. That light flashed again, and he focused on a long pipe, pointing down past the waist of the man who held it. That was the longest flute he had ever seen.

The man turned it, pointing the pipe directly at Zair.

Nobody else was playing music right now. The shouting and cheering were so loud, music couldn't have penetrated it. So why was he playing?

Zair raised his hand to point at the man and opened his mouth to ask Shaleen what she saw. The man turned, following them as their horses passed the building.

A story flashed into his mind. A story from the thick volume of tales of Shadows. Pendrake had given it to him to help him understand all the many ways someone could try to hurt, kidnap, or kill Anwir. Something just like this had happened. A man had died in the story.

Zair yelped, "On the roof!" and leaped from his horse, wrapping his arms around Shaleen.

She cursed and raised her arms, and he thought in that split second she would strike him, but she twisted so they went down between their horses.

"Roll," she shouted, as the people around them shouted and screamed and the horses shrieked and snorted and the guards cursed. Shaleen wrapped her arms around him and turned so they rolled directly under her horse's hooves. One clipped his shoulder, a glancing blow that left a bruise that made him ache for a week. Shaleen kept them rolling.

Her horse shrieked and reared back, lashing out with its front hooves. More soldiers shouted and cursed and Zair looked up, past Shaleen, as her horse lost its balance and came down on top of them. She screamed and for a few heartbeats he could see nothing but the dust raised by the horse's fall.

Then they were surrounded by guards, cursing and shouting orders and fighting to shove the downed horse off them. Gregor, one of Anwir's guards, slung Zair over his shoulder and ran with him, into the closest building. Two more guards followed, carrying Shaleen. She was pale and sweating and weeping silently and struggling to breathe. Gregor settled Zair in a corner of an interior room and stayed right there, an arm around the boy, putting himself between him and the door. The other guards cleared a long table of papers and scrolls and inkpots with furious sweeps of their arms, spread their cloaks on it, and laid Shaleen on her back. Someone shouted for a healer.

"No!" Magnus shoved his way past two guards who tried to block the door. "That's the last thing we need."

"It's clearly broken, my lord," Captain Grebus barked. He stepped back, gesturing at Shaleen's leg.

Zair had just enough room to look around Gregor and see Shaleen's left leg. It twisted so her foot pointed to the right.

"Yes, I can see that, and I can deal with it far better and faster than any healer. Who will tell the world what happened to the princess. And have enough magic in her to see through the illusion." Magnus jammed his fists into his hips and glared around the room. His gaze landed on Zair and some of the sternness faded. "Are you all right, lad?"

"Saw the assassin before I did," Shaleen said, her voice a raspy sort of whistle.

"Did he now?" Magnus nodded. "We can discuss that later. I need to mend this before rumors start flying."

"Already are," Grebus grumbled. He turned to nod to Zair. "Well done, lad." Then he frowned. "What exactly did you see?"

"A man with a pipe. But nobody else was playing music and he pointed it at us," Zair said. His face heated as he heard the shaking in his voice.

"Blowpipe." The captain growled out a few curses in another language. He snapped out commands and several soldiers hurried out of the room.

Magnus peeled off his cloak and long vest. He rolled up his sleeves as he approached the table.

"Horse?" Shaleen started to push herself upright, braced on her arms. Her leg flopped to the side. She went white and hissed, and two soldiers on either side of her hurried to grip her arms and hold her flat to the table.

"Dead before it hit you," Magnus said. "Hold still."

Shaleen bit her bottom lip, flinching and digging her fingernails into the cloaks cushioning the table. Two soldiers worked to unlace her boot and slide it off her foot. Soft, high-pitched grunts escaped her with every rapid rise and fall of her chest.

Zair tried not to move, stunned by the shimmering green and gold haze that spilled out of Magnus's hands where he gripped Shaleen's twisted foot. He turned it. She tipped her head back, breathing light and fast. Zair dug his fingers into the bench beneath him and refused to look away or even blink, despite the sweat spilling down his forehead into his eyes, so they burned.

Please, please, A'theosius, don't let her hurt any more.

"Good lad," Gregor murmured, and tightened his arm around Zair. "Sorry to say, you'll probably see much worse than this in the years ahead of you."

Magnus staggered a little when he lowered his hands and the glow faded. Shaleen's leg was straight and her foot pointed upward again. He sank down on one of the benches against the wall. He beckoned for Zair, and questioned him about what he saw, while the soldiers hurried around, bringing in wine for him and Shaleen. Other soldiers reported on the chase that captured the assassin. Town officials called from the doorway, apologizing and begging for mercy and for a chance to speak with the princess and her son.

Grebus wouldn't allow that, and Zair was grateful. He wanted to peel away the illusion magic that seemed to stick to his skin like a layer of itchy, burning-cold dirt. He wanted to yank off the illusion that covered Shaleen, because he still saw Princess Jillian lying there on the table, still pale and sweating, gulping wine directly from the pitcher and flinching as the soldiers carefully but quickly wrapped her leg and put her boot back on. Magnus gulped wine while Zair talked, and the color returned to his chalky skin.

Not until that moment had Zair ever thought that magic took something from the one who used it. He had been startled enough when that spell for his eyes made him so miserable. Magic was more complicated than he had ever guessed, and he wished Viza was wrong, and magic wasn't awakening in him, like some vile parasite. He felt sick, wanting to laugh and shout at the same time. For most of his life, he had wished for some magic, just to get revenge on his brothers and the village bullies, or to do his chores quickly so he could go adventuring with his friends.

Grebus appropriated an enclosed wagon from the village, hastily cleaned out and scrubbed and padded with cushions, for Shaleen and Zair and Magnus to ride inside, out of sight. The coach they had traveled in had gone on ahead to the palace already with the party protecting Jillian and Anwir. The borrowed vehicle rocked from side to side and hit every rut and rock, and creaked so Zair could barely hear himself think. He was glad for the distraction, because he was left with nothing to do but think, sitting in the stuffy darkness. Shaleen and Magnus slept for most of the ride.

Magnus woke first, just about the time the rocking and banging of the wagon changed to the steady rumble of wheels on cobblestone streets. He groaned and sat up and threads of green magic wove around his head for a few seconds. It looked almost painfully bright in the thick darkness of the wagon.

"Don't know what's worse, the illness or the cure," he muttered. Cloth rubbed against cloth as he adjusted where he lay on the bed of the wagon. "Awake, Zair?"

"Yes, sir."

"Feeling like a hero?"

"Wish I could. Did they catch the man who killed Shaleen's horse?"

"If they didn't before we left, they've surely caught him by now. Enough people were infuriated at the injury to the princess, and impressed by your heroism — sorry, Anwir's heroism — they'll turn the man in soon enough." Magnus shifted around a little more. "I will be very interested to see what results from today's little adventure. There could be long-lasting influence, many years into the future. The question is how to handle the situation now, to create the impact we want," he said, his voice ending in a whisper.

"I wish I could go home," Zair admitted.

"So do we all." The man sighed. "Magic and royal blood catch us up like a fishing net that hauls us away and dumps us out onto a fate and destiny none of us would have chosen. If I could let you go home, I would." He chuckled. "But I daresay that if you could go home, you would very quickly wish to be back here. Home will seem painfully boring and restrictive, after this."

The soldiers had gone ahead and cleared the road, driving away the cheering crowds and musicians and dancers who had been waiting to greet the princess and her son as they entered the capitol city. The wagon trundled through the palace gates and rolled from one courtyard to another, until it finally went inside, into a tunnel, spiraling downward, so when Zair climbed out and he and Magnus helped Shaleen climb out, and step through a doorway, there was no hint of the sunset that spilled across the city. The torches crackled softly and flickered in the damp air and turned the waiting king's thick mane of white hair to gold.

No one had accompanied the king to greet them in the unfurnished room with stone walls and floor and ceiling, other than a few men in the black and red uniforms and armor of the Red Brigade. King Joben didn't sit or lean on a cane. He stood straight, hands clasped behind his back, as the three took a few steps before bowing to him. Shaleen leaned on both Magnus and Zair. He felt abandoned when she took her hand off his shoulder and gave him a nudge, pushing him ahead of her.

"I thank you, me and mine," the king said. His voice sounded thin, but not weak. "I could wish there was no need for your services, but you have proven to too many doubters that I am not a doddering fool listening to ridiculous fears." His voice tightened, threatening to crack. His calm expression never changed. "You have given the throne to Anwir this day, Shadow boy, and you have my gratitude." A tiny snort escaped him. One corner of his mouth twitched up. "You made him a hero, leaping to protect his mother. Yes, and we shall need you to help build that legend, so our enemies will not dare to strike him when he sits in my place. Well done, all of you." He turned, his gaze brushing over them once more. "If I could, I would ensure that such heroics are never needed again, but kings know more certainly and more bitterly than anyone else that such is not possible."

"With A'theosius's grace," Magnus said, his voice pitched soft.

Zair thought perhaps the king didn't hear him, because he didn't pause, didn't look back, but a grumbling sort of snort echoed back as the door swung open for the king to leave.

That started a thought that he didn't dare to speak until many days later. Even then, he whispered it, and only to Shaleen.

Gresibel and Tonia taught Zair all the skills he needed to navigate the complicated world of the palace and court and nobility. Shaleen taught him to be a warrior, a spy, an assassin, a thief, and a Shadow. Zair had learned quickly he could ask Shaleen questions that Pendrake ignored and earned him stern looks and silence from his other keepers.

"Doesn't the king obey A'theosius?" Zair asked, after more than two weeks of gnawing on the troubling idea, until he could finally put it into words. He still felt like he had done something wrong by asking. He had waited until he and Shaleen were alone in the isolated tower room where they went early in the morning and late at night to practice tumbling and leaping and twisting. Despite the softness of his voice, it still seemed to echo off the stone walls.

"The king... obeys where it benefits Dorwain," Shaleen finally said.

"He goes to worship, he kneels for prayers, he asks advice from the priests and holy advocates, he studies the holy words, he lives an outwardly virtuous life…" She sighed and settled down on one of the narrow benches on either side of the doorway. "But I think he has no hope of A'theosius's justice or blessings." She shrugged. "Good men are sometimes the hardest to convince of their need for help and forgiveness. Healthy men are the hardest to convince of their need to stop doing what will eventually make them sick."

Zair couldn't think of what to say to that. He would have to think on what she had said for a long time. They resumed their practice for another half hour, then went to their rooms to wash. She went to have breakfast with Jillian and decide which public appearances required the princess's Shadow. Zair ate with Anwir and they studied maps of the other side of the world, and learned the history of the kingdoms there and the names and politics of their kings. Later, Magnus came to discuss the differences in philosophies and practices of magic on that far continent. And Zair gnawed on what Shaleen had told him.

~~~~~

Four weeks after arriving in the palace, Darngrell wove a spell between the boys that allowed Anwir to share everything Zair heard and saw and smelled during the sessions when he took the prince's place. Zair thought that was cheating. He had to sit through one boring meeting after another, fighting not to fall asleep or scratch or make any noise that would remind people he was there, while Anwir got to read or nap or find something fun to do. After that spell was successfully woven, Zair spent three hours every afternoon sitting in a niche in the king's council chamber, pretending to be Anwir learning how to be king by watching and listening as his grandfather dealt with nobles and ambassadors, criminals and secretaries and messengers.

Then again, Zair told himself he was better off, and it wasn't like Anwir could pry into all his memories and thoughts. He had to wear a browband with charms on it, to facilitate the recording of those memories. All he had to do to keep his mind his own was take off the band.

Someday, though, Anwir would have to go into those meetings and participate. That meant after every session where Zair sat in for him, Anwir had to wear the band to put those memories into his head, and he had to talk with Pendrake or one of the five tutors charged with teaching him statecraft, to analyze them. Zair didn't have to think about what he heard. Everything passed from his ears and eyes to his memory. No one expected him, disguised as Anwir, to ask questions or answer questions or give his opinion. None of the magicians could come up with a spell to let Anwir talk through Zair without risking the bond becoming permanent between the boys and turning them into twins. Knowing they
~~~~~

didn't have the skills or the resources to create such a spell comforted Zair more every time he thought of it. That and the private lessons he had with Shaleen made up for the boring duties that came with taking the prince's place.

She taught him useful skills such as untying rope bonds put around his wrists and ankles, wriggling free of nets wrapped around him, picking locks or picking pockets, or climbing supposedly sheer, unclimbable walls. Shaleen taught him how to hear the breathing and even the heartbeats of people in hiding, to smell the fear or anger of people waiting to attack and feel vibrations giving away the presence of people in a room that looked empty. She taught him how to look around a room with a single glance, go away, and come back a short time later and spot the details that had changed. Even something so small as a flower that had lost some of its petals, or a carpet that had been moved slightly. Even to notice the change in the smells of a room when a window had been open for less than a minute.

Those lessons had to be kept secret, Shaleen told him. Half of a Shadow's protection came from being mysterious and generating just a touch of fear in those who served alongside them. A Shadow who depended on magic charms and spells to help him do his job was at an automatic disadvantage, because those things could be counteracted, the charms destroyed or simply stolen. The less a Shadow depended on outside assistance, the more invulnerable he became. Enemies wasted time and effort trying to find and destroy or steal or counter-spell those things. And if they couldn't find those charms and spells, they became afraid, convinced the Shadow was more powerful than them, and perhaps gifted with innate magic of his own.

Besides, Zair liked knowing some things Anwir didn't. The prince smirked far too often when he had an advantage over him, even in small things like treats or knowing the answers when Zair didn't, in their shared lessons.

Until Darngrell was done layering all the spells that bound the boys together, Zair stayed in the royal family's apartments and shared a bedroom with Anwir. The prince hadn't seemed to mind at first, but by the time spring brought them some freedom to have lessons outdoors at night, his attitude toward Zair had soured. The sooner Zair moved out of the royal family's quarters and began his apprenticeship with the Red Brigade, the happier everyone would be. Anwir resented sharing his lessons and bedroom and meals, though he had the alertness and wisdom not to say so, even under his breath, when his mother and their teachers and caretakers were around. He had temper tantrums every time he thought Zair was wearing his clothes, and sulked when Gresibel or Tonia proved duplicate clothes were still in the prince's dressing room.

Zair caught Darngrell muttering to Anwir every night he came to weave another spell between the boys, telling him how unfair this was for the prince, how demeaning it was to share quarters and food and anything else, and how ungrateful "that filthy Shadow boy" was for all the privileges granted him.

The night Zair heard the magician telling the prince that he wasn't even worthy of the privilege of dying for him, his fury grew strong enough to wake Viza. The mirror always put herself into a deep sleep so no one working magic could sense her presence, on those nights Darngrell spelled the boys. She left a hair-fine trail of magic behind her that Zair could follow in his dreaming mind, to hide his inherent magic from detection as soon as he fell asleep.

His fury, the aching hunger to do something, anything to slap Darngrell through the wall and down to the pavement three stories below shot through Zair like a flame in a stream of strong wine. Viza woke swiftly, with a burst of energy that scorched through the growing connection between the boys. Anwir sat up in bed with a yelp. Zair went stiff, losing his breath so he couldn't make a sound. He lay still, sweating, waiting for Darngrell to follow the trail of that magic to him, and discover Viza's presence.

Chapter Ten

Darngrell muttered and dashed in and out of the bedroom several times, more frustrated and cursing a little louder with each trip, and clearly unable to figure out what had happened. During that time of distraction, Viza examined the first layer of the spell the magician had tried to lay down in tonight's weaving.

Well, that's just what I would expect of a nasty like him. If he can't tell I'm here after that fuss I made, I think I can get away with some reworking. Let's see if he's aware enough to realize what I did. She chuckled, and the sound soothed the scorched feeling inside Zair's head.

What is he doing to us tonight? He grinned with relief when the effort of thinking to her didn't add to the ache in his head.

The original spell he and his idiot cohorts totally shredded and rewrote is to create a sharing of wellbeing. Essentially, if Anwir gets hurt or sick, some of your health and strength is drawn away to speed his healing. The original spell is mutually beneficial, meaning that when you're injured on the practice field or say you're out on exercises so long that you miss a meal, some of his energy reserves are drawn away to help you. The rewritten spell destroys the mutuality, so that all benefits go to Anwir. They destroyed all the safeguards, too, enabling him to drain you dry, and preventing you from resisting, even at the cost of your life.

I can just see this one when he's a few years older, going out drinking and carousing all night, inflicting all the nasty results of overindulging on you, and getting so drunk he jumps out a window and breaks a leg or his back or even his neck. He walks away without a bruise, while you could end up crippled or even dead. Well, that is not happening while I'm here, you can be sure.

Darngrell came back into the room for the last time, slammed the door, and was upset enough he snapped at Anwir to lie down and "stop asking all those foolish questions about things you could never comprehend." Zair's sense of Viza's presence faded, but he thought he heard her chuckling, just faintly, as he went to sleep.

In the morning, Zair didn't feel as drained and bruised, inside his head, as he normally did after a spell-working.

The next morning, the boys went for their usual pre-dawn ride. They traveled the usual path underneath the palace, emerging half a mile away, into a meadow surrounded by trees to protect them from sight.

Moments after they settled into a trot, Viza whispered, *Sorry. They do need to be taught a lesson.*

Zair lurched out of the saddle, landed on his head, and tumbled head over heels across the dew-drenched grass.

Anwir yelped and folded up in the saddle, clutching his head.

Zair felt nothing but surprise. Until Viza laughed, and he understood.

Did you turn the spell around completely? He gets hurt for me?

Sorry, the mirror said. *I could only pull on enough threads to re-open the connection between you, so pain and healing go both ways. But won't that set the silly old crows in a tizzy. They'll probably spend the next week shrieking at each other, trying to lay blame elsewhere and put someone else's neck on the chopping block.*

Her exultant words were more true than either of them could have guessed. Magnus came to examine the boys and the configuration of the latest spell between them. He consulted with Lazius and reported to the king. No spellworking was done on the boys for more than two weeks. During that time, any lessons and exercises that might lead to one of them getting injured were either suspended or reduced. When the spellcasting resumed, Darngrell was gone, and according to the gossip Zair overheard, he had left the palace.

His work, which had been done solo before, was now handled by three young magicians under the supervision of Emrastus, the oldest of the magicians. His robes gave off a cloud of sour-smelling dust whenever he moved. He spoke in a whisper, but sparks leaped from his eyes and bit at all three of his underlings whenever they did something wrong. Anwir found it amusing. Zair kept quiet, wishing himself a thousand miles away, or that all this would turn out to be a bad dream. Any moment now, Emrastus would turn and look at him and sense Viza, no matter how deeply she had retreated into sleep within him, and those sparks would bite him. And maybe do far worse things.

The magicians came back every three days to try to remove the spell Darngrell had bungled, but they couldn't. It was too deeply rooted in both boys. They repeatedly failed to reweave it, and their efforts caused Anwir just as much pain as Zair. After nearly three weeks of trying, Anwir complained enough that the king heard about it. He ordered that the removal efforts stop, and all future spell-working should be designed to work around and counteract the spell. Later, after Zair finally revealed Viza's presence to Magnus, they laughed together about the trouble the mirror had caused the magicians. The enchanter revealed that Anwir had pestered his grandfather so many times the king had threatened to replace him with his Shadow, who certainly knew how to "take a little discomfort like a man and a prince should."

After that, Anwir refused to sit at the same table with Zair at lessons and meals. Shaleen intervened and made Zair part of her daily ritual of exercises and study. More tutors came in, and Pendrake focused solely on teaching Zair. The only time he saw the prince after that was on the nights the magicians came to weave another spell between the boys. The other nights, he gladly avoided the bedroom they were supposed to share and curled up in a nest of blankets by the fire pit.

Viza's intervention did have a negative result. None of the magicians could identify where the interference and rewriting of the spell had occurred, but they agreed that some outside force was partly to blame. Emrastus created a barrier around the spells connecting the boys, making it harder for Viza to touch the weaving and decipher what each new layer of spell was intended to do. The barrier grew thicker with every new spell and drained the mirror of what little energy she regained during her periods of retreat. This resulted in Viza spending more time asleep and silent. The weakness of her voice and the sense of her presence frightened Zair.

He begged her to stop trying to penetrate the barrier, to conserve her energy. He refused to ask if she could die, because he didn't want to admit the possibility, even to himself. He had come to depend on her witty comments and her advice. She absorbed the contents of books when they were within arm's reach of him, then passed them on to him, so he learned more than Pendrake taught him. She taught him history and fables and rules of magic. She taught him discipline, to find the slowly growing kernel of magic within himself and hide it from the magicians without her help.

That last became increasingly necessary as the roots of the spells they wove between him and Anwir dug down deeper into Zair's mind and body. He felt them growing and sometimes woke from dreams of them strangling him in his sleep. Zair learned enough magic from Viza that he had a good idea what the magicians would do if they discovered the hidden core of magic inside him. They would either drain it for their own benefit, or they would kill him outright, considering him a danger.

Magnus no longer came to oversee the spell-weaving process and ensure Zair wasn't hurt. Emrastus was skilled enough the enchanter couldn't protest his involvement. The king sent him on errands dealing with magic throughout the kingdom, and out of the kingdom. His visits to check on Zair's welfare and encourage him grew shorter, and farther apart.

As the months turned into a year of tedious, repetitive spell-working, Zair thought about Magnus's promise to help him escape. He had turned fourteen some time back, and no one had cared. Would he turn fifteen and sixteen, still living in the palace, a weapon and tool, with no future to look forward to? When the last spell necessary for his work as a Shadow had been woven into place, then he would leave the royal family's quarters and begin his training with the Red Brigade. What were his chances of escaping then, with the most elite, dangerous warriors in the kingdom surrounding him?

Shaleen took full responsibility for his training and in later years, Zair reflected that she became a mother to him. More of a mother than Traysa had been, certainly. She taught him the finger language the soldiers used, to speak to each other when enemies were dangerously close and silence meant survival. Early in his second spring in Andorwain, she presented him with a ring that went invisible just moments after Zair slipped it onto his smallest finger.

"This could be the most important weapon in performing your duties," she told him, with a somberness that made Zair shiver, and at the same time feel like a heavy, smelly old coat had fallen on his shoulders. They were out riding under the stars, far enough from the palace that they could be sure no one could overhear them.

"This needs time to become part of you," she continued, "and no one else can know that you have it. Magnus gave me the ring to give you. The king gave a command that from now on, no one can work any spell weaving on you boys without the permission of Nostrados. Oh, Lazius and his black-robe crows didn't like that. Magnus and I both fear they will try to work some spells on you, separate from the approved ones they weave on Anwir. Just because someone told them they couldn't. That's the kind of nasty children they are, despite their wrinkles and decades."

"What does it do?" Zair said, holding out his hand. If he concentrated, he thought he could see a faint glimmer of light, where starlight would have glanced off the edge of the ring if it had still been visible.

"It warns you when someone tries to slap a spell on you. Those old crows insist on doing things their way, instead of listening to those who have centuries more experience with things magical." She muttered something that sounded like a curse and spat into the darkness. "They've been slapped for trying to add some spells that make both you and the prince believe whatever they say. Since he was already in disgrace, they put all the blame on Darngrell. Rumors say he didn't get exiled, Nostrados incinerated him."

Zair shivered, surprised at the brief, pleased jolt he got from that news. He had hated Darngrell. He hadn't thought he could hate someone so much he would want him to die brutally and painfully. Later, he realized that news would please Anwir, but he didn't want to be like the prince.

Shaleen explained the ring, after they turned their horses to go back to the palace. The warnings it gave depended on the strength of the spell cast against him, the intended effect, and even the distance from which it was cast. The ring could tighten on his finger, turn hot, turn cold, or tickle or give an impression of teeth sinking through his flesh. Only time and experience could teach him how to interpret those signals.

"A handy tool that can become a weapon, if you are sensitive enough to interpret what it tells you. At the very least, a necessary shield for one in your position," she added.

"How long?"

"How long what?"

"How long will I have to be his Shadow? Pendrake said something like ten years, one time. I won't be needed once Anwir becomes king, but could he become safe enough before then, that he won't need me? When can I ..." He laughed at the sudden realization that he really hadn't wanted to go home for a long time. Even the longing to see his father had died. Everything that had happened to him had changed him too much.

Shaleen had taught him enough, he could be a warrior. He wouldn't particularly have to stay in Dorwain. Maybe once the illusion spells were unraveled and removed, he could let his inborn magic release, and start learning how to use it? Maybe he could travel to kingdoms where enchanters lived and studied, where inborn magic was understood. He could find a teacher and read the books that dealt with magic the way A'theosius had intended it to be. Maybe he and Viza could find the desert canyon she had told him about in dreams, that protected the magic-infused sands used to make magic mirrors. If he could get there, maybe the enchanters who made the mirrors could give her a new body?

He would go to other kingdoms and find a better king to serve. King Joben was strong, but he was not loved, he was not good. He was feared. Pendrake had been trying to guide Anwir into being a good prince and a better king than his grandfather. Now that he only taught Zair, who knew what those other tutors were teaching the prince? Would those lessons stick in Anwir's mind and heart, and do any good?

"You can't go home," Shaleen said, her voice weary and sad coming out of the darkness. "This adventure you didn't choose has changed you too much. To help you play your part, you will have the best education possible in the entire kingdom. The best training in arms, and the sort of tricks and defensive skills that nobles and merchants never learn. When you are free of the illusion spells, how can you return to the home and the family you left behind? You won't fit in." She sighed. "I learned that the hard way. My family were minor nobles. They knew when I was taken to be Jillian's Shadow. Yet I came back so changed ... I could never be the pretty little toy they needed to create political alliances. No man wanted a woman who could kill him with her bare hands. For the likes of us, starting a new life with a new name and new home and new friends, that is the only bearable path to take."

"But they will let me go, like they let you go, didn't they?"

"I don't know. My situation was different. Jillian stopped being a princess when she left Dorwain. Anwir will never stop being the crown prince, until he becomes king. I doubt it will matter how safe and stable and kind the kingdom is when he no longer needs you. I advise you to go to another kingdom. And don't wait for permission. There will always be many who will see you as a threat. You know so much about the kingdom, you have gone disguised among them, learning about their lives, their beliefs, overheard their schemes and scandals. They must kill you to protect their secrets and sins or convince Anwir you are a danger."

~~~~~

Magnus came for one of his brief, rare visits just a few days after that talk with Shaleen. He and Zair managed to be alone in the royal apartments for a little while. Zair told him what they had discussed, and a new idea that had come from continuing the discussion with Viza.

"You keep saying the spells they're weaving on us are full of flaws, and they've rewritten so many old spells that have gone bad through age and abuse ... what if the spells go wrong just like you've been warning, and Anwir starts to look like me, instead? Nobody will really know until the spells are unwoven, but what happens then, when his face changes, not mine? Or we both still have the same face?"

Magnus didn't respond for some time, other than a snort and a shake of his head. His eyes took on a distant light as he gazed into the fire pit. Finally, he met Zair's gaze, just for a few heartbeats.

"I fear that the very ones who have convinced the king that I am wrong about their ability to remake and rewrite and control all those multiple layers of ill-advised spells will convince him that you and I are both traitors. Nostrados is no friend to me, though I have always deferred to him. I save my energy and time by letting Lazius and his gaggle of crows waste their energy and destroy their credibility by opposing him. Their kind will always see opponents and enemies where no resistance is offered, because they can never feel secure in their power. They constantly look for accusations and justification to attack."

"Then what can we do?"

A crooked smile twitched up one side of his mouth. He continued looking into the fire, and Zair had the oddest feeling Magnus was looking to another time and place.

"You can do nothing, and perhaps that is the wisest course. Let them keep weaving their mangled spells until everything collapses and tangles and erupts in catastrophe and utter humiliation for them. Despite their years of study and effort, that kind has no respect for magic. Generations ago, there was a purge of true magic learning and training, all the thousands of books of magic generated through centuries of practice and refinement. Those who call themselves practitioners of magic nowadays
~~~~~

have no concept of what true magic is, as it was gifted to us from the mind and heart of A'theosius. They don't realize that the oldest magic has a mind of its own.

"There are so many layers of magic throughout Dorwain, residue of spells and magical battles, the echoes of spells gone horribly wrong, and the outcry of magical objects that have gone ... well, if they have any intelligence, any awareness, I would hazard to say those objects have gone insane in their way. They are old and lost and wounded from misuse, or worn out, demented ... well, all that noise from the war on magic, the destruction of enchanters and seers and their libraries ... it affects how new spells work. Or more accurately, ensures the new spells from this new generation of magic practitioners don't work.

"The larger the spell, the more noise that spell makes, and that in turn attracts the attention, I suppose you could say, of those broken bits and pieces of wandering magic, the sour notes. And more important and concerning, the attention of other users of magic. The ones who have retreated into themselves and hidden away. The ones who value silence in the magical atmosphere above any other kind of treasure, because they have realized too late what damage, what chaos they have created. Eventually, the spells Lazius and his kind are weaving will make so much unbearable noise, and draw so heavily on the magical atmosphere, it will draw too much of the wrong kind of attention. It will draw down on Dorwain the wrath of those hermits who want nothing but silence. And when magic users of that much age and experience and power decide to interfere and intervene ... only A'theosius knows what will happen then."

"Can't you do anything?" Zair said. "Maybe I should try to run away before the spell is complete?"

"Oh, lad ... if only it were that simple. I was able to feel your presence and find you that first night. Now, the old crows have attached so many leashes with their spells, you can never escape without a great deal of help. The poisoned threads of that magic must be snipped, one at a time, slowly and carefully, to make as little noise and backlash as possible. Take what comfort you can from knowing that our princess has foreseen the dangers, and she has tried from the first to create an escape for you if that day comes. In fact, I fear for her safety, and her influence over her son, if the king and prince realize how she resists them to protect you."

"They wouldn't hurt her, would they?"

"I fear so. And we must prepare for that day, to defend her and spirit her away to safety, because your fate and mine are bound up with hers."

"Then what can we do?" Zair felt like an idiot, asking the same question, but Magnus didn't seem to be irritated.

"We wait, and we watch, and we study. Play your part and continue being obedient and a good influence on the prince."

"How? He won't let me be around him, except for the spell-working."

Magnus sat up and turned to look at him, gazing into his eyes so intently, Zair thought maybe he would finally feel the presence of Viza.

"I did not know that," the enchanter murmured. "Their influence is even more pervasive than I feared ..." A weary sound, partly a sigh, partly a chuckle, and partly something Zair couldn't interpret escaped him. "If you are unable to influence him for good, as our lady had hoped, then the less Anwir sees you, the better. Those crows need to protect their influence over him, so they need to make him unwilling to trust the one who should be his closest friend and ally. The sooner you are out of here, completely out of his sight and training with the Red Brigade, the better for all of us."

Chapter Eleven

That night, Zair made his bed on the floor of the room where he studied. He tried to talk to Viza. She didn't respond, though he felt a slight whisper like a breeze across his forehead, her signal that she heard, but was unable to speak. Either she had worn herself out in the constant battle to stay free of Emrastus's spell-weaving, or she was caught up in some new task that she hoped, prayed, would eventually lead to their freedom.

When Zair dreamed, he saw himself riding down the road to his home village, dressed as a prince. Just as he reached his home and his father smiled and held out his arms in welcome, a fierce storm pounced on them, shredding the village and casting Zair into dizzying, bottomless darkness. He woke sweating, hearing Anwir's laughter in the back of his mind.

He couldn't do anything to repay Anwir for his thousand tiny slights and abuses and complaints, but he could escape and take his life out of the hands of his captors. The question was how. He knew enough to disguise himself and ride hard and hide effectively, but Zair understood more of magic now, thanks to Viza. Lazius and his magicians could use the bond woven between him and Anwir to find him, no matter where he went, no matter how far away he ran. They might even use it to drag him back to them, like Ward had used the seeking spell, wrapped around his blessing band, to pull him out of the tree.

Common sense said he needed to reveal Viza's presence and confide in someone with powerful enough magic to break the bond between him and Anwir. Did he dare to trust Magnus?

Yet who else could he turn to?

He spent much of the morning worship time begging A'theosius for knowledge, for allies, for strength enough for Viza to break him free. Shaleen had told him, several times, that if A'theosius stood with him, then nobody could stand against him. Right now, Zair found that hard to believe strongly enough to find any comfort. Yet what could he do but pray, and study, and watch for the right moment?

~~~~~

Just after the midsummer festivities, Zair returned from washing up after his pre-dawn weapons drills to see servants he didn't know putting breakfast out on the dining table. They only put out dishes for one person. He thought for a moment that Anwir had decided to sleep in today, but
~~~~~

echoes of his bad dreams warned him that he couldn't be so lucky to escape the prince's presence. Princess Jillian had left yesterday on another diplomatic mission for the kingdom, so that explained her absence. And Shaleen's. But what about Pendrake, Gresibel and Tonia? Why weren't the women setting the table, and why wasn't Pendrake settling down with a scroll or book, to slip more lessons in over the meal? If Anwir wasn't eating with him, then Zair would eat with his three keepers. Where were they?

The unknown servants left, without introducing themselves or even looking at him. Zair retreated to the little closet off the study room where Pendrake had advised him to store his few possessions. His journals, a growing stack of sketches he had made with memories of home, a few gifts from the soldiers who trained him such as throwing knives and a lodestone and star charts. It wasn't wise to leave the few things that were truly his in a chest under the bed that he was only allowed to use every third or fourth night.

Soon after the wellbeing spell went so painfully wrong, Anwir had had a temper tantrum and accused Zair of being a thief and cheat. That had very clearly been at the instigation of the magicians. They were always whispering to him, accusing Zair of disloyalty, plotting against him, or disrespect. A servant searched Zair's chest, with the prince watching and smirking, until nothing was discovered that didn't belong to him. Anwir then demanded that Zair leave the chest unlocked. Likely the prince had tried to take the few things Zair valued and he couldn't get into the locked chest. Pendrake gave him the advice to put his possessions elsewhere soon after that.

Any advice? Do you know what's going on? Zair thought.

I didn't overhear anything, Viza said, when he expected her to be silent. That didn't ease any of the growing tension in him. *Best to prepare for change, though.*

He folded up the clothes he had gotten sweaty and dirty in his dawn training session and dug out a sack to hold the changes of clothes that were entirely his and not duplicates of Anwir's. Zair put the small chest in the bottom, covered it with his dirty clothes, and put the clean on top. Then he went out into the central room of the suite. Anwir was eating. So, he had been wrong, thinking the breakfast was for him. Zair wasn't surprised.

A wax tablet sat in the empty spot at the far end of the table where Zair usually sat. He didn't look at the prince as he approached the table, picked it up, and retreated to the fire pit to read it.

You're done. No more idiocy and mangled spell-weaving! Viza cried, before he could read more than halfway down the tablet.

Zair couldn't wrap his mind around the instructions until he had read through the tablet twice. His hands shook a little, and his eyes felt hot and wet, but he wasn't about to cry. He wanted to cheer.

He was ordered to report to Captain Grebus, who would take him to the Red Brigade's quarters, where he would live from now on. He was to train and make himself useful to the Brigade and stay within their quarters except when performing his duties as Shadow.

Zair was sure that last part was Anwir's idea. Just in case there was a chance that Zair might be able to have some fun. He grinned, fighting down a pressure and thickness in his chest that threatened to erupt as a cheer. The prince could have no idea what good news this was to him. Being separated from Anwir by several stories of the palace and whatever distance lay between the Brigade's quarters and the royal family's wing, meant Emrastus wouldn't be weaving any more spells on the boys. The illusion spell was finished.

And if A'theosius was gracious and merciful, Zair would never have to see Anwir or hear his voice, ever again. Acting as the prince's Shadow meant he would be wherever the prince was not, except when he was traveling. That suited him perfectly.

He got up, careful to keep his back to the table where Anwir was still eating. Noisily. Zair grinned, remembering the times Princess Jillian had commented on what good table manners he had, and compared him to her son. He supposed that if he ever ate in public, acting as Shadow, he would have to remember to gulp and chew with his mouth open and snort and put his elbows on the table and lick his fingers.

Then again, Anwir was just nasty and clever enough to deliberately be a slob at the table to trick Zair into acting that way. Likely he had been given that advice by Lazius, just to make Zair look bad as Shadow.

He ignored the prince and went back to the study room and his closet, retrieved his sack, then stopped and looked around the room. He had been happy there, more than any other place since being taken from his home. A stack of books sat on the corner of the table where Pendrake usually sat. Zair couldn't remember if the tutor had left them there yesterday after his lessons. He picked up the first book, and a sheet of paper slid out from under it.

My lad. The note was written in Pendrake's distinctive square, light handwriting. *I must bid you farewell. Friends have warned us that we are being sent away and that making farewells will be unwise. Silence is the best protection for us all, though I fear we are not being retired as a reward for faithful service, but punishment for crimes others imagined we have committed. I once was friends with Yancob, commander of the Red Brigade, and I have risked all our lives to request that he take you under his protection. Trust him. Trust Magnus. Trust Shaleen. There are no others I can recommend to you. May A'theosius guard and guide and bless you, and lead you away to safety quickly, before the well-deserved storm falls upon this kingdom. Complete your lessons. Remember us fondly, and in your prayers.*

The note wasn't signed. Zair shuddered, understanding what risks Pendrake had taken just writing what he had. He thought for a moment, then slid the note down to the bottom of the sack, inside folds of his dirty clothes. He hesitated for a few more moments, then slid the stack of books into the top of the sack. He could say truthfully that he had been instructed by Pendrake to finish his studies in those books. Anwir would let him take the books just because they were worn, their covers faded and unworthy of a prince, as Lazius had said quite often. Thinking a few moments more, Zair removed the clean clothes from the sack, put the books in the bottom with the chest, then the dirty clothes on top, to reduce the chance of the sack being searched. If he knew Zair was taking the books, the prince would take them from him, just because he valued them.

He slung the sack over his shoulder and stepped out of the study room. He held the wax tablet in his free hand, to show if Anwir questioned him and tried to cause trouble. No sounds of eating reached him. He dared to look at the table. Anwir was gone. The question was where he had gone, and if he would ambush Zair before he could escape the suite.

Silence followed him to the door. He tugged on the latch to open it, braced for some last bit of cruelty, an accusation of stealing, an order to stay.

Nothing.

Zair didn't look back as he stepped through the door and pulled it closed behind him. All the good memories of that suite had been taken away when Pendrake, Gresibel and Tonia vanished. He focused on the light at the end of the corridor and the dark niche behind it that hid the door to the servants' stairs. He prayed for safety for his keepers as he walked.

When he reached the bottom of the stairs, he paused and listened for sounds of people at work, talking, moving past. Zair had learned by now how servants gossiped and how quickly stories flew through the palace. The fewer people who saw him trudging toward the guards' barracks with a sack of belongings over his shoulder, the fewer stories to go racing in all directions. He was the prince's Shadow, after all, and the fewer people who remembered him, the better. He wouldn't put it past Anwir or Lazius to accuse him of treachery, just because an unsafe number of people knew he existed.

When the corridor had quieted, he stepped out of the stairwell's shadows and headed for the door out into the servants' courtyard and the short walk across to the barracks.

"Couldn't wait to escape?" Grebus greeted him when Zair stepped outside. He chuckled when the boy stumbled backward and nearly dropped his sack. The guard captain lounged on a bench in the sunlight, with a tankard of foamy ale in one hand and a massive meat pie in the other. He beckoned with a jerk of his head and slid over on the bench to make room for Zair. "The Brigade is out for the day, either guarding the king on a riding tour of the city walls or training in the foothills. Nobody will be back until late, and the sentinel spells won't let anyone in or out of their quarters until nightfall."

"Then why did they tell me to go now?" Zair put his sack down on the cobblestones and settled on the front of the bench.

"They didn't. That message is supposed to reach you after dinner. We figured you didn't need that young snot making you miserable. Arranged for the tablet to be delivered early. Yancob is a good man. He's seen enough of the prince that he doesn't have any use for him, and he likes what he's seen of you when you've been playing Shadow." Grebus grimaced and spat. "Truth is, he's ready to like you, just on principle."

"So … what do I do all day?"

"Oh, we'll put you to work. Never waste an extra pair of hands." He tore off a portion of the meat pie that hadn't been touched by his teeth and handed it over to Zair.

The boy grinned and nodded his thanks and dove in. The portion Grebus gave him was more than enough for a meal by itself. Zair's insides were calming down enough from all the changes that his stomach's protests were turning loud and painful. He wondered if the lack of breakfast was on Anwir's orders, or the new servants didn't know he was there.

Well, he wouldn't be there anymore, so what did it matter?

Grebus lived up to his word, giving Zair dozens of small chores in the barracks and stables. The boy was achy and sweaty and dirty by dinnertime, but he had enjoyed himself tremendously. He knew all the soldiers in the palace guard because they had been his teachers. They included him in jokes and told ridiculous, exaggerated stories and even taught him thoroughly filthy, sometimes bloody songs and chants having to do with battles and the celebration of life afterward. He washed quickly, his stomach twisting from emptiness despite the generous noon meal he had thoroughly enjoyed. He wished he could linger in the massive tubs of scalding hot water filled with healing herbs. That was another improvement on sharing quarters with Anwir. No waiting until the prince was done and hoping there was enough hot water.

The tingling of the ring Shaleen had given him jerked him upright, out of a half-doze. He scrambled out of the tub, cold with the certainty that someone was coming for him. Some magic had touched him. Someone tried to work magic on him. If they had succeeded, he didn't know. He wished Magnus were here, so he could ask. Who else could he trust?

Maybe he could ask Grebus and some of the soldiers who had been training him.

By the time he had dried off and dressed in the trainee's uniform put out for him, Zair talked himself out of that hope. What would soldiers, even soldiers assigned to the palace, know about magic? What could they do, especially if the magic-users who came for him were in the service of nobles who had the authority to order him around? He wished he could run to Shaleen, but she was with Princess Jillian.

In the mess hall, the soldiers' cook filled a platter for him and laughed at the boy's wide-eyed reaction to twice as much food as he thought he could eat. Hunger helped distract him, enough to let him enjoy his dinner, and some of the teasing from the soldiers he had been working with all day. Part of Zair wished he could stay here in the barracks, working his way upward in rank, accepted by those around him, so he wouldn't have to be afraid anymore. A useless dream, he knew. As long as the illusion spells to make him look like and sound like and move like Anwir were rooted in him, he couldn't go anywhere.

His ring tingled again before he had half-cleared the platter. Zair considered the exits from the room and how quickly he could duck into shadows and find a small nook to hide. But what if that magic stretching out tendrils, seeking him, latching onto him, led his pursuers right to him?

He hated magic. He thought maybe he understood, at least a little bit, why some kings several generations ago had tried to purge Dorwain of magic that they couldn't control. They couldn't quite eradicate those who were born with magic in their blood, just drive them over the border to other countries. They destroyed the magic libraries so the history and lore couldn't be taught, and so the only magic in the kingdom was under their control. No one could become a magician without permission from the throne. Magic wasn't allowed to be wild, to spring up in unpredictable places, from unpredictable people. There was a strong allure to that kind of certainty. A sense of safety. Zair could understand that, especially now, facing unknown magic that tried to work on him.

Yet at the same time, where would he be without Viza to guide him? Granted, she needed to hide her presence to keep him safe from Lazius and his followers, but at least he knew she would be there when he truly needed her.

And now that he thought of it, if magic hadn't been reduced and forced into hiding so many times, he and Anwir wouldn't be suffering from all that bungled magic inflicted on and woven around them. The ones doing the weaving would have been taught from the oldest, most stable magical principles, instead of, as Magnus had muttered multiple times, "making it up as they go along."

"Lad." Grebus came to the end of the long table and gestured for Zair to get up. "Time to go."

Was that a reprieve? Zair hurried to take his platter to the hatch in the wall where he had seen the soldiers depositing their used dishes and cups, left it, and hurried back to the barracks to get what few possessions he had been allowed to keep. While he had been working, and then washing, all his clothes had been taken away, replaced with several changes of uniforms. He had his chest, the books Pendrake had left, the ring on his hand, and nothing else.

When he reported to Grebus's office, another tingle of magic tightened the ring and he nearly stumbled. A tall man in a hood and cloak waited outside the door. Zair knew, as if he could see the tendrils of power between the man's hand and his ring, that zap of power had come from him. He tightened his grip on his sack and prepared to swing hard and run.

The man's hood slid back, revealing Magnus's weary smile. He and Grebus exchanged nods, then the enchanter held out a hand, beckoning for Zair to follow. The boy bowed to the commander, who nodded somberly back to him, slung his new uniform cloak around his shoulders, and followed Magnus out the door.

They were silent, trudging through the evening shadows, through a narrow door, then up even more narrow stairs, to come out on top of the outer wall surrounding the palace. Magnus tugged up his hood before they stepped out into the fading daylight. Zair did the same. They walked slowly for maybe ten minutes. His ring tightened almost painfully and Zair flinched. He managed not to gasp or stumble or make any other reaction.

"That should do it," Magnus murmured. He gestured at an alcove with two benches a dozen steps ahead of them. Zair followed him and sat down and waited. "We're shielded now. Someone was attempting to attach a leech spell to you. The tug-war for influence and power over you has begun. The fools don't realize that the Red Brigade has more magic in their thumbs than all their slap-dash, self-made magicians can offer."

"What does ... it's supposed to drain me, like a leech?" Zair guessed.

"A properly made leech spell, yes, but I dare even one out of a hundred magicians in Dorwain to know how to do any spell properly." Magnus's mouth pursed like he wanted to spit. His anger faded quickly, and he leaned back against the short wall of the alcove. "The spell is to drain the power being focused on you by other parties trying to control you. It turns out Lazius and his crows have even more rivals than I guessed, trying to sow their seeds of influence over Anwir, against the day he becomes king. If they control you, they think they'll have power over the throne. Some of them want to prepare you to take his place. Some of them want to destroy you, so their own puppet can move in and take your position. Palace politics is a grievous waste of energy and time, but it keeps the idiots busy, so they don't have half the power they believe they do, and they stay out of the way of those who keep the kingdom safe."

"Did they succeed? Putting the spell on me?" Zair hurried to add, when the enchanter raised an eyebrow in question.

"No. And I wove skillfully enough, revealing the rivals to each other, they'll be focused on fighting each other instead of trying to decipher who is protecting you. All leading to petty squabbles and more waste of time and energy over the next few weeks. Until the Red Brigade's enchanter has woven shields around you and made you safe." He sighed. "And we can begin the long, involved, tedious task of freeing you of all those ridiculous, dangerous, badly woven spells. Without the crows realizing what is happening."

"How long will that take?"

Magnus could only shrug. "There is no telling, because the magic was so badly woven, and interwoven, and roots allowed to dig deep into you, when the illusion spells should simply be wrapped around you, like a cloak. It will take time and delicate care to unweave and untangle. Not only do we need to free you so you can't be tracked, we need to turn those spells back on the ones who cast them at you. Reveal the spells to the rivals of the casters, so they constantly attack each other, blaming each other for the failure of their spells. Then, while they're distracted ..." He shrugged. "Set you free."

"How much and how far?"

"Oh, lad ..." Magnus chuckled. "When you have escaped at long last, I will miss that clever mind. Anwir has robbed himself, and the kingdom, by acting the petulant snot and blaming you because he doesn't measure up. What a king he could be, if he would make you his friend and confidant, and follow your example." His brief amusement faded and he sighed. Then he added, so softly Zair nearly didn't hear him, "If only it were safe enough to reveal your bloodline and put you on the throne. I fear Dorwain will be ground to dust before a true-born prince takes his rightful place. If I am A'theosius's instrument to free you of the enchantments trapping you, my life will be well spent."

Chapter Twelve

When Zair thought of those words later, and the implications, he shivered. Mourning and death shadows hung at the back of the enchanter's words.

Magnus and Zair left the shelter and walked along the top of the wall. Shadows followed them, on the ground and along the tops of intersecting sections of the city walls. Zair tried not to react to every flicker of movement. The surest way to trick the enemy into making mistakes, Gregor had taught him, was to pretend to be less alert than he was. If they thought they didn't have to work so hard to stay unseen, then they would relax, giving him opportunities to escape or launch his own attack.

He and Magnus walked along the city wall into full night, when the shadows melted into darkness. The enchanter led him down a winding staircase built into the wall, to a room that made his ring hum with the strength of the magic filling the stones. There, Magnus showed him maps of all the swiftest and most secure routes to escape Dorwain, when the day came. He had lists of allies in various cities on the other side of the border, in each kingdom that Dorwain touched. There were stores of clothes, for disguises, and purses filled with coins, and various charms holding simple magic spells for healing and disguises.

"What if someone finds this room?" Zair blurted, when hope and fear combined so strongly he thought he would choke.

"They won't. The magic protecting this room is old, part of the stone itself, an illusion so steady and well-established, only someone who knows this room exists can detect that it isn't solid stone here. Most important, the magic sleeps, so the music at its core can't be heard. Again, except for someone who knows it's here." Magnus gave him a grim smile. "It isn't right that you need to think about such things, but you will survive and thrive." The light of satisfaction in his eyes faded into weariness again. "I need to show you this, if anything happens to me, if I'm not here to give it to our ally."

He bent and unwrapped a small trunk hidden under four layers of cloth that shimmered at his touch. Flickers of magic made Zair's ring hum and pinch several times, and he understood that magic filled the cloth, protecting what was under it.

"This is the most valuable weapon we have against the enemy. Eventually, it will provide us the tool to loosen the deepest root of the spell that imprisons and tethers you." Magnus opened a small box, revealing a double handful of silvery dust that sparkled in the light of the single lantern. Fragments of what looked like carved ebony wood poked through the dust.

Can it be? Viza cried.

Her voice shimmered and shattered inside Zair's head, so he stumbled backward, nearly tripping over a bench before he could sit down. He pressed his hands against his temples, fighting the sensation his head would split open. Nausea spun through his insides for a few heartbeats, then settled down as quickly as it had come.

"What was that?" Magnus said, his voice a strained whisper. He stared at Zair.

Tell him, the mirror whispered. *I'm sorry, Zair. It was such a shock. That's ... that's the remainder of* **me** *in that box. Oh, if I could regain that much of myself, I could start to uproot the perfidious spell from inside you!*

"Viza." Zair pointed at the box the enchanter had put down on the small table. "There's a magic mirror ... alive in me. She sleeps most of the time. She's been hiding. She's trying to help me, protect me from Lazius and everything his magicians were doing ... what?" His voice cracked when Magnus trembled and gripped his shoulders and sat down on the bench facing him, staring, in a mixture of wonder and horror. "Magnus, what is it?"

"It's true. What we thought, what we feared those two idiots had done ... the resemblance ... A'theosius, protect us, now more than ever." His voice cracked.

"What is it?" Zair demanded, and didn't care that he shouted. Common sense told him that a room sealed and soaked in magic and illusion would be protected from sound escaping it, too.

"How long has the mirror been with you?" The enchanter's expression grew grave, when Zair said she had come during that first testing spell the magicians had performed on him. "It is as we feared, and prayed we were wrong. They have woven much of their magic with the mirror as the foundation, claiming they obeyed and wove illusion around you, but they had to know all this time ..." He closed his eyes, clenching his jaw so the muscles visibly rippled under his beard.

"Despite all the warnings, despite the lectures from Nostrados himself, they decided they knew better. Or what is more likely, and more dangerous for both you and Anwir, they are working under the orders of others. The spell is no illusion, do you understand?" He opened his eyes and shook Zair for emphasis. "They are not just changing your flesh, to make you Anwir's duplicate for as long as you serve as Shadow, but they are making the change permanent. All the signs, all the clues ... we couldn't believe they were able, or brave enough to do it, so we have believed all this time that they were arrogant, misguided, fumbling ..." A snarled, foreign word escaped his lips, making the light flicker for a moment. Zair trembled at the strong lash of magic.

"You must understand what they have done, so the mirror can help you work free of this insidious snare. It is vital for the sake of your sanity and your soul. Their warped reweaving of the spell required continuous small doses of the mirror's dust be given to Anwir. When I stole the box with the dust, there was a ruckus throughout their ranks, but only briefly. I dared to hope that meant they weren't performing the mirror enslavement, that they were using the dust for other magics, creating other tethers ... If they regularly dosed Anwir when they wove the spell around you two, their intent all along has been to give him control over you. Over your flesh and your mind. To drain you of your health and strength and inflict the payment for his excesses and injuries on you. To use you as a library for all the things he needs to learn and remember, making no effort himself to study. You would be emptied out, to supply him everything he needs to perform as king, without any effort on his part.

"Yet for the mirror to speak to you, to be strong enough in you from the first dose ... the timing is dangerous for us all. We suspected that you had royal blood, and the inherent magic that comes with it. That magic is far stronger than any of us have guessed, if you can talk with the fragments of mirror, and allow it to remain conscious. Has the mirror been hiding your strength?"

"Her name is Viza, and she put me to sleep every time Emrastus wove more spells on me, so they wouldn't find her or sense my magic."

"Good, good. A'theosius blessed us from the very start. Be sure, you teetered on the knife's edge of disaster. If your friend had been unable to hide her presence, and your magic, all would have been lost. Pendrake and Gresibel and Tonia would have been destroyed with you. No wonder those two scoundrels fled as soon as they turned you over to them. Ward and Gabe suspected you were of the royal bloodline, the true bloodline, when they found you. Pendrake agreed with them, and we all fought hard to ensure you became Anwir's Shadow to keep you safe, so no one would ever suspect. Hidden behind the very illusions they have been weaving to make you useful to Anwir. It is more vital than ever to free you, as swiftly as possible. And to move as carefully, as delicately as possible."

"Can you fix Viza, put her back in her mirror?" He gestured at the box with the mirror dust and what he guessed were pieces of her frame.

"No, that would take a greater power and skill than even I possess, even combined with our ally ... and too much of Viza has been embedded in Anwir already. If she isn't speaking to him, from such a large quantity of her dust ... can you know, Viza, if part of you is speaking to Anwir?"

Tell him I have caught echoes of that young snot's thoughts, but I try to ignore him, and I try to keep my magic from helping him. He's thoroughly despicable inside, utter contrast to how he looks on the outside, the mirror responded.

Magnus let out a dry chuckle when Zair reported her words. "Another reason to move swiftly. Eventually, Emrastus and his people will have to conclude that it isn't just lack of the magic of royal blood in Anwir that keeps him from benefiting from the mirror dust. They will investigate. They must, for the sake of their own lives. Enough failure could move Nostrados to become more involved in the weaving, and A'theosius protect us from that. He wears the label of wizard, but I am sure he is a sorcerer of greater strength than even he realizes. He has the sensitivity and skill to guide him to you and the truth, Zair. We need to smuggle this dust out of Dorwain, along with you two, and find a way to the oasis of the sands that are made into magic mirrors. Then create a new body for her. I have no idea if it is possible to destroy the dust within Anwir, before he learns how to access and use the power those crows have been trying to give him. Or worse, Nostrados will tether the boy and enslave him as he hasn't been able to enslave Joben, and become the power behind the throne."

Ask him if he can try to give me back a little more of myself, Viza urged Zair. *The more of me there is inside you, the better I can serve as a guardian. More alert. More strength.*

Magnus was thoughtful, frowning at a distant point, for nearly half an hour after Zair passed on her request. Then he pulled out sheets of paper and ink and pen and scribbled calculations and muttered to himself for just as long. When he was satisfied with the results, he put Zair to sleep, to better talk with Viza. The boy felt as if he sat in another room, hearing their voices in conversation through the wall, unable to make out a single word. When he woke, shortly before dawn, he felt as if he hadn't slept at all. Magnus looked exhausted and pale, with dark circles under his eyes. The dust in the box had gone down by half.

"Is that good?" he asked both enchanter and mirror.

It's hard to be sure right now, Viza answered. Her voice sounded stronger in his head. Or perhaps that sense of energy came from a giddy, bubbly sort of tone.

Magnus promised to fashion the fragments of her frame into something Zair could wear or carry with him, for safekeeping. The pieces would be useful in creating her new mirror body, when that day came. Then they put their cloaks on and climbed out to the top of the wall and resumed their interrupted walk from last night. Zair needed to be in his new quarters before the city began to awaken.

Some of the shadows followed them. Then they seemed to slither up a nearby wall and leap down from a higher section of wall, becoming three men in the black and dark red uniforms of the Red Brigade. The most frightening aspect of the Brigade, Zair decided, was that they rarely wore their armor. They slid through the shadows and stood on display around the king, around the Council of Lords, marched in parades, escorted nobles to war, with nothing but their uniforms to protect them against arrows and boiling oil and catapults and a dozen other weapons that could strike from afar.

"Is your unweaver ready?" Magnus asked, after the two sides contemplated each other for several long minutes.

They were all of similar build and height and coloring, with broad shoulders, narrow hips, long legs, and closely trimmed, dark beards. The only difference between the three men was that one man had gray-blue eyes, one had hazel, and the third had black.

The gray-eyed man nodded to Zair. "Seeking spells are roaming, loose and raising a clamor, which just attracts more. Best to get you under cover, inside the barracks' shields, before your enemies find you."

"I'll be down to see you when it's safe," Magnus said. "Go quickly." He turned before the boy could respond and hurried back the way they had come.

Zair wondered if the enchanter was going back to that hidden room, to study the remains of Viza's dust. He tried to keep his legs steady as he crossed the gap to the three warriors.

The gray-eyed man rested a hand on Zair's shoulder, making him flinch, and guided him along the wall, into a guard shelter, and down a staircase so narrow, the boy was surprised any of them could navigate it without getting stuck. It felt almost too tight for him, and his shoulders were still as narrow as Anwir's. Zair wondered if his shoulders would be as wide as these warriors', from all the weaponry practice he performed every day, if the mirror spell hadn't been reshaping his body.

He tried to mark every feature in the shadowy stairwell and then the winding tunnel it opened into at the bottom, which was just as narrow. Everything was uniform, unchanging, even the stones paving the floor and lining the walls and arched ceiling were the same, in size and shape, a deep gray that somehow seemed to glow. There were no torches, so perhaps the faint light did come from the stones. Zair kept silent, trying to control his breathing and how he put his feet down, until it seemed like he heard nothing but the steady, deep beats of his heart. He was sure the warriors in front of him and behind him heard every time his heart skipped and raced a few beats.

"What's an unweaver?" he asked, once the winding, narrow tunnel opened into a meeting room. It was large enough for several hundred men, with rows of tables, and lanterns on the dozens of pillars that supported the ceiling made of massive slabs of stone.

"She shreds spells," a rusty-sounding voice responded from the far side of the room. A huge, hairless man wearing a long apron stained with blood and what looked like gobs of dough appeared in a wide doorway. "But carefully, so those who wrapped them around you never know what's happening until everything rebounds on them, and they have no chance to flee the backlash." He grinned wide enough to reveal several gold teeth. "Are you any good at cooking, boy?"

Zair hesitated. He had the awful feeling that everything these men said around him would have double and triple meanings, and every question would be a test.

"I don't know, sir. I helped the cook when we were traveling, and nobody got sick or complained. He always said that just meant I would never be allowed to be an assassin."

The three men now standing behind him chuckled, one raspy, one whispery, one crackling like there was something wrong with his throat. The big man, whom Zair guessed was a cook, nodded, studying him with narrowed eyes for several seconds. Then he tipped back his head and let out a guffaw that seemed to rattle the nearby lanterns. He held out a huge hand, beckoning.

"Come try not to poison our breakfast, then." He stepped back through the doorway, into what Zair guessed was the kitchen.

He was right. He hurried to find the basin, huge and shallow, sitting under an iron spigot that dripped hot water from a massive vat that radiated heat, and washed his hands. He turned around to see the big man watching him, nodding.

"You've served in a kitchen before. Let me guess, younger son, left behind by your brothers to help your mother?" He nodded when Zair did. "What's your name, boy?"

"Zared, sir. I'm called Zair."

The man gestured with a sweep of his hand toward a long table topped with a sheet of polished stone. Zair found it covered with neat, identical gobs of dough. It smelled of honey and yeast and studded with something dark that he guessed was raisins or maybe currents.

Somewhere in between pinching off uniform bunches of dough and rolling them and flattening them on a dozen long baking sheets, the man told the boy his name was Yancob. He waited until Zair had scrubbed out the mixing bowls and utensils and was busy stirring spices into the butter and putting hefty portions in stone crocks, before mentioning, casually, as if it didn't matter, that he was the commander of the Red Brigade. He chuckled when the boy went stone still, so he didn't even breathe.

"Trying to decide if I'm a madman, or just testing you?"

"Why would the commander of the Brigade make breakfast?" Zair said after discarding a handful of other responses.

"A'theosius himself told us, in the visions of seers and prophets and when he himself visited our world, that the best leader humbles himself to serve, and is glad to do it." Yancob settled down on the edge of the stone table he had just finished scrubbing clean. "Besides, it saves us the trouble of testing our cooks and kitchen workers, to make sure some enemy hasn't slipped in an agent or spy or cast a spell to make one of them poison us. We all share our chores here, no one man any more elite than the next. My men trust and respect me, because they know I will do my utmost to bring them back from any mission, alive if not unharmed." He chuckled. "But they love me for my fruit biscuits and sugared fruit drops."

Zair laughed, startled by the sound escaping him. And grateful for the sudden loosening of the tension all through his chest, so his lungs hadn't been able to fill completely ever since he first stepped foot in the Brigade's quarters.

"Believe that all you want." The woman's voice came from the shadows on the far side of the long kitchen room, beyond the rows of beehive ovens where their breakfast now baked. "I still say your firebreath stew is what keeps them loyal." She moved into the light of the long row of lanterns hanging from a bar down the center of the kitchen. "Through fear, if not suicidal adoration of the wretched stuff." She wore a long cloak. The hood kept her face in shadows from her nose upward. Her voice had ripples that matched her crooked, mischievous grin.

Yancob barked laughter. "I wondered when you would show up. How much have you done?"

"Oh, I've barely started. The unskilled weaving is more difficult to untangle, especially when the fools don't know how to enforce their own barriers, and one spell tries to melt into another. Pull one strand," the woman said, as she reached the table and leaned one hip against it, "and you end up pulling on ten more, and alerting everyone in the entire knotted mess."

"That's a good thing, the enchanter says." He gestured with his chin at Zair. "Boy, this is my daughter, Encobi. Lass, this is Zair, the brat's Shadow."

Encobi's grin and Yancob's words got a sighing bubble of laughter from Zair. He admired them and envied their freedom to call Anwir a brat. He was afraid to even think it, and more judgmental words, just because he could never be sure what spells the magicians might try to wrap around him next. If they felt it necessary to suck up all Zair's skills and strength to benefit the prince, while inflicting injuries and illnesses on him in return, why not try to look into his mind and control his thoughts?

With her hood pulled down, the resemblance between Yancob and Encobi wasn't as obvious when all Zair could see was her smile. She was lean and elegant like a hunting dog, where her father was all muscle and power. Her hair was such a deep black it looked blue, bound in multiple braids and wound around the back of her head into a cap. Her skin was warm olive, when her father's, while tanned dark and crisscrossed with scars, was the color of wet sand. Her face was long and smooth, while his was all snub angles. Their eyes, though, marked them as blood-kin.

Encobi explained that she was the secret enchanter, and more importantly, the unweaver for the Brigade. She undid all the spells that enemies flung at them, to hamper them in their duties.

The entire time Zair had been working with Yancob, focused on the breakfast rolls, she had been studying him, following the tangle of the first, outer layer of spells enfolding him. Such work was much easier to do when the person caught in the knots of competing spells didn't know it was being done. Awareness could awaken protective magic, either woven into the spells or inherent in the victim. Any awareness of probing and testing and uprooting spells usually resulted in an unconscious resistance. Zair would in some sense defend the same roots of magic he needed to have removed.

"I feel like an old tree covered with air vines," Zair complained.

She chuckled. "That's a more apt description than you can guess. The tree benefits from the water and food the air vines bring in, even as they penetrate bark and healthy wood and drain the very life from the core."

Chapter Thirteen

Encobi didn't stay for breakfast. Now that Zair knew she was there, he would be on the alert, trying to sense her at work, and that would block her. She gathered up a basketful of the fruit buns as soon as they came out of the first oven and headed for the tunnel entrance.

"What's the judgment?" Yancob called after her, before she was out of sight of the kitchen doorway.

"Oh, I didn't say?" She pressed her flattened hand over her heart and widened her eyes, as if in shock. When her father shook his head, muttering under his breath, she grinned. "The first few strands were the easiest to remove because they are the most recent, and they come from different, highly competitive and antagonistic sources. They haven't rooted in him. How long the various spells continue competing as I dig down will determine how easy it is for me. Eventually, I will come to layers that are anchored and working together harmoniously, and those could be alert enough to be on the defensive. Perhaps even defending each other. Then, we will have trouble. I recommend Jaspron work on reinforcing the barracks' shielding spells, so the creators don't follow the death song of their spells down here and find him."

Zair decided to see her assessment as encouraging. He hoped that most of the magic she found woven around him consisted of spells from multiple sources, fighting each other, and too busy to notice when Encobi attacked them.

He stuck close to Yancob during breakfast, staying alert to run for more butter, more spiced morning brew, more mulled wine, and massive bowls of the firebreath stew. The sweetness of the fruit rolls countered the painful intensity of the spicy stew.

The warriors watched him from the corners of their eyes as he moved among the tables, filling plates and bowls and cups, but never seemed to pause or change their conversations. Zair tried not to meet anyone's eyes, while at the same time not look like he was avoiding them. As Gregor had taught him, the first sign of weakness or fear just encouraged attack. These warriors might never like him, and that wasn't important, but his life would be misery if they despised him. He needed their respect.

~~~~~

Almost a month later, Zair woke with the sensation of someone calling his name. He lay still on his cot in his tiny closet of a room,
~~~~~

listening, waiting for the voice to speak again, and trying to keep breathing evenly and shallowly, as if he were still asleep.

There. That same voice. Clearer now.

His mother's voice. He knew her voice from his dreams, though he could never remember anything about her when he was awake. She had died when he was only a few months old.

To hear her voice now could not be good.

He flung off his blankets and rolled onto the floor and yanked one of his practice daggers free from where it was strapped to the underside of his cot. He hunkered down, held his breath and listened, reaching out with all his senses. The sweat coating his bare chest and back chilled as he waited.

No sounds came from the room beyond. It was too early for Demetrio to come for his turn at kitchen duty.

The bruises he had gained during yesterday's brutal yet exhilarating exercises, involving leaping from one galloping horse to another, now woke up and punished him for his frozen position. Zair tried to focus on the mental exercises to silence the aches in his joints. Especially the bloody streaks of bruises in his ribs where he had fallen and been kicked when he tried to roll out from under the horse. Salty sweat beads rolled into his eyes. He swore under his breath and raised his knife hand to wipe them dry.

This was useless. He stood up, eyeing the dark gray blot where the blanket covered the doorway. Now was the perfect time for an enemy to attack, while they thought he was distracted.

Nothing happened. He pulled on trousers over his breechclout and a shirt, all the while keeping his knife ready in his hand. Then he put on his boots and crept to the doorway. Still, all was silence in the massive meeting room beyond. He wished he had a cot in one of the long rows of cots and chests in the soldiers' sleeping rooms, rather than isolated in this little nook of a room. He strapped the knife to his upper right arm, to keep it out of the way but more handy than in a sheath at his waist.

Since he couldn't go back to sleep, he got to work in the kitchen. Demetrio always made the same thing every time he had kitchen duty. Grilled cakes filled with chopped pork and onions and cheese, and vats of a brew made with gingerwort, a tangy yellow herb imported from Alfordia, on the other side of the world. Zair filled every spigot pot with water to boil for the brew and got the onions and meat chopped and dumped into the wide pans on the cooking fire.

His communication ring, a gift only three days old, from Magnus, pulsed in the opening sequence for the tap code he and Encobi had created. To set a trap for their enemies, they had created multiple versions of the tap code, wrote them down, and the enchanter had allowed the papers to be discovered in various places, and stolen by spies for their enemies in the palace.

Anton.

Code for *we must meet*. That was the same in several versions and couldn't identify the specific enemy magic user.

Dawn.

Code for *come now, urgent.*

Cloth merchants court.

He shuddered at this proof that enemies were trying to lure him out. It didn't really matter if they planned to kill him, or capture him, or try to bribe him to support them. He snarled at the sender and turned to pick up an enormous, slotted spoon, to stir the meat and onions that had started to sizzle and sputter. He wasn't stepping foot out of the Red Brigade's underground quarters until every strand of badly woven magic had been removed and he wore his own face.

"They're loud," Encobi said, stepping into the kitchen. "That's a good sign they can't detect we've removed more of their spells." Her somber expression twisted into nasty delight. "You need to respond before they realize you don't believe them. Where should we send them, so they get caught?"

He suspected his expression matched hers, when he immediately thought of the perfect place. A few seconds of thought, and he slipped the ring off, turned it around and slid it back onto his finger. Then he turned it right and left and right in long and short sequences, to spell out his response.

Mud, he sent the soon-to-be-identified enemy.

Code for *can't go to you.*

My room.

Next to Silver. Code for *Anwir.*

~~~~~

The ruckus that unfolded in the royal family's quarters five floors above the Red Brigade's domain had far-reaching implications.

The enemy trying to lure him out to the market square were in the employ of the ambassador from King Pelodon of Marcocia. They had inserted some of their own people into the ranks of the servants in the palace, using illusion spells much better than the ones wrapped around Anwir and Zair. The magicians and wizards of Marcocia treasured the ancient books that taught true magic principles and rules, and hoarded every magical artifact they could find. They were generations ahead of the magicians of Dorwain by the simple fact that they didn't burn books or grind up magic mirrors or hunt talking beasts to extinction.

The disguised servants had replaced servants who had inherited their duties from their parents. Meaning they had grown up trained to be
~~~~~

utterly, unswervingly loyal to the throne. Meaning they were trusted, and the last to ever be suspected of treachery.

Those spies, accompanied by two minor wizards in the employ of the ambassador, acted quickly when they got Zair's response through the ring. They went up the servants' stairs, approached the doors of the royal family's quarters, spelled the guards at the doors, put them to sleep, and went into the suite's common room.

Anwir rose earlier than usual that morning, or else hadn't gone to sleep yet. He wouldn't say. The servants had stern orders from his mother to limit his drinking. Several servants among the nighttime workers regularly hid jugs of wine in the suite for the prince to find. Anwir was just settling down with an unopened jug when the invaders arrived.

The enemy's men wrapped a silence spell around him before they shattered the guarding magic on the door and entered the suite. They assumed the prince was the Shadow they hunted, because all the servants knew Anwir preferred to sleep late. They would have succeeded in carrying him away, but Magnus had received Encobi's warning and followed the invaders up the stairs with six members of the Red Brigade. He overpowered their spells by snapping his fingers, crumbling all the magic charms they carried, and with another flick of his fingers sent their bags of sleeping powder into the pitchers of wash water.

The capture was relatively silent. Few people would have known what had happened, except Anwir had the loudest foul-mouthed temper tantrum of his life the moment the silence spell died. He flung himself bodily at the men who had been trying to pick him up and carry him away. His shrieks of fury and demands that they be executed immediately brought servants and guards running from other floors and apartments.

Zair and Encobi were both slightly disgusted to learn that Magnus painted Anwir as a brave, fierce fighter who would have rescued himself if he hadn't been outnumbered by the kidnappers.

To capitalize on the positive stories that immediately spread out from that incident, King Joben sent Anwir on his first diplomatic mission, west to Syntych. It was a small, subservient kingdom with a reputation for fawning on Dorwain for the sake of every bit of military assistance Joben cared to send. Syntych was the source of a large number of herbs the magicians needed for their many potions.

Magnus didn't accompany the boys, but he met with Zair and Encobi the night before the company rode out, to test for any changes in the spellwork tangling him. He commented that he found it suspicious that somehow, Syntych didn't realize just how valuable their harvest of herbs was, in terms of magic. If they ever learned, they might be foolish enough to start making demands, or even rebel.

Zair learned later that Ysobet, the new queen of Syntych, was only thirteen years old. King Joben wanted Anwir to impress her, if not begin the process of a royal courtship. Princess Jillian was not in favor of the match. Her uncle, Justan, the oldest of Joben's brothers, had offered her to Syntych's king as an alliance bride during his five months as king. She had been twelve at the time and had made plans with Shaleen to run away. Fortunately for her and Dorwain, Justan had drunk himself to death before his ambassador returned with King Yargo's answer. Syntych's king disliked Justan and had refused the offer. The general consensus was that Justan expected the refusal, and the offer had been made as an excuse to declare war on Syntych.

No one was sure if King Joben's plan was to annex Syntych through marriage or by declaring war over insult when Anwir was rejected. He merely told his grandson to make a good impression on the young queen. As Zair learned later, Queen Ysobet and her court were never given any warning that Anwir was on his way.

As far as anyone in Andorwain knew, Prince Anwir was still in the palace. King Joben didn't send his grandson out with an escort from the Red Brigade, but with the company of soldiers, headed by Captain Grebus, who had escorted Jillian and her son from Ambrecht. As far as anyone knew, the soldiers were being sent to a post on the southern border, to reinforce a fort at the confluence of the River Twye with the Sandflood. Zair and Anwir rode out disguised as trainees. Their company changed direction at the point where the road south skirted the Ombodway Desert, and headed west, across the desert, to Syntych.

They made good time in the crossing, with none of the expected dust storms to slow them and reached the border with Syntych half a day ahead of schedule. Grebus ignored Anwir's demands that they travel ten miles north to the most important border crossing station and make a grand procession over the border. The king's orders were to arrive in the capitol with all speed and stealth, to impress on the ministers and lords of Syntych that Dorwain could do whatever it wanted, and no border crossing stations or a scattering of soldiers on patrol could stop its might.

Besides, as Grebus commented to Zair on their return journey, everyone in the company knew Anwir's tendency to whine and complain and blame everyone around him for his boredom and discomfort. The sooner they arrived in the capitol of Syntych and he became the center of attention, the better for everyone.

The company approached an unwatched portion of the border with Syntych at twilight. Anwir was still sulking, so he unintentionally obeyed Grebus's order for everyone to ride as quietly as possible. Sound carried exceptionally well at night across barren landscapes.

Something is ... odd, Viza said, breaking into Zair's discussion, entirely in finger-talk, with Alryc and Aryc, twins, on the finer points of knife throwing.

They rode near the tail end of the procession. Grebus had the questionable honor of riding beside Anwir at the front of the column of fifty soldiers and three wagons of luggage. There was always a chance that despite their precautions, someone patrolling the border of Dorwain and Syntych would see them and come to investigate, meaning Anwir would have to be ready to perform. Just in case.

How? Zair almost spoke aloud. Something in Viza's voice inside his head made him itchy. She sounded uneasy. Or did the itch come from the strengthening buzz in her voice?

My dust in the brat is starting to sing, reacting to some spells entangling him waking up.

Why would that happen?

I don't know. I'm blinded in far too many aspects of the magic those fumble-brained idiots have been weaving together. She sighed. *I'm sorry, dear boy, but I fear that our tactic to hide your magic and my presence from them has contributed to this blindness. And I also fear that if something is happening to the brat, then it will happen to you soon.*

Why?

I don't know! Her voice echoed inside his head, with a feeling like sharp-edged rocks rattling around for a moment. *I hear several notes reverberating from him and reaching through the air. I fear they are seeking you, to lock in the connection between you two. It has something to do with the usual guarding spells implanted in the ground at the border, which makes no sense to me. I don't think we, and I mostly mean you, should cross that border. Tell them to stop!*

"Something is wrong with the prince," Zair said.

"What gave you that idea?" Aryc said with a grin and pointed to the front of the column.

Zair heard shouting. He had been so busy listening to Viza, the fuss hadn't registered until now. One of those voices was a girl's. Why was a girl riding with them? Or had the front of the group encountered some travelers and done something wrong? He heard Princess Jillian's voice in his head, asking him to look out for Anwir. With a sinking feeling, Zair dug his heels into his horse's flanks and tugged on the reins to move out of the column and race up to the front.

He was halfway there when he passed a marker pillar on the side of the road, indicating he had just crossed the border into Syntych. A cold, stinging sensation flashed over his skin, startling him but not hurting. Zair didn't stop.

That's it, Viza said. *Crossing the border triggered a spell. It's so badly tangled and mangled, I can't discern what it's trying to do.*

"Why would the Syntychans put an attack spell on their border?" he said, and didn't care if anyone heard and thought he was speaking to himself.

They didn't. It triggered a spell on you, just like I feared. Oh, this is going to be a sloppy, ugly, ridiculous mess by the time we figure out what happened!

The sting sank through his skin and itched in his bones, just for a moment. Zair reached the knot of soldiers surrounding the source of the shrill, cracking voice.

"Stop it! Just stop it! Which one of you did this to me?" the girl shrieked.

Zair saw Anwir's horse standing to one side, the reins in the hands of a soldier, the saddle empty.

"Where is the prince?" he shouted.

The soldiers blocking his way stepped aside, revealing Grebus struggling with a kicking, wriggling girl in his arms. He held her from behind, pinning her arms to her chest, and kept leaning back to flip her legs up in the air.

"I'm right here," the girl shrieked, followed by a stream of curses.

She wore Anwir's clothes.

A heartbeat later, nausea twisted through Zair's belly. The sting returned to his skin, but pressing from beneath. The bones of his face ached, like they were being squeezed. His scalp itched, so he yanked his helmet off to scratch.

Long curls fell down nearly to his shoulders.

"Oh ... lad," Grebus said, eyes wide, and so stunned he put down the girl.

She stared at Zair, startled enough she stopped fighting the captain.

"Get down now, before you fall," Grebus ordered. He shoved the girl toward one of his men and reached up a hand for Zair.

He started to swing his leg over the saddle to dismount. His boot slid right off his foot. His clothes sagged on him, suddenly three sizes too big. More nausea twisted through him and he became dizzy and fell sideways. Grebus caught him.

"Why are we both turning into girls?" the girl shrieked.

I would wager it has something to do with the illusion spells woven between the two of you, Viza said. *And all those spells they were told not to use. Those idiots deserve ... I can't speak all the wretched, painful, embarrassing punishments they deserve!*

Later, Zair wished he could have laughed, but he was nearly breathless with the realization that the girl was indeed Prince Anwir. Not only had both of them turned into girls, but they were identical girls, as confirmed by Grebus, and later Alryc and Aryc and other friends among the soldiers.

Fortunately, Grebus had ensured they would cross the border alone.

There was no one within hearing range of the shrieks, no one to witness the consternation through the company of soldiers.

Grebus checked the dozen or so charms scattered through the company, attached to the wagons and saddles, for self-defense and guidance on their journey. His frowning confusion and deepening worry didn't change, so whatever the charms were supposed to do, they were of no help. Finally, he ordered the company to cross back over the border into Dorwain.

That sting flashed over Zair again as soon as he walked past the marker pillar. Anwir was sniffling and whimpering and insisted on riding his horse, even though Grebus advised against it. Common sense anticipated the same sensations as the first time they crossed the border. Zair caught at least half the soldiers fighting to hide their grins when Anwir let out a shriek and jerked forward, his arms over his belly, and fell off his horse. Grebus had assigned two men to look after the prince and the one on the left caught him. The captain walked with Zair, an arm around his shoulders to keep him upright. A groan escaped him when the stinging, twisting, bone-shredding sensation shot through his belly. Zair comforted himself that he managed not to fold in half and embarrass himself.

By the time the company made camp, a good ten minutes of walking away from the border, both boys had started the transformation back to their own faces and bodies. Speculations filled Zair's head, distracting him from all but the worst of the sensations as his body changed, filling out his clothes again, shortening his hair.

If he had turned into a girl identical to Anwir, how much of the face he wore now had been reshaped, in flesh and bone, to be Anwir's face, and not just an illusion covering his face, to make him look like the prince?

How long ago had the magicians been disobeying Magnus's advice and orders, weaving together magic to change Zair's body rather than anchoring an illusion in him? Had it started with Darngrell, or had Emrastus made the decision? Lazius? Or was it possible Nostrados was involved in this?

Who would be punished for this debacle? Zair desperately, furiously wanted someone punished for this.

Chapter Fourteen

The healer for the company dosed Anwir to make him sleep, without asking permission. Several men called out their thanks, when the prince slumped sideways and toppled off the folding camp chair he had been sitting in. His complaints and whimpers and muttered threats died away instantly.

"How are you, lad?" Grebus asked. He dropped down on his haunches to look Zair in the eyes. "Care for something to blunt the sharp edges?"

Zair muffled a chuckle. He shook his head, grateful when the movement didn't make his head throb and pound like it had been doing since the first transformation began.

It's definitely something written into the framework of the illusion spells, Viza said. *Which, I am chagrined to realize, are not illusions. I'm sorry, dear boy. I didn't realize more illusions were wrapped around the spells to hide their true purpose. What bad timing, to finally gain enough mastery of their bungled magic to fool a mirror. Even one as damaged as I am. And worse, they had enough skill to fool Magnus! I prefer to believe it's all one huge mistake. They didn't know what they were doing. If A'theosius is merciful, they still don't know what they're doing. Because I shudder to think some of those idiots have figured out the foundational laws of magic, and they do know what they're doing.*

The spells are remaking your body, not anchoring an illusion on you. I can't narrow down the wording, because it's so jangled and muffled and twisted and tangled and ... there are fragments, but they make no sense. Why would the illusion spell specify the face and form of the true king? Well, actually, the wording is more accurately translated the true ruler, but ... She sighed. *I'm sorry, dear boy. I should have been paying better attention.*

"That's all right," Zair muttered, as a horrifying, and yet strangely amusing thought crept up from the back of his mind.

"What is it?" Grebus said. He caught Zair's chin in his hand and tipped the boy's head up to study his face.

"What does Queen Ysobet look like?" he asked, before he lost his courage and confidence in the idea.

"Why?"

"Stupid mangled illusion spell and trying to sneak one past Magnus, and a dozen rival magicians working against each other and trying to merge their spells with everyone else's to steal their power and ..." Zair gestured at his face.

Grebus slowly stood up, mouth pressed flat as he studied Zair's face. Then he nodded and turned sharply and stomped away. The last of the aches and dizzy feeling and itching in his scalp had faded enough that Zair just felt worn out and drained. Alryc came over with a wineskin and dropped it in his lap, along with a fist-sized lump of cheese and half a loaf of bread from the midday meal.

"To hold you until dinner is made. You look pale enough, someone would think you'd been in a bloody, bruising battle." He clapped Zair on the shoulder. "Just not fair, whatever broken magic is tying the two of you together. Why should you suffer for the snot's mistakes?"

Zair thanked him with a nod and filled his mouth with the cheese. His stomach twisted painfully, making him feel as if he was entirely hollow. He untied the mouth of the wineskin and took a large mouthful between each bite of bread, followed by a bite of cheese, then more wine, then more bread. He barely chewed, with a growing desperation to fill that void inside before it turned around and devoured him.

He was down to his last mouthful of bread when Grebus returned. He held a small framed portrait at arm's length, eyeing it like he would a quiet snake that might wake at any moment and bite him.

"All I can think is that someone doesn't want Ysobet and Anwir to meet, either to protect her or try to steal a courtship march on him." The captain handed the frame to Zair.

The portrait looked almost exactly like the shrieking girl Anwir had been half an hour ago. Granted, the young queen's hair was neatly curled and woven with jeweled clips. She had a sweet smile on her face, and laughter filled her eyes instead of terrified fury.

"What do we do?" Zair said. "Will we change again if we cross the border again?"

"Can't take that risk. Although ..." Grebus took a step back and rubbed his bearded chin as he looked Zair over, head to foot. "I hate to ask it of you, lad, but if we don't try to solve this riddle, the king won't be happy."

"That's putting it mildly," Alryc muttered.

Zair could guess what the captain was going to ask of him. They camped within sight of the border for the next ten days, waiting for a courier to reach the palace with the report and return with instructions. Twice a day, in dawn and dusk shadows, he stepped across the border and waited just long enough for the transformation to begin. Each time, he took on Queen Ysobet's features, with no variations. Which just verified Viza's theory.

Why didn't my ring react when the spell triggered? Zair asked, during one of the rare moments when the mirror had the energy to speak to him. She spent most of those days trying to work her way through the tangle of spells to make some sense of them.

The ring warns of magic being enacted on you, spells being cast from a distance. It's just more proof that the transformation is magic that is part of you, embedded so deeply in your flesh and your inherent magic that the ring, which is looking for attack from outside sources, does not recognize that particular magic as being outside.

What can we do? How do I get free of it?

I don't know. I'm too tangled in all of this to see clearly.

The response from King Joben was just what Grebus expected. They were ordered to return to Dorwain, as swiftly and secretly as possible. The only good news in the entire debacle was that no one had warned the young queen and her advisors that Prince Anwir was nearby and had been intending to come visit. Grebus had no need to lie and apologize and deal with the embarrassment of the failed mission, because as far as anyone was concerned, there had been no diplomatic mission, and the prince and his Shadow had never left Andorwain.

~~~~~

When the company returned to the palace, arriving after midnight, on a cloudy night that Zair suspected had been arranged by magical means, Magnus and a short, rotund, jolly-looking man dressed all in deep purple, waited in the guards' barracks. Grebus stiffened and went pale under the grime of travel. The captain turned and growled orders to the men following him and the two boys, so no one else entered the barracks. The door shut softly. Then Grebus went down on one knee and bowed his head to the two men.

The short man stepped up and his jolly expression drained away as he looked back and forth between the two boys. His tongue clicked in disappointment and he looked Anwir over, head to foot, his eyes narrowed. Zair watched the prince from the corner of his eye. A chill filled him when the prince trembled at the man's examination. Anyone else, he would have been stomping and whining and muttering threats over the rudeness and lack of respect. This man terrified him. Even King Joben didn't frighten Anwir like this. Who was he?

"You did warn us, didn't you?" the man muttered, glancing at Magnus. "I warned them, but they are just arrogantly foolish enough to think they know better." His voice was thin and dry and tight, totally betraying his formerly jolly expression. "This knot is so huge, how shall we untangle it without killing both boys at the same time?"

"Kill?" Anwir yelped. "Why? Can't you just kill him and free me?" He waved negligently at Zair.

"Stupid boy," the man whispered, and Zair imagined a snake leaping out from behind the man's fat face to bite Anwir, maybe snap his head right off his neck. "Haven't you learned anything from all the times one
~~~~~

of you suffered the other's injuries? Those imbeciles and all the other fools who played their idiotic games have tangled the two of you so tightly together that nothing can happen to either of you without it being mirrored in the other. It will take us years to unweave this mess. Go to your room and consider how you played into the hands of the mentally defective workers of worthless magic who did this to you."

"I didn't play into anyone's hands!" the prince retorted, flushing red and then going pale just a heartbeat later.

"Yes, you did. All has been revealed. We had more than enough time to investigate and uncover the truth while you were scurrying back here with your tail between your legs. You assisted them. You took charms and books on magic from the royal archives that no one but royal blood should ever touch. You gave them to Emrastus and his brainless cohorts in exchange for complete control over your Shadow." He flicked his fingers at Zair. "A stupid, selfish child's whim. How can you rule a kingdom when you cannot rule yourself? They failed you, and none of you realized that when their spells failed, it indicated a strong, defensive magic inherent in his blood. They should have investigated where that magic originated, at the very least."

His gaze slid sideways to Zair, just for a moment, and the boy felt as if he had inhaled liquid ice. He kept his mouth shut and his legs stiff and straight, when he wanted to pick up his feet and run, as far and as fast as he could.

"Go to your room. Spend your days and nights considering how to repair your ways. Be grateful this mess was discovered before the roots of the spell became permanently part of you, body and soul." He pointed at the door.

To Zair's surprise, Anwir turned and fled, nearly running into the door frame. Who was this man who could command not just obedience from the spoiled prince, but fear?

"You wonder who I am, do you?" the man said, his voice gaining some warmth. "If we had met earlier, perhaps much of this mess could have been prevented ... I am not pleased, Magnus, in having you proven right. Although it is amusing to contemplate the terror of those fools. There is much housecleaning to do in the magical domains of Dorwain. Your loyalty to the throne, however, has never been questioned. I know I can trust you to work on this ugly tangle from the boy's side and not work against me. That is beneficial for you both." A chuckle escaped him. The sound didn't ease Zair's tension. It was just a shade too cool for his restored jolly expression.

"In answer to the question you are cautious enough not to speak, Shadow-boy, I am Nostrados. I see much potential in you, and many mysteries to resolve. We will work together in the future, I think. You will become my ally in protecting the throne. Take him, Magnus." He flicked his fingers at Zair.

Bowing, Magnus caught hold of Zair by the shoulder and turned him and hurried him from the room.

Zair thought he finally took a breath for the first time, once they were entirely out of the barracks and hurrying down the first tunnel that would take them to the Red Brigade's barracks.

"The sooner we can get you entirely out of Dorwain," Magnus whispered, keeping his grip on Zair's shoulder and bending so close his breath brushed the boy's ear, "the better for all of us."

"Is he—"

That dangerous? Viza finished for him. Fifty times more than you can imagine right now. He senses the hints of your royal blood. He is likely already wondering if the spells binding you boys together have been changing Anwir to look like you, rather than changing you to look like him. You, dear boy, have a greater claim to the throne of Dorwain. You are the rightful king.

"Well, that's helpful," Magnus said.

"What is?" Zair asked.

"While I'm touching you, I can hear Viza. Interesting. Proof of how thoroughly interwoven you two have become ... and unfortunately, we now theorize that the mangled, bungled spell forces the image of the rightful ruler on its victims. I wonder how many heads will roll when the king realizes he can't send Anwir out of the kingdom for any reason. If Emrastus and his followers have any sense at all, they are already running for their lives."

~~~~~

Over the next twenty days, Yancob kept Zair with him every waking moment. He personally oversaw the boy's training, pushing him in the riding ring and in the sparring circle until Zair wobbled on his feet and felt like one massive bruise from scalp to little toes. When he wasn't learning every self-defense skill in the Brigade's arsenal, he was in the kitchen. Yancob told him, only half-teasing, that when Zair ran for his life, he would need a skill to earn his daily bread, so why not make the bread himself? Always wise for a man with a price on his head to ensure that no one else touched the food he ate.

Every hour they spent in the Brigade's kitchen, Encobi was with them, studying the threads of the spells tangled around Zair or searching ancient, previously forbidden books of magic for a spell to untangle and unravel what Emrastus and his followers had woven. She often read aloud what she found, bits of history or fragments of spells, slowly and stumbling when she had to translate foreign books. Yancob was also a gifted linguist. He had studied other languages as a hobby, just as he learned baking, to have a clean break from his warrior duties.
~~~~~

"We have an enormous handicap here in Dorwain, when it comes to magic," Encobi explained on the second day. "There were several eras when over-zealous types decided that because those who rebelled against A'theosius's laws depended on magic to the point of worshipping it, even giving over their minds and souls to one dark, demented overlord after another, therefore all magic was evil. So it was outlawed, schools were closed, books were burned, and those born with magic were either killed outright, or drugged to block their gift. Those who were allowed to live were castrated to prevent them breeding more magical abominations. Most went into hiding. Far too many turned into the very monsters they were accused of being.

"That only lasted for a generation, until people got tired of invaders and bandits coming over the border, aided by magic they didn't have any defense against. Then magic would return to favor, and all sorts of newfangled, idiotic, complicated ideas would be taught as solid fact, which just made magic even more frightening, and drove even more magic-gifted folk to other kingdoms, in search of a proper education and acceptance."

She paused to shudder and took a long draught of the sweet, spicy cold drink her father made just for her. One time, Zair thought he'd sample it. Yancob caught him just before he gripped the handle of the pitcher, swatted his hand hard enough to make it tingle, and nearly knocked the pitcher across the table.

"Those with magic in their blood stayed in those kingdoms, even when the most recent reasonable king offered them all sorts of wealth and privilege to return. Well, yes," she said, and wrinkled up her nose at Yancob, who was turning from the hearth with a massive spoon dripping with firebean sauce. His mouth opened as if he was about to say something. "There were some who did return, because yes, they did want privilege and power, and to get some revenge on the self-righteous slimeworts who drove them or their parents out of the kingdom. That sort were held up as proof that magic was indeed evil, the next time the loudest voices decided to eradicate it again.

"This is why there are very few good, solid enchanters and sorcerers in Dorwain. My magic comes from my mother, who was the daughter of the ambassador from Cammerlang. Magnus's parents belonged to a traveling group of inspectors and justiciars for the Enchanters' Court. They found a pretty little river valley on the border with Kaskagarde and Dorwain and settled there to raise him and create a sort of holiday retreat for their fellow inspectors. Magnus made the mistake of displaying magic at the wrong time, saving the wrong royal officials and for a while was highly regarded by the king and most of the court. He's been falling slowly out of favor for years. He should have gone home years ago, but he always said he had a vision guiding him." She reached for the pitcher of her spicy drink, then paused, glanced at Zair, and then away, her gaze going distant. "His lack of desire for power or influence makes him safe, and yet at the same time highly suspect. Let's hope all his warnings that have been proven correct will not be used against him, and you both have enough warning to escape when the time comes."

"Meanwhile, my girl has been studying magic in secret, and she's the foundation of our success and the fear everyone holds for the Red Brigade," Yancob added, punctuated with a satisfied grunt. He heaved the pot of firebean sauce off the iron arm in the hearth and set it with a *bang-thud* on the worktable. "No Dorwain magician can unravel the spells she makes for us because no one knows who our enchanter is, or the school of magic she follows. They can't come up on her from behind, so to speak, and steal the source of her power." He snorted. "No one reads the few remaining books of true magic because they don't know those books exist. Self-destructive idiots. The kingdom gets saddled with self-satisfied idiots like Lazius and his ilk, while the king listens to dangerous sorts like Nostrados, with ice water for blood."

"The few holders of real magic spend most of our time on quests to retrieve the lost books and rescue the thinking, aware artifacts like magic mirrors and rings. We avoid the places where the magicians with their badly woven magic congregate, and we try to stay invisible and silent. Sooner or later, it's just simpler, easier, safer, to leave the kingdom and stop trying to teach the old, proven, clean, intelligent ways of magic." Encobi shrugged. "Real magic is born in the blood, a gift from A'theosius. Magicians attain magic through discipline and study and effort. Enchanters and sorcerers are born with magic in their blood. You could be an enchanter if you wanted to devote your life to magic. If the call of royal blood wasn't so—" She broke off with a yelp when Yancob leaped from several steps away and slapped his hand over her mouth.

"Even down here, with all your shielding spells, do you truly think we're safe, girl?" he whispered harshly. He met Zair's gaze from across the table, waiting, his gaze ordering the boy to be silent, to hold still, until finally his daughter nodded. He closed his eyes, bent his head, and pressed a kiss into the part in her hair. "You know I'd break all my vows to the throne if you were threatened, don't you? But don't take silly risks, I beg you." He moved his hand off her mouth and patted her cheek.

"Sorry, Papa," she whispered.

Yancob squeezed her shoulder and went back to the new pot he was filling with water. Encobi managed a lopsided grin for Zair. She shrugged and took a long drink, then pulled her shoulders back.

"Where were we? The death of magic in Dorwain and the growth of false teaching that will lead to disaster. If it already hasn't. King Joben's great-grandfather disbanded the schools for enchanters, and royal orders will prevent them from ever being reinstated. Until a new royal line takes the throne. The purges resulted in thousands of records of magical teachings and just as many magical artifacts being destroyed in fire. Or worse, buried in deep caverns. All that loss of knowledge, all the cautions, all the mistakes previous generations made, recorded and discussed to help their successors avoid repeating those mistakes and inflicting curses on themselves ..." She wrapped her arms around herself, shuddering fury, and what Zair suspected was fear, too.

"Dorwain was one of the few kingdoms where masters in magic sought out those with a gift for magic and assembled them into schools. Other kingdoms don't approve of schools. They hold to the tradition of one or two students for each teacher. Still, there is a hierarchy to ensure proper teaching, and guidance, and some way of recording the signature of each magic-worker, the scent of their magic, so those who use their gift for evil can be tracked and stopped. During the purges, the enchanters learned the hard way why other kingdoms don't approve of schools. Large numbers make it easy for enemies to find them. They didn't learn how to survive in solitude. They lowered their shields to reveal their weaknesses to those who betrayed them for the sake of survival." She frowned and shook her head, her gaze focused on something far away. Perhaps in time as well as distance.

"Now, the lack of communication and anything resembling a hierarchy or sense of authority means we end up with clusters of idiots like Lazius's crows, or dictators like Nostrados. There's no way to identify or correct the idiots, the ones who do more damage than good because they don't understand the price that magic exacts, the traps it can create, the damage it can do if it isn't handled properly, with fear and respect."

Chapter Fifteen

After weeks of tense waiting, someone made a proposal that both King Joben and Nostrados agreed on. After that, Lazius and a team of six magicians Zair had never seen before held him and Anwir captive every evening, studying the boys. That was all they did, dusting them with powders and sprinkling them with potions, for two hours at a time doing nothing beyond studying the tangle of spells. The two boys had to sit perfectly still and silent, until Zair's muscles ached. Viza had to hide. She retreated so deep inside him, he felt as if a hole had been pierced through his chest and head, allowing an empty, chill wind of loneliness to blow through him.

Zair's fifteenth birthday passed and he didn't notice, until Lazius and his minions missed their nightly torture sessions, three nights in a row. Viza emerged into his dreams on the fourth night, and wished him blessings. She laughed when he didn't understand what she meant right away. Then she apologized, when a hot, sharp thread shot through him, at the realization that he had lost two years of his life in captivity. When would Magnus fulfill his promise and find a way to free him?

The magicians didn't come back, which was a relief and a blessing. Except just as Zair let himself start to relax and looked forward to long nights of dreaming and catching up on his lessons with Viza, she went silent again. She wouldn't do that unless they faced some danger of a magical nature. He paid more attention to the shadows in doorways and down corridors as he performed his duties. He took Anwir's place at some sort of meeting or ceremony or public appearance outside the palace nearly every day.

Nostrados moved in those shadows. Once Zair became aware of him, he felt the brief, tiny pulses of tingling in the warning ring Shaleen had given him. No wonder Viza hid. The wizard did nothing but study him, so the ring didn't react more strongly than it did. Most likely the wizard only studied the multiple, tangled layers of spells wrapped around Zair, nothing more. But what if he suspected the magic potential hidden and sleeping deep inside him? How could Zair evade that intense searching, day after day, without rousing suspicion? Nostrados wasn't the self-taught, arrogant fool that Lazius and his magicians had been. He would solve the riddle and puzzle of the broken, tangled, warped magic that bound prince and Shadow together. When he did, then Zair's magic would be revealed, and then what hope did he have? How could he escape the palace and Andorwain and the kingdom before Nostrados sank his magical hooks into him, and destroyed him for the threat he presented to the throne?

Not even Magnus and Encobi and all the hidden magic they guarded could save him. What could he do?

There is a magic deeper than anything you've studied or Encobi has taught you, Viza said, when she finally returned to speak in his dreams. That was a good sign, meaning the intensity and length of Nostrados's regard had decreased. *How often have you asked A'theosius to save you, to help you break free? Start now, and don't stop praying until we're both far away.*

Zair laughed at the simplicity of the answer. He laughed at himself for not thinking of it before. He laughed because he suspected if he didn't, he would scream fury. The slightest display of anger or distress would no doubt be reported to Anwir, and he refused to give the other boy the slightest bit of satisfaction. The more Zair appeared to enjoy his life, his strenuous training, the more he could irritate the prince. And nowadays, that seemed to be the only satisfaction he could find.

When the change came, Zair doubted it did so because of his increased prayers, morning and evening and when he woke from nightmares of doom. King Joben decreed a long tour of inspection for his heir, to learn the land and people of Dorwain in his blood and bones and heart. That was the public reason for the journey lying ahead of the boys, which could take two years.

The true reason was to take Anwir and Zair out of the reach of all the magic that competing political forces continued to throw at them. Distance might weaken the hold all that conflicting magic had on the boys, which would help in untangling the weaving that imprisoned them. Magnus and Encobi tentatively agreed with the theory. Their efforts so far hadn't had much better effect than what Lazius's magicians and Nostrados had tried.

In preparation for the journey, Zair's lessons changed, the intense physical training reduced. Now he spent hours studying maps of the kingdom, all the highways and remote villages. Darben, who kept the archives and oversaw the care of the Brigade's specially bred horses, taught him how to read the wind and the sky to predict the weather, and navigate by the stars to find his way around the world. That skill would be necessary if some disaster struck and separated Anwir and Zair from the mixed company of their regular assigned guards, led by Captain Grebus, and the outriders composed of Red Brigade soldiers.

Zair briefly found some amusement in contemplating Anwir's discomfort and dismay at his grandfather's orders. The prince hated traveling. He would complain and whine and sulk in the coach that would be his living quarters for much of the journey. That suited Zair fine, because if Anwir traveled in hiding, that left him free to ride with the soldiers.

His amusement faded when it occurred to him that everything he did that was upright and mature and well-mannered would add up to a good reputation for Anwir. That was the entire point of the tour, Yancob said, when Zair spoke his thoughts. By the time Anwir returned to the capitol, every citizen of Dorwain would know his face and his voice, and they would trust him, because they would see him in action, and he would know his kingdom as intimately as his own flesh. Even more frustrating for Zair, the people of Dorwain would consider Anwir their hero and defender. The troops escorting him would inspect the kingdom's defenses and improve them. They would eradicate any bandits and bands of criminals they encountered, and deal with invaders who dared to come over the border to plunder and attack the helpless and innocent.

"The most important part of the plan," Magnus told Zair, the night before their traveling party left the palace, "is to separate Anwir from everyone who has been influencing him since he came to Dorwain. Good and bad influence. Politics and magic. You will spend the winter at an outpost sitting the farthest from the capitol of any point in the kingdom. I have friends who live just over the border, who will smuggle potions to you, to start loosening the roots of the spells in your flesh. Your task will be getting the potions into Anwir's food. If he knows we're setting out to break the bond between you two, he will resist. He sees you as armor and shield and sword, and we know how badly he takes care of his weapons."

Zair was still chewing on those ideas when he and Anwir slipped out of the palace and the city in the pre-dawn gloom the next morning. Zair rode beside Grebus, dressed as the prince, while Anwir slept, securely hidden inside his coach. Their route out of the palace took them past a courtyard with high walls that was always full of crows, either perched on the walls and towers or circling overhead. The gates were open, and torches provided enough light to see more than a dozen bodies, hanging from bars extending from the walls into the courtyard. All were robed in black. Some of the bodies moved, and Zair held his breath in horror, until he realized that movement came from crows perched on the bodies and pecking at them.

~~~~~

Four times within the first month of their journey, heading out to the farthest flung reaches of Dorwain, Zair felt twinges in the ring, warning him of a spell trying to dig its teeth into him. Each time, Anwir smirked and preened, and the next day performed a training exercise perfectly that he had failed on the previous day. One Zair had just mastered.

He considered deliberately making mistakes, just so Anwir wouldn't use whatever spell talismans the magicians had given him before they
~~~~~

were all hauled away to be hung. He had too much pride to pretend not to be his best. He reasoned that Anwir mirroring his skills, even if it was cheating, and taking advantage of the broken magic, was his own way of defending the prince. After all, as long as he was a Shadow, he had a duty to protect the other boy, and that meant ensuring Anwir could defend himself when necessary. Attacks would come. The prince was too arrogant and selfish to be protected forever by respect or fear.

So he worked harder, and if Anwir also suffered bruises and aches and strained muscles and had a hard time rolling out of his blankets in the morning after using the mirror spell, Zair tried not to smirk too much.

Zair told Grebus about the ring Shaleen had given him, each time it twinged and bit at his finger, and Anwir appropriated his new skill. The guard captain was not happy.

"We came out here to get away from all that magic, and here the snot brought it with him. Whoever gave him those charms gave themselves a way to track wherever he is. That's the nature of the kind of magic those crows were using. The king killed them, to cut their ties with the boy. The problem is, if they're all dead, then the spells they attached to those charms should be dead, too. So who is feeding those charms power?"

"So one of them is still alive? Or someone else is using the same magic on Anwir?" Zair guessed.

"Likely. But how do we send word to the palace, to start an investigation, without alerting our enemies? There's no telling who has stepped into those magicians' place. Anyone with any schemes for power could use this to get all of us removed from our post, maybe killed for failing this assignment."

"That's not—" Zair stopped himself. He knew better. Hadn't the last two years of his life taught him at least that one bitter lesson?

"Not fair?" Grebus snorted. "Since when does 'fair' have to do with the throne of Dorwain?"

~~~~~

Payter, a courier, caught up with their company, near the end of their second month of travel. They had penetrated the foothills of the sky-scraping mountain range at the northern border of Dorwain. While the fall rains hadn't turned into day-long deluges, the skies were constantly dark gray, and dropping temperatures threatened snow. After greeting Grebus and handing over two thick pouches full of documents and coins to pay for supplies, Payter strode over to the other side of the camp, where Zair was sharpening his daggers. He bowed, which stunned the boy. Usually the couriers greeted him with a thump on the arm, like they greeted each other. The man held out a small pouch with Princess Jillian's seal. Zair caught his breath, realizing the mistake.

"No." He held out one hand, palm forward, to push away the pouch
~~~~~

and looked around for Anwir. None of them needed the temper tantrum that would result if the prince realized Payter had mistaken Zair for him.

The other boy had been in a bad mood for the last three days because, as usual, he couldn't manage the new riding trick Martyn had been teaching them. So far, Zair hadn't mastered the entire exercise, so the prince hadn't used another charm to snatch that skill for himself. The boys had to slide down off one side of the saddle while the horse raced along, put all their weight and balance on the one foot resting in the stirrup, bend over, and scoop items off the ground. A box, a length of rope, a piece of cloth. The horses barely moved at a trot, yet Anwir couldn't manage to keep his foot in the stirrup before he reached the place where the item waited. Zair's problem was in the timing, bending down at the right point to snatch up the item.

"I'm Zair," he added, after a glance around the camp assured him Anwir was still down at the stream, with a curtain of bushes between him and the camp.

Payter took a step back and went very still, and his eyes narrowed. "How do I know you're you and not the prince?"

"What's that supposed to mean?" Grebus said, joining them.

"Shouldn't that magic be over and done with? You don't need the illusion spells out here. That's why the king killed those magicians, to end it. Nostrados will have a working, controllable illusion spell ready by spring. Don't envy you or the ones who have to escort him out to meet you and implement it." The courier shuddered.

"They don't look alike."

"The boy hasn't changed. He shouldn't look like the snot so much." Payter pointed at Zair.

"The boys don't..." Grebus' mouth pressed into a flat line. "You can't linger here long enough to see them together, to see the differences, but I do swear on my sword, the boys don't look alike. Except ... Every time that snot uses one of his charms on you, Zair, then yes, you two do look alike again. Just for an hour or so. Should hear him sniggering like a drunken lout when that happens," he added in a muffled, growling tone. He slapped his thigh, hard enough it sounded like a muffled explosion.

Zair bit back a demand to know why no one had told him that. He thought he understood, and warmth spread through him at this proof the soldiers did like him. At least enough to spare his feelings. The warmth turned to a brief flicker of anger, at himself mostly, when he decided he should have sensed there was more magic going on than just stealing his skills. His skin always prickled when he woke up the next morning, and sometimes his bones ached, but he had blamed that on rocky ground or an extra chill in the air or extra bruises and falls during his lessons the day before.

"Why does Zair still look like the prince, if you say the boys aren't twins any longer?" the courier said slowly.

"Because those idiots mangled their magic so badly, they made the prince look like the Shadow, instead of the Shadow look like the prince!" A wry chuckle escaped him on a breath. "Lad, you're in trouble."

Zair put down the dagger and the whet stone before the two men could see his hands shaking. As long as they thought it was mangled magic at work, and not the remnants of the mirroring spell revealing that he had more powerful royal blood than Anwir, then he was safe.

Viza?

I heard, the mirror said. *What worries me is if this courier reports what he saw, and the wizard sends someone with a better grasp of magic to investigate. Yes, the weaving of all those badly made spells is coming unraveled, but slowly. The process isn't as much cutting the threads as it is water running over stone, to wear it away. It's difficult for me to push from the inside, as it were, to help you. I am eager for Magnus's potion to help us. I fear for you, when we return to the palace in two years.*

~~~~~

Snow pelted their traveling party when they were still two days of travel away from their destination. The altitude and the steepness of the trail had slowed their pace more than anticipated. Anwir used the mirroring charm twice, stealing Zair's stamina and threatening his ability to breathe, when the altitude made every step an exhausting effort. They had to walk because the horses had a hard time traveling in the final week as they made their slow climb upward. The steaming brew that they inhaled every morning and every evening helped their bodies adjust to the thinner air, but not nearly fast enough for the prince. If he had had the breath for it, he would have whined and threatened for the entire journey.

Just before the first pounding storm of the winter, the troop reached the garrison outpost. The stone fort perched so high in the border mountains, some of the soldiers joked that even birds couldn't fly high enough to sneak over into Dorwain.

Rasselus, a tutor sent out by the king, was waiting when they arrived. He was a narrow-faced man who greeted Anwir with a bow and nearly drowned him with questions as to his welfare, if the soldiers had tended him correctly. He also apologized profusely about the enormous trunks full of books the king wanted his grandson to read and understand over the winter. Zair thought of Pendrake and ached for those blissful days of lessons with the old scholar who fed his ravenous hunger for knowledge. He told himself he was grateful when Rasselus ignored him for the first few days. He didn't want to learn from the obsequious little man, anyway.

For the first three days after they reached the garrison and settled in, Anwir stayed in his quarters. That left Zair free to creep about and learn
~~~~~

the layout, find the shortcuts to the lookout points, and make friends with the big, silent men stationed there.

The jugs of potion that Magnus had promised and his friend had smuggled to Andru, the garrison's healer, were waiting when the boys arrived. The brew tasted foul. Zair wished he could force the magicians to drink it and suffer with him. He could barely get the third mouthful down to finish the first dose. It coated his tongue with a greasy, prickly feeling, and tasted like the stench of a stable full of sick horses. Andru suggested that Zair mix it with his morning hot spiced beer. When Anwir complained about the taste in the food, the healer glibly said that the altitude affected his tongue. He would have to wait until he adjusted before food tasted right.

Zair found some petty amusement, knew it was petty and didn't care, when Andru took to putting the potion in Anwir's wine and beer. After several days, the prince didn't complain about the taste anymore. Whether his tongue had grown numb or he just drank enough not to notice, Zair supposed it didn't matter. What did matter was that they were both getting regular doses of the potion, loosening the roots of the tangled spell-weaving. The spells weakened, so that those who cast them wouldn't know when Zair broke free. Eventually, he would be able to escape, with nothing to help his enemies track him down.

On the fourth day, Grebus took the boys around to every post, every soldier, every room, and made sure they knew the layout of the garrison and the men who protected the one navigable pass through the mountains into Dorwain. When they finished the tour and turned to head back to the guest quarters, the prince's expression showed he was about to give the captain a tongue-lashing.

"Think. For once, think," the soldier snapped. He had the enviable talent of making his voice penetrate without echoing off the frozen stone walls all around them. "This is too small a place for one of you to be immured in a dark room all the time. You need to move about and perform your exercises. Daylight and moonlight, you need to be ready and alert, because attack could come without a flicker of warning. These men don't need even a heartbeat of distraction, if attack comes and they have to escort you back to your room and bar your door. You will join in the defense, because the difference of one less bow or one less hand on the catapult could make all the difference in warding off invasion."

Anwir sulked, but surprisingly said nothing. No threats. No complaints.

Zair hoped maybe the months of travel and living without luxuries and people tripping over each other to do his bidding had forced the prince to grow up. Maybe the lack of village girls to giggle and adore from afar, and no officials or elders to be impressed and flatter him and beg for favors, might finally teach Anwir the lessons in kingship that King Joben wanted for his grandson and heir.

But he doubted it.

~~~~~

Years later, looking back, Zair considered that the most pleasant winter of his life, both before and after Ward and Gabe kidnapped him. Grebus's soldiers had always treated him like one of them and pushed him hard to be the best at every warrior skill. The soldiers of the garrison made him prove himself. Even better, they regularly mistook Anwir for him and expected the prince to perform just as well as the Shadow. Which frustrated the other boy to no end. That was fun, especially when no one quailed in fear of his temper tantrums, and no one hurried to soothe his injured feelings and his pride.

Even better, the twitching and tingling of the mirror spell stopped. Zair braced himself for the assault the first time he learned a new skill to perfection, with Anwir lagging behind. The ring didn't alert him to a spell at work. Viza didn't sense threads of magic coming from a far distance, tracking Anwir's use of whatever charms he had hidden in his belongings. Nothing happened, and Anwir sulked for several days afterward. The potion was more effective than Zair had allowed himself to hope. Or perhaps Anwir had used up all the magic charms given him. Or maybe Grebus's message had reached Magnus and he had identified the magician still pulling strings to control Anwir from the other side of the kingdom. Or perhaps Magnus had shared the message with Nostrados, and the king's wizard had done some seeking and dismantling of magic himself.

When Zair mentioned the change to Grebus, the guard captain just grinned. He pressed a gloved finger to his lips, signaling silence. Then he tugged up the tail of the thick fur vest they all had to wear, even indoors, now that winter had settled into the mountains. Five flattened rings were strung on a thong, tied securely to the man's thick belt. The boy laughed, understanding. Anwir couldn't work his charms if he didn't have them in his hands.

Now he could settle in to really enjoy the winter.
~~~~~

Chapter Sixteen

Zair did enjoy the winter, for the most part. As ridiculous as that seemed, when he thought back on it later. No one could enjoy blinding snowstorms and winds that threatened to pick him up off the wall when he walked watch duty and lift him higher than the peaks. Nor the cold that made his fingers and toes and the exposed skin on his face ache for an hour after he had come indoors again. Still, there were benefits to the isolated, uncomfortable posting at the outermost limits of the kingdom. That list started with such intimate quarters with the soldiers at the garrison that they quickly learned to tell the boys apart. Either the potion Magnus had sent was having an effect, or Anwir's mannerisms and sulky tone of voice made it easy to identify him, even bundled up in thick layers of fur. Zair sometimes daydreamed about the shock that would spread through the palace when they returned to Dorwain and Anwir wore his own face, while Zair looked as he always had. Were there any magicians left of Lazius's gang of crows to punish for this huge error in their calculations, and proof of their lack of magical mastery?

The speculation amused him for only two days. Then renewed realization of the danger he was in bore down on him. If someone besides Magnus untangled the badly woven spell enough to realize that it had specified the image of the true heir to the throne of whatever kingdom they were in, they would guess Zair's dangerous secret. Either they would accuse him of trying to steal the throne, or they would try to use him to put themselves into power.

The question was if King Joben or Nostrados understood the implications.

Zair included a petition in his morning prayers that the winter would last twice as long.

The soldiers took pains to teach Zair skills that they thought would come in handy someday, including dirty in-fighting tricks. They gifted him with coins embedded with short-term spells to expand his senses in dangerous situations. They liked Zair and made no effort to hide their disdain for the prince. Then again, they had little use for anyone who expected everyone around him to consider his comfort before the security of the kingdom. They amused themselves by pretending they still couldn't tell the boys apart. They treated Anwir exactly as they treated Zair when he was serving watch duty, or running errands for them, or when they put him through sword drills. Meaning they were rough with him, pushing him hard, and swatting him when he slacked off. They shouted and sang filthy songs and pretended they couldn't hear, every time Anwir whined and insisted he wasn't Zair. They made up several new training exercises that didn't teach any warrior skills, but did test Anwir's nerve and the steadiness of his stomach and proved them both to be sorely lacking.

Zair thought the exercises good fun, despite the bruises he got, and despite knowing the prince would eventually make him pay for being better than him. Especially now that Anwir didn't have the charms to steal Zair's skills for himself. Several of those exercises included two of the tallest soldiers tossing Zair as high up against a cliff face as they could, with a rope tied around his waist. His task was to climb up the icy, sheer rock face, and fasten the rope at the top for the soldiers to climb up. The soldiers took to calling Zair "spider-boy," he did so well.

They were there in the garrison for just over four months. Anwir soothed his wounded pride by smirking about how oblivious the soldiers were, how easily they were fooled by the repaired illusion spell. The only person he seemed to consider a friend was Rasselus. Zair had feared for a while that Rasselus was in league with Nostrados or whoever had replaced Lazius. Then he noticed the tutor made a habit of sitting with the off-duty soldiers when Anwir was sleeping or sulking and wanted no one around him. Rasselus seemed quite comfortable with the soldiers, drinking and chuckling, and talking quietly. They always went utterly still when Zair approached them, until one of the soldiers said something under his breath and nodded to Zair. Then they relaxed. Especially Rasselus. The tutor never played favorites with the boys, but he always gave Zair far more interesting books to study, and twice as many as he assigned to Anwir. He constantly made snide little comments that made Anwir laugh, and tricked the prince into believing the tutor despised the entire garrison and sympathized for all his discomforts and inconveniences.

Anwir still thought Rasselus was devoted to him after their traveling party left the garrison in the spring, despite the tutor spending every moment he could manage out of the prince's company. Then again, Anwir preferred to sleep when he traveled, and probably didn't notice he was the sole occupant of the coach. Zair wondered how the prince could rule Dorwain when he became king, if he was so oblivious now.

It frightened him in those moments when he thought, just for a few seconds at a time, that he would make a much better king, and Dorwain would be much better off.

~~~~~

The spring rains followed them out of the mountains, and nearly every day started with a chill drizzle before dawn. The clouds hid the
~~~~~

sunrise and the steady downpour rarely let up before noon. Zair preferred riding for hours wrapped in a wet cloak, rather than retreating to the coach and enduring Anwir's company. He felt sorry for Rasselus, who spent every morning in the coach, teaching Anwir. He hoped the tutor kept the prince busy reading, when he wasn't sleeping.

Late one morning, their troop crossed a saddleback ridge and headed down into a valley that seemed to be entirely mud. Every person they passed, every horse and dog and sheep, was coated with mud. They were all in good spirits, and finally curious, Grebus asked why. Several people who answered all agreed it was because the raging river floods that had cut their valley into three parts had finally gone down. There was rebuilding to do, but the people who chose to live here were used to that regular occurrence every spring. When asked why they didn't move to higher land, they laughed. They had a system of levies throughout the valley to guide the floodwaters and protect their homes. The flooding that did escape their control was a small price to pay for the resulting richness of the soil.

Alarm horns sounded in mid-afternoon, just before their troop was about to cross the second of the three rivers. Signal mirrors flashed further down in the valley, followed by the clatter-boom of message drums banging out code.

Cairson was driving the coach that afternoon. Rasselus was free of Anwir, who was sleeping again, and rode ahead of the coach, chatting with Malchus and Nedden about poetry. They were both in the Red Brigade, and kept the soldiers amused around the campfires with new, witty, sometimes filthy verses every few nights. Zair rode on the right of the horses, ready to help urge them to pull harder if the coach got stuck again. The driver went alert, his face stern.

"What's wrong?" Zair asked.

The soldier raised a hand to silence him. A moment later, more drumbeats.

"Captain!" Cairson shouted, and stood up, yanking on the reins to stop the horses. "Flood's broken through a levy wall ahead. Children are trapped, and water's rising faster every second."

"How does he know?" Rasselus said, slowing his horse and looking back at him. Malchus and Nedden dug their heels into their horses and sped up, heading for the front of the column of muddy horses.

"Grew up in this valley," Cairson said. "Yo, Obrey, switch with me."

He leaped down into calf-high mud, splattering it everywhere. Obrey, who had been riding on the left of coach, swung a leg out of the stirrups and over the side of the saddle. He climbed up into the driver's seat, then Cairson took his place. The man dug his heels into his horse's side and raced down the side of the road to join Grebus at the head of the column. Zair followed. This situation was part of the reason the king had sent this troop with Anwir. To make Anwir's face known to the entire kingdom and build a good reputation for him. Granted, Anwir preferred to sit at the head of feasting tables and dance with pretty village girls, as opposed to helping pull wagons out of ditches and transport the ill and elderly to the healer in the next village.

As Zair found out later, listening to Grebus talk with the locals so he could put together his report, the levy had two purposes. First, to guide the soil-rich water to the fields to prepare for spring planting, and then to keep the village dry. The children had been having their lessons in a building also used for sorting and drying the many herbals the village produced. The children were taught on the ground floor, and the harvest from the fall before was stored on the second floor. The village headman and elders had been concerned that the water was still running fast and not going down as quickly here as in other parts of the valley. They had been gathering to discuss what reinforcements to make to the levies, and where, and whether to open an emergency channel that hadn't been used in nearly fifteen years. The meeting hadn't even begun when the main levy broke, with such speed and force that the water ran over and then shattered three subsequent levies. The sorting building was in the lowest part of the valley.

By the time Grebus and his men reached the side of the flood that separated them from the building, the water had already covered the top of the door. The walls visibly shook, taking a pounding from debris from the shattered levies and other buildings already torn down by the force of the water. Sections of mud brick wall had washed away, revealing the beams that reinforced them.

"The horses can't swim against that current," one soldier said, as the troop studied the raging water. "They're too smart to go in, even if we beat them." Even as he spoke, the water swept away more solid ground, surging up so quickly it wet the toes of the boots of the soldiers standing there before they could jump back.

"Arrows, with rope tied to them. Hit the beams, have the children slide down," another suggested.

Visually sizing up the children huddled in the rain on the tile roof of the building, Zair could see that only the oldest would be able to do that. The smaller children shivered so much, they wouldn't have the strength to hold on.

"We have to try to send somebody across, but how can an arrow dig in deep enough, weighted down with a rope thick enough to hold a man's weight while he's working his way across?" Cairson said. Then he stiffened and turned to look at Zair. Several other soldiers turned to him too.

"No," Grebus began, but stopped himself, the agony of the choice wrinkling his face.

"You have to try," Zair said. His voice cracked a little, and he felt hollow. "Now, before the water gets any wider." He gestured down to where the churning edge of the widening stream had climbed higher toward their feet. "Too bad I'm not small enough to attach me to an arrow," he offered, trying to joke.

"You've grown over the winter," the captain said. "Last fall, yes, it might have worked. You've put on muscle and height. Maybe you don't see it—"

"Sorry, captain, but that might be the only workable idea," a man behind Zair said. "Forget the arrow, throw the boy."

"Malchus," he began, a growl in his voice.

"Why not?" Zair said. "The soldiers used to throw me straight up twice that distance. Wouldn't it be easier to throw me as high as you can, and forward instead of up, so I'm still going forward while I'm falling?"

"Lad, you're worth twice that lazy ..." He shook his head, but Zair sensed the captain had already accepted the idea.

Grebus adjusted the plan, moving farther up the banks of the muddy, thick flood. Just in case Zair didn't make it all the way across, he could try to swim toward the building as the current carried him along. They attached several ropes to him, six for the men throwing him to hold, and two ropes for Zair to pull across. The rest of the soldiers got to work jury-rigging harnesses for the children to slide down the ropes to safety.

Zair lay face-down and tried to breathe evenly and not close his eyes as the men holding the ropes swung him back and forth, building up momentum and counting down. He held his head up, when he wanted to tuck it in, and not see what lay before him. On "one!" he swung up high and flew. He nearly forgot to put his arms forward, to try to guide himself.

He hit the water hard, a full horse's length away from the crumbling side of the building. The impact shoved water up his nose and drove air from his lungs. Zair fought not to open his mouth as he struggled up to the surface. The corner of the building seemed to lunge at him and he nearly flung up his arms in automatic defense, to ward off the coming blow. He kicked and paddled and clawed at the building's side as the water slammed him against it, then tore him away.

He clutched at the slick mud bricks. Chunks came off in his hands. Zair scrambled to hold on, dig his fingers in, climb up the wall. Anything to keep from being swept away by the current. The ropes tied around his limbs dragged on him, and for two heart-stopping seconds, he thought the weight of them would drag him down, under the thick, churning stew of mud and debris.

Children's voices cried out and he looked up. There was a window, just above his head. Could he reach it? Zair dug his fingers into the mud bricks. More chunks came off in his hands, and his fingernails tore. He scrambled and clawed and somehow brought his feet up against the side of the building, despite the force of the water yanking on him. Entire bricks collapsed, falling out of the wall. Zair cursed and jammed his hands into the sloppy mess, desperate to catch hold of a beam.

From what sounded like miles behind him, the soldiers shouted and chanted battle cries, their voices penetrating the roar of the water. He grinned despite the water and mud covering his face, threatening to spill down his throat. They cursed him and taunted him, daring him to succeed and prove them wrong. As if he were one of their own.

His fingers jammed between two beams. Zair let out a choked cry of triumph and hung there for several moments, catching his breath. Then, aching, he pulled his body in close and got his feet as secure as he could amid the water and mud. He pushed upward, digging his bleeding fingers into the mud of the half-dissolved bricks. Left hand. Right hand. Raise a foot. Hold on. Raise the other foot. Push higher. Left hand. Right hand.

Slippery wood met his fingers, and he pried his eyes open to see the window frame. He hauled himself up onto it, landing hard on his belly. The impact brought up some of the water he had swallowed. He spat and gagged, hanging there, breathless, his top half inside the building, his bottom half hanging just above the reach of the water. Zair gave himself ten seconds to catch his breath, while the soldiers shouted and cheered and a few of the children echoed them. Zair wanted desperately, painfully, to slide down into the building through that window and find the stairs to the roof. But that would mean untying the ropes that would get the children off this building. He turned himself over, aching, shaking, feeling like he would never be warm and dry again.

The windows were tall and narrow. One shutter was gone, but the other seemed solid and secure. Zair tried not to imagine what would happen if he was wrong. He wiped his muddy fingers on his wet jacket and dug them into the gaps between the thick slats.

"That's right, lad!" Malchus shouted. "Just like on that cliff face. Easy as spitting."

Zair pressed his face against the wet wood and tried to swallow. Despite the drenching he had taken, and the rain battering his backside, his mouth and throat were dryer than sand. He pulled himself up, left arm, pause, catch his breath. Right arm, pause, catch his breath. Again.

A hand wrapped around his wrist, painfully tight. He looked up, into the wide eyes and pale face of a young man only a few years older than him. Another hand snagged his other wrist. A bald, wrinkled man just as drenched as Zair nodded to him. He and the young man pulled, and Zair thought for a moment they would pull his arms out of their sockets. Then he fell sideways, the ropes snagging on the edge of the roof.

The two man were the schoolteachers for the village. While Zair had been climbing, Gregor had shouted instructions to them. They sliced the ropes to get them off him. Drenched and full of mud, untying them was impossible. They fastened the ropes to roof beams they had uncovered by prying up the roofing tiles. They pulled up the drenched harnesses and rigged more out of the ropes used to fling Zair through the air. As quickly as possible, they sent the children down the two long ropes now held tight and steady by teams of soldiers on the opposite side of the growing flood. The smaller children went two and three to a harness. When they ran out of rope and harnesses, they ripped up their jackets, then their shirts, and Zair's jacket and shirt.

The village had twenty-two children. By the time the last five slid down the ropes to the soldiers, the walls of the building shuddered and swayed. Any moment now, they would collapse right off the foundation. Zair cut one rope and tied the end around the two teachers. He helped them slide down the shutter until they were in the water, then he signaled the soldiers. They pulled hard and fast, marching away from the edge of the widening flood. Zair sawed at the remaining rope. He wanted nothing more than to curl up there on the roof, in the rain, and close his eyes for just a few minutes. Every part of his body ached. He thought he could go to sleep there, with the rain hitting his face, so tired that even the bumpy, slick tiles would be as comfortable as his bed in the barracks.

The building shuddered and dropped underneath him, so Zair fell to his knees. Shouts came to him through the thundering of his heart. The rope snapped. The loose end slithered away from him. Shouting a strangled prayer for help, he stumbled after the rope. It jerked and leaped as if alive, up into the air and vanished over the side of the building.

Zair threw himself after it. He didn't think to take a deep breath before his face hit the water. The fingers of one hand caught on the rope. It slid through his grip, burning and scraping. He brought his other hand up, fumbling blindly and caught hold of it as it tightened and jerked, as if fleeing him. He held his breath until he thought his chest would split open, then water filled his mouth and raced down his throat. Coughing and twisting, he held onto that rope until his hands cramped.

Then suddenly hands were pounding him and gripping his wrists and voices burst into his ears. Zair thrashed and coughed and choked and spat and the mud all around tried to drag him down. Then air filled his lungs and he coughed more, stunned by the sharpness of it, the sensation of scratching as he coughed up more water.

Grebus had Malchus and Regan hurry him away, wrapped up in blankets until he almost couldn't see. They made camp on high ground, rather than accepting the grateful hospitality of the village.

Zair didn't even learn the name of the village, Norwent, until several days later. He slept long and hard. The troop's healer, Aron, dosed him against waterlung, until Zair thought he would lose everything in his belly.

When he woke fully, two days later, he heard Anwir talking. Zair groaned, recognizing that self-satisfied tone of voice even before he could make out the words. He was alone in the coach. It stank of wine and the pungent incense Anwir used to clear his mind after a night of drinking. The prince, fortunately, wasn't talking to him, but was outside, addressing a group of villagers.

He was accepting their thanks and deep gratitude for rescuing their children. Zair listened, too tired to be upset. Later, when he heard Rasselus had drowned while helping in the rescue efforts elsewhere in the village, a slow burning settled into his belly. The unfairness of it choked him more than the muddy water. Anwir would always take credit for the risks he took, the rescues he performed, the bruises and broken bones he suffered. If he couldn't break free soon, would he have to ride to war in Anwir's place, give orders, fight his battles, and always stand in the shadows while Anwir was praised, and his name was recorded in the history books as a skilled warrior and great leader?

The burning took on sharp edges when the search party returned, long after dark, having finally found Rasselus's body that had been swept away. Anwir whined that it was about time, could they please leave this cursed wet place now? Grebus was silent a long time. Zair stayed in the shadows just out of the edge of the firelight and trembled for the captain. Would Grebus finally reveal how much he disliked the prince, how little respect he had for him?

"Certainly, Highness, we can leave right now if that is what you want. But consider the repercussions if you leave the honor of burying this hero, your former tutor, to the people of Norwent. What will they think of you, for leaving before the funeral rites are finished? What report will go back to the king? What will your grandfather think of your actions?"

Chapter Seventeen

"I am sick to death of always having to worry about what everyone else thinks!" Anwir shrieked, pounding the air at his sides with his fists. He nearly bent over, so Zair imagined how easy it would be to tap him and send him face-first into the wet dirt. "I don't care! Do you hear me? I don't care!" He stomped away from the firelight. "Do whatever you think best. Nobody cares what I think anyway!"

Then he vanished into the darkness, with his footsteps loud, squelching in the wet dirt. Zair waited until he heard the creaking of the coach door opening, then closing. He muffled a chuckle, picturing Anwir's fury that he couldn't slam the door. It hung too heavy on its thick wood and leather hinges to allow slamming or any abrupt movement.

"I know you're out there." Grebus held out his hand, beckoning, and smiled wearily as Zair stepped out of the shadows. "Tell me, lad, if you were the prince, what would you do?"

"Besides whip his sorry backside until he learns some respect?" one of the soldiers on the far side of the fire circle said. Several chuckled, barely covering the mutters of several others.

"I think Rasselus wouldn't want a monument or any big, fancy tomb," Zair said after a few moments of thought. He felt sure that this was a test. "He'd want to be buried at home. Maybe give some money in his name to help rebuild from the flood?"

"Be careful, lad," Malchus said. He gestured for Zair to take a seat on a folding camp stool between him and the captain. "You might end up doing all the prince's thinking for him, and his choosing, and maybe even his eating and sleeping, not just wearing his fancy clothes."

"A'theosius help him if he has to do the prince's marrying, too," someone else said. Several soldiers laughed at that.

"We all need to be careful here," Grebus said. "Yes, we're tired and the tutor was a good man we all respected, and we're grieving and angry. That loosens tongues, even without a few cauldrons of mulled wine. But do we all trust each other that deeply, to speak so freely and recklessly? All we need is one hint of what was just said to reach the scandalmongers and the schemers and more screeching crows trying to get the king's ear. We'd all be strung up without a heartbeat of warning. And what about our lad, here? He left the palace a boy, but he's become a man among us. What crime has he committed? Think of his neck, even if you don't care about your own."

Zair held perfectly still and tried not to look anyone in the eye. His face warmed, despite the chill settling in his belly. Wouldn't he make a better king than Anwir? Then he pushed the thought away again. It certainly wasn't safe.

~~~~~

Grebus bought a cart from the village and arranged for Rasselus to be taken home, high in the mountains surrounded by the Sandwind Desert, in the southwestern corner of Dorwain. Until the soldiers parted company with the cart and its escort, Zair rode alongside it. He had no trouble portraying the grieving, respectful student. Anwir slept and sulked in the coach. Zair's ring tingled from time to time, warning him that someone was trying to work magic, either on the troop, or focused on him or Anwir. Did the prince have some charms Grebus hadn't found and confiscated? Or were the schemers back to work, with the king's approval? Maybe Nostrados was handling this task binding prince and Shadow personally? Zair's fear grew to an aching in his stomach, when Viza admitted she couldn't discern where the magic came from. The touches were so brief, so faint, she couldn't trace them.

The warnings of magic at work stopped when the cart and its escort separated from their troop and headed south. The remainder of the soldiers and the boys headed east and south. News of Zair's heroism went before them. He considered it his heroism, even if the people called out Anwir's name. He let himself enjoy a little of the acclaim. Why not, since he rode in public and they saw his face? Too soon, though, the need to smile and wave and look dignified grew wearisome. He resented not being able to enjoy the sweets and small pastries that the wives and daughters of village headmen pressed into his hands whenever they stopped for a loyalty-building visit along the way. Anwir always had to have first choice. He smirked whenever he reminded Zair that those gifts were for the prince, not the Shadow.

The story of the rescue at Norwent raced ahead of them, and soon, calls for help were coming in from every direction. The first time, Anwir grumbled, until Grebus reminded him that was the purpose of their long journey around the kingdom: to make him look good and earn the people's love. By the sixth race to assist in some crisis, Anwir grew excited whenever a messenger on foot or horseback caught up with them. He took visible pleasure in sending his soldiers, and especially his Shadow, to deal with the crisis.

Zair rode out every three or four days in answer to pleas for help. Tracking roving bands of bandits. Providing protection for a caravan of healers or merchants escorting precious herbs and other ingredients for healing potions and salves. Helping to track down and capture and kill
~~~~~

rogue beasts created through magic that had broken free of their restraints and were threatening innocent villagers. Every call for help, no matter how small, Anwir insisted on responding. Which meant that Zair rode out in his place.

Sometimes, Zair wondered if Anwir hoped he would be killed. Then again, wouldn't that put the prince in a bind, if he had been seen lying dead in some accident, and then appeared in public an hour later, perfectly fine? Maybe Anwir just wanted him brutally injured, crippled, at the very least in agony for a few days.

Didn't the prince think things through to their logical conclusion? What if the magic binding them together hadn't been weakened enough for the most dangerous ties to snap? The ones that made prince and Shadow share what they experienced. Wouldn't Anwir be surprised if Zair broke bones or suffered deep, bloody wounds, and he felt the pain? Or even suffered the breaks and cuts himself? The shrieks of fury and pain and terror would be hard for the soldiers to muffle. Especially if there were witnesses.

And even if Anwir didn't taste some justice by sharing what he inflicted on Zair, there was the problem if bystanders saw him go down under his wounds and saw the prince a short time later, unharmed. He would be revealed as a fraud. Not just a fraud, but a coward and a cheat.

The pleasure of anticipating Anwir's humiliation if the truth ever came out didn't last long under the weight of common sense. Zair knew he would be punished for the prince's loss of adoration and respect, and the people's justified fury if they ever learned the truth. He held fast to the prayers he made to A'theosius every day for safety for their entire troop, freedom from the tangled spells binding him to the prince, and a chance to escape. He trusted Viza to soothe his aches and bruises, and prayed he would never need to depend on her limited power to heal him from worse injuries. He chose to enjoy responding to the calls for help, just because the hunt got him away from Anwir.

~~~~~

Just past summer solstice, a call for help turned into an ambush. Men clothed in black capes and hoods leaped out from under and behind the wreckage of a merchant caravan. Zair's ring bit at his finger, warning of strong magic in use. He shouted the signal word to Grebus, to warn him. At the same moment, the captain lunged forward, aiming at a tall man with a cloud swirling around him in a putrid shade of yellow. The man shouted words in a foreign tongue and pointed his sword straight at Zair.

The boy's horse stumbled but kept its feet. Cairson put himself between Zair and the men racing toward them on foot. Following the pattern established by long months of intense drilling and preparation, Grebus and the others raced forward. Zair fell back and circled around
~~~~~

and away from the traveling party and the coach where Anwir rode. Probably in another drunken sleep.

Someone had at long last come after Anwir, to kill the heir to the throne.

As the prince's Shadow, Zair needed to lead those assassins away and find a secure place to hide, find some way to distract them, keep them busy, until the soldiers could disarm them.

All their focus was on Zair as they sped forward on foot, faster than ordinary men could run. Definitely aided by magic. They were so intent on Zair, their leader didn't see Grebus on the attack. The captain easily slashed him with a sword, halfway severing his head from his neck. Several soldiers went down under the nearly maniacal slashes of swords from black-garbed attackers, three to a man. As soon as they fell or were disarmed, their attackers moved on, as if they had become invisible.

Cairson shouted and tossed Zair the end of a rope. He twirled his gloved hand. The boy understood. They turned their horses, riding circles around three men, tangling them in the rope and knocking them to the ground. They struggled and cursed, until Cairson dismounted, yanked off their helmets, and clubbed the backs of their heads with the hilt of his sword.

The attackers shouted in some foreign tongue, clearly curses even if the words weren't recognizable. They kicked and spat and punched when they were disarmed, and kept moving, trying to get to Zair even after they had been slashed so brutally, they should have collapsed in pools of their own blood.

Obrey, the coach's driver today, stood up and swung a bag that glowed with a pulsing silvery light. He flung it over everyone's heads to Grebus, who winced when he caught it. He untied the knot holding it closed, then turned his head away. He swung his arm, holding onto the bottom of the bag, and spread a powder through the air that glowed with the same silvery light.

The powder gathered itself up in a cloud and spun down and around all the writhing, kicking bodies that should have been still already. A *whoomph* sound, like dragon powder thrown into a fire, erupted with a flash of black light. The bodies lay still, and Zair gagged as a smell of corruption gushed out from them.

Several last flickers of that silvery powder swirled around, sending out seeking tendrils. A large tendril found the three men Zair and Cairson had captured. The men twitched and the light enclosed them, lifting them until they hung upright, with their feet dangling at knee height above the ground. Their heads lifted and their eyes opened, and that silvery light gleamed in their eyes.

Grebus stomped over, wiping blood spatter off his face, studying the men with narrowed eyes.

"They're not dead, but I'll swear before the Enchanters' Court, they aren't alive, either," the captain said.

"Wonder what kingdom is desperate enough to come after the prince," Cairson growled. He rested a hand on Zair's shoulder and shook him twice. "You did good, lad. When I was your age, I would have run for it and wet my trousers while I was at it."

Grebus snorted. "When you were his age, you were already making the rest of us wet our trousers."

Cairson snorted and nodded, his answering grin only a brief flicker.

"Who do you serve? What king? What wizard empowers you?" Grebus asked. The men shuddered but didn't answer. The two soldiers exchanged puzzled, worried frowns.

"Shouldn't that powder compel the truth from them?" Obrey said, moving up to join them.

"Maybe they don't know?" Zair offered.

Grebus snorted and nodded. "Who knows the answer to my questions?"

"Angrus," the three said in unison.

"Anyone else think that's more than a little unnatural?" Obrey muttered.

"Where is Angrus? Who is Angrus?" Grebus said.

"Shokamal's fires," the one facing them said, at the same time the one on his left said, "Bittram's pit," and the one on the right said, "The outer darkness."

"Huh." He took a step back and glanced around at the bloody battlefield.

His gaze landed on a pile of rotted clothes and rusty armor and bones, all that remained of the tallest man of the group. Zair's stomach knotted when he realized that had been the man with the yellow cloud of magic. When and how had he decayed so quickly?

"That tells us much, and nothing useful," Grebus said.

"Meaning?" Cairson growled.

"They're mercenaries, from all over the world. Their leader is in whatever eternal punishment each of them believes in, and he didn't trust his men enough to tell them who was paying them to come after the prince."

He walked around the three bound men once, scowling and rubbing his jaw as he always did when he was thinking hard about unpleasant things. Zair didn't like it when Grebus did that, because the decisions he came up with were usually rough on their entire troop, and hardest of all on him as their leader.

"Do you know why you were sent after the prince? To kill him or just capture him? To enslave him with magic?" Grebus asked.

The three prisoners said nothing.

"Shouldn't they at least say no?" Zair said. His voice cracked.

"They should." Cairson nodded.

"So. I didn't ask the right question," Grebus said.

"What's the right question?" Zair clenched his fists, hating the growing sense of pressure in his chest. "What were you looking for? Why did you attack us?"

All three men turned their heads to focus on him. He held still, when he wanted to duck behind Cairson, who was certainly big enough to hide him. Zair had the awful feeling those glowing silver eyes could see him no matter where he went, no matter what he hid behind, and no matter how far away he ran. He was sixteen, and the soldiers had celebrated his birthday with an ox roast and a night of bloody and bawdy storytelling, but he felt as if he were only eight years old now.

"Why aren't they answering?" Obrey said. "Still the wrong answer?"

"Maybe I'm the only one the spell compels them to answer," Grebus said. He repeated Zair's questions.

"Catch the Shadow," the three men said in chorus. Their hands twitched and their arms flexed, straining against the ropes binding them. One man's hand snapped at the wrist in the effort to reach into the pouch at his waist.

Zair gagged, but made himself stay still, watching, listening, despite the thundering of his pulse in his throat.

"What were you supposed to do when you caught him?" Grebus asked. He stepped over and gripped Zair's shoulder. "What's in your pouch?"

"Spells. Talismans. Enslave him. Kill the prince and put the Shadow in his place," one man said.

~~~~~

Before Zair went to bed that night, in the coach, with soldiers posted all around it, Grebus sent the fastest rider to Andorwain with a report. Zair couldn't sleep, though Anwir certainly had no trouble, once he got over complaining drunkenly about having to share the coach. Usually, Zair slept outside, perfectly content to roll up in a blanket beside the fire, among the soldiers, or camp under the coach when rain threatened. The prince snored, until it seemed like the fittings inside the coach rattled with his every breath. Zair kept startling, twitching his blanket aside or even sitting upright every time he thought he heard someone trying to get into the coach. Or worse, imagined he heard someone scratching at the bed of the vehicle beneath him, trying to get up through the wood with a sword to kill him.

How could Anwir sleep, even drunk? Didn't he understand how bad
~~~~~

things were, what danger he was in? These mercenaries had been sent to kill the heir to the throne and put another in his place. Didn't Anwir care about the danger to himself?

Long after the guard shift had changed for the second time that night, Zair finally wore himself out with startling and thinking and managed to say a few prayers. He considered praying aloud, in hopes Anwir would hear him and wake up and have a temper tantrum. The prince had made it clear that he shared his grandfather's true feelings about A'theosius and prayers and reading the holy words. He refused to participate in the soldiers' morning prayers or listen to the short homilies provided every few days by Abyl, the troop's cook and friar-in-training.

Zair curled up on his side and whispered his prayers. Mostly they consisted of, "Please, A'theosius, keep us safe. Please make any other enemies out there blind, like in the story of Andrus who smuggled copies of the holy words through the blockade at Mercocia. Please ... if I can't go home, if it still isn't safe for my family, can I get out of Dorwain? Please?"

He repeated himself until he relaxed enough he fell asleep.

He woke at the dark between moonset and dawn, with Malchus shaking him awake, a hand over his mouth to keep him silent. Zair climbed out of the wagon, resisting the temptation to "accidentally" kick the sleeping prince on his way out.

The entire camp had been packed up and everyone was mounted, ready to ride. Zair found his mount, saddled and waiting next to Grebus. He rubbed his eyes, nodded salute to the captain, and climbed up into his saddle. He barely got settled before the entire company moved out.

They rode into the dawn. Abyl trotted up and down the column, passing out cold meat pies and small water flasks filled with a spicy herbal brew that would help them stay alert. No one banged on the door of the coach to feed Anwir.

"Sleeping potion in his evening wine," Grebus said, after Zair had looked back down the column at the coach, and the prince had yet to bang on the roof and shout his usual demands for food, hot wine, wash water, attention. He grinned, and it was not a nice grin.

"Where are we going?" Zair asked after several long moments. The only sounds breaking the quiet were the clop-thud of hooves and the whisper of the wind through the short stalks in the vivid green fields that surrounded the highway as far as the eye could see.

"Back to Andorwain. It's the only logical response to that threat. If one enemy knows the prince has a Shadow, then many others will know." Grebus shook his head. "I'm not waiting for the king's council to dither and argue and put your life in danger. I've seen them delay decisions in the hopes that others will act and take the need to decide out of their hands. You're worth ten of Anwir, and every man of this troop would face a lot worse than those puppets we killed to ensure you live long enough to be an even better man. If the throne of Dorwain wasn't protected with a wretched spoilsport's curse, I'd be tempted to put you in that young, filthy puppy's place, permanently. Our kingdom would be much better off."

"Please don't talk like that," Zair whispered. He shivered, feeling his guts twist around the meat pie that felt like a brick inside him.

"No, never again. That's why it has to be said now. Once we ride through the outer gates of the city ..." Grebus sighed, and the light faded from his eyes. His mouth settled into grim lines. "Even innocent, you'll be considered the ringleader of every plot that appears from now on. I don't doubt you'll be watched and isolated for the rest of your life, to keep schemers from contacting you and keep you from plotting to take what, by all rights, should have been yours all along."

Chapter Eighteen

Their company took every back road and cut across barren plains and generally avoided the expected route to reach the capitol with as much speed as possible. Zair played with the idea that Grebus chose that route just to make the journey as uncomfortable as possible for Anwir. Then he discovered that Abyl drugged the prince's wine every night, so he always slept until halfway through the morning. If Anwir caught on, he didn't complain or threaten anyone. He did, however, demand his wine earlier every evening, and more of it.

Their company split up, a day out from Andorwain, and came into the capitol from multiple directions. Grebus led the small escort trusted with Anwir and Zair. They came from the north, using the route and gate normally reserved for couriers. They exchanged the coach for a wagon piled high with crates to create a hidden space for Anwir, who slept the entire time. The soldiers removed their uniforms and disguised themselves as emissaries with a wagon of quarterly tribute collected from several small, minor vassal kingdoms hidden among the mountains. There was no parade, no welcoming crowds. When Grebus explained the plan, Anwir sulked until Abyl gave him a skin of wine. Then he finally climbed into his hiding place. He muttered threats and complaints until the drug took effect. Most of those threats had Zair's name, sometimes the only coherent word. Apparently, the prince had decided now that everything was his Shadow's fault.

They entered the palace through a long tunnel that began more than half a mile away from the city walls. Zair wondered just how many of these hidden passages there were under the capitol city, and just how firm the foundations of the large buildings could be, with so much cut out of the rock beneath them. He thought of the hints of danger for the seamstresses who had made his wardrobe to match the prince's, more than three years ago now, and wondered if anyone who had dug those tunnels had been allowed to live long past the completion of their work.

The seneschal waited for them, to take charge of Anwir. The prince tumbled out of the wagon in a cloud of wine fumes. In the shadows of the underground chamber, Zair couldn't clearly see the seneschal's face, but he could have sworn the man looked amused by the prince's condition.

The seneschal thanked the soldiers for their time of service, expressed the king's gratitude for their loyalty, and dismissed them. Then, as Grebus turned to lead his horse away, the man tossed over his shoulder, "And take the Shadow back to the Brigade. They are his keepers, after all."

Zair tried not to flinch at being treated like an afterthought. Going back to the Red Brigade, to Yancob's care, was a good thing. He would be more worried if someone else was in charge of him now. Of course, common sense said that he might never leave the Red Brigade's underground barracks, even to fill in for Anwir at some boring council meetings. He might just be waiting until the king decided if he was a threat or merely a tool that no longer served its purpose.

Would the Red Brigade be charged with disposing of that tool?

~~~~~

Yancob and a good third of his most trusted and skilled soldiers were gone, when Zair crept into the barracks long after midnight and found his room. The ones who were awake smiled and welcomed him back, but there was a restraint in their eyes and voices that worried Zair. Had Yancob fallen out of favor? Had Nostrados discovered Encobi had magic and studied the forbidden magic books, using all her skill and knowledge for her father's benefit? True, serving the Red Brigade with magic was serving the throne, but Zair felt sure that the politicians and nobles and power players would twist the discovery around to paint Encobi as a traitor for not offering her inborn magic to the king.

He wouldn't find out anything until morning, if he was lucky. Zair dropped his pack of clothes and weapons in his tiny closet of a room and shivered at the sudden understanding that washed over him. He had never been put into the barracks with the other soldiers, and that had to mean something. Either he was considered a threat back then, or he was in more danger than anyone was willing to admit, as the prince's Shadow.

Would he be allowed to leave the barracks and go visit Shaleen, and Magnus? Would they be able to tell him anything? He wasn't certain he could remember his way to the shielded room where Magnus had hidden the remainder of Viza's dust. Could he hide in that room if the situation turned dangerous?

Morning came far too soon, which was bitterly amusing, because he thought he wouldn't be able to sleep. When he went to get his breakfast, he asked about the residents of the palace. Magnus had been gone from the capitol for a month now on errands for the king. Princess Jillian had been in semi-retreat since last fall. Shaleen had gone back to the Firebird Guild. The princess never left the palace, and since she attended few public gatherings or occasions, there was no need for her Shadow. The Red Brigade provided her protection, when Magnus was not at her side.

Zair didn't like that news. He felt as if all his friends and allies were being removed. He wondered if Anwir had reported to his grandfather yet on the grand tour, what he had done and said, how he had made
~~~~~

himself popular with the people. He felt Anwir would claim all the heroic things and hard work Zair had done as his own. Would the king know Anwir lied? Would the king even care?

You think very loudly, Viza said. She chuckled softly when Zair flinched, nearly dropping his mug of mulled wine.

She had been silent for longer periods of time as the company grew closer to Andorwain. With some kind of magic always being flung around for defensive purposes, or other magic triggering his ring, alerting him to someone spying, it simply hadn't been safe for the mirror to be awake. The more active Viza was, the easier she would make it for the remaining magicians to find Zair through the magical "noise" he gave off.

We're safe here, the mirror assured him.

How do you know?

Because my remaining dust is here. That girl is lovely. Clever, with a nasty sense of humor, and brave and so very considerate. Yes, before you ask, I have been talking with her ever since we arrived here last night. That's why I've been silent. Magnus gave her the box of dust last winter. She has been seeking a way to reunite me and find a mirror to be my new body, all the time we've been out there, hiding and making that snot look like a decent man.

Girl? Encobi? She's safe?

Indeed she is. But not for long. That wizard has come sniffing far too often. She's had to abandon Magnus's shielded room and rarely comes down to visit her father. Ten men who have been added to the Red Brigade since you left stink of controlling magic. If they aren't voluntarily spying for that wizard, then they've been enslaved, so he can look through their eyes and hear with their ears and smell magic at work.

But it's safe for you to talk to me now?

Not for long. Magnus is preparing to fly. The princess is in danger. That filthy wizard has turned her father against her even more than she feared. She has been in mourning. Word came in the fall that her husband, Phoebus, died in a shipwreck. Magnus sensed too many people in the inner council weren't surprised. Some of his diplomatic trips for the throne took longer than necessary, so he could investigate. He learned the ugly truth. Phoebus was murdered. Even worse, he died two winters ago. All the letters the princess has received from him have been forgeries.

"Why tell her now, if they kept it secret so long?" Zair whispered, losing all sense of caution in his shock. He flinched and looked around. None of the soldiers scattered among the tables, having their breakfast, seemed to notice.

So she can be officially named a widow. The king intends to sell her as an alliance bride as soon as the minimum time of mourning has ended.

Anwir doesn't know. He'd have destroyed the coach with his tantrum if he knew.

Don't be too sure. That boy has been under too much of the wrong kind of influence. He hasn't asked about his father once since he and his mother were summoned to Dorwain. Whenever she read him her letters from Phoebus, he felt shame at having a merchant for a father. I wouldn't be surprised if he not only approves of his father's death, but he won't even think to go to his mother to comfort her. The truly wretched part of the whole cruel scheme is that the king intends to sell her to Encruestia.

Zair shuddered, even before he could recall the details he had learned about that far off northern kingdom. His breakfast turned foul in his stomach as the worst details rose to his mind: Encruestia had outlawed all worship of A'theosius. They practiced a bloody worship to fuel their form of magic and burned human sacrifices alive. They were rumored to have breeding farms to supply infants for sacrifice. Princess Jillian would not last more than a few days in a kingdom like that. She was devoted to A'theosius, and even if she was bound and gagged, she would still worship. Her new husband would kill her within days.

We think the king intends for those vile creatures to kill the princess, to justify war, and take over Encruestia's wealth, Viza offered in a sad whisper.

"When do we leave?" Zair said, his voice a rasp of fury. He clenched his mug so tightly, the wood creaked.

Encobi will try to remove some of my dust from the snot. If she succeeds, she will try again. Until she has it all, or no more comes out.

"Or she is caught?" Zair shuddered.

Yancob won't let that happen.

Zair hoped that was true. But what happened if Encobi was caught before her father returned from the mission that took him and his most trusted men away from the palace?

He clenched his fists and prayed, and even though the words were nearly incoherent inside his own head, he knew A'theosius heard.

He had to believe the All-Maker heard.

~~~~~

At midnight, two nights later, Viza woke Zair with the news that Yancob had returned, and he was to meet him and Encobi in an inner, shielded room. She also showed him how to find and open the secret passage that Encobi used to enter the barracks without anyone noticing.

"Why do you sound louder?" Zair whispered, once he had crept down the passageway far enough no one in the barracks could have heard him if he shouted. His head seemed to ring a little, so he found it hard to form the words inside his mind.

That lovely girl. Viza giggled. That ringing grew louder.

"What did she do?"

She freed some of me, and that spoiled brat didn't notice a thing. I expect that vile wizard to notice, though. I've felt him poking around among all the tangles of spellwork, removing the badly made spells and trying to tighten other
~~~~~

threads of magic to gain control over Anwir. I caught fragments of thoughts about assassination attempts on the king, and how he can't allow that just yet because the prince doesn't trust him. And yes, before you ask, I warned the girl and she told her father. If it's safe for him to warn the king, who knows?

"Why wouldn't it be?" Zair almost ran into the solid wall at the end of the passageway before he realized he had run out of passageway.

Just how does he explain to the king how he learned what he's reporting? And how does he prove the wizard is guilty?

"Oh." He felt more than a little stupid. "How do we get out?"

She's coming.

The ringing sound grew stronger, louder, and threatened to make his teeth itch. Zair stepped back, sensing the stirring of magic before he saw the line of light draw an oval in the stone wall, from floor to ceiling. With a soft grating, scraping sound, the oval of stone slid outward, then aside, and lantern light spilled golden and warm into the passageway.

Zair stopped himself just in time from exclaiming that he had been able to see in the dark but hadn't realized it until just that moment. He hoped he could blame being awakened from a sound sleep for the slow pace of his brain. He stepped into a small, low-roofed room carved out of the bedrock. The walls and ceiling shimmered in soft bursts, in a color he couldn't name, or even describe, when he thought about it later. Encobi and Yancob sat at a long, narrow table, with a deep tray of water in front of them that flickered and sparkled with light. The ringing sound, Zair realized, came from the water. Or maybe that wasn't water?

"Is that some of Viza's dust?" he asked, as he stepped over to join them. He nearly stumbled and missed the mark, when a new thought struck him just as he lowered himself onto a bench opposite Yancob. "Am I going to have to drink that water?"

How else, he wondered, would Viza's dust be joined to the dust of her that was already inside his body?

Encobi shook her head, her weary smile widening. She probably thought he was being silly.

"Just put your hands in the tray and let me sort of slip in through your skin, dear boy," Viza said, her voice coming from the water, with accompanying sparkles of green and blue and purple. She chuckled when Zair flinched. He wasn't used to hearing her voice with his ears.

"She's been filling us in on all the things she's been learning, all the things Anwir's hopeful masters were telling him, twisting his mind and soul, turning him a traitor to his grandfather," Yancob growled. "She couldn't talk to him, like she could to you, because he doesn't have a lick of magical potential. Nothing for her to anchor to. But the dust could hear everything that stupid boy did and said and thought and heard."

"They put three times as much of her dust on Anwir as they did on you," Encobi said. "Hoping to awaken magic in him. That's not how it works. Oh, the awful, stupid, entirely untrue things they've been teaching him, promising him all sorts of magic when he becomes king. It serves them right, getting their tongues cut out and then hanged up for crow bait like they did." The fierceness of her voice made Zair shudder. "What do you expect, with the loss of all the magic schools and books and the destruction of traditions? People have been figuring out magic on their own, and unable to warn anyone when something goes wrong and they get themselves killed. And all those ridiculous, illogical theories that keep perpetuating through the decades, because everyone comes up with a dozen reasons why a spell worked for someone else but not for them, and—" She squeaked when Yancob put a huge hand over her mouth.

"Enough, lass. This handy little time pocket of yours will only last so long. It's draining you too much as it is," her father said.

"Time pocket?" Zair asked, intrigued.

"I'll explain later," Viza said. "Oh, there is so very much to teach you." The light shimmering across the surface of the water in the tray darkened and swirled with angry-looking yellow and black sparks. "It's distressing, the depths to which the levels of magic have deteriorated in this kingdom. Someone should really make an official report to the Enchanters' Court. I find it hard to believe they don't know."

"I've never asked," Yancob said. He braced his arms on the table, leaning forward slightly to look down into the water. "Why are there no magic mirrors in our kingdom?"

"We have plenty of legends," Encobi said, "and many of them are so ridiculously frightening, it makes me wonder what crimes previous generations of enchanters committed, to make mirrors turn against them, to generate those stories."

"I'm too far away from the web of magic mirrors, to ask and get a definitive answer, or at least send a request for a historical archives search," Viza said. "Even when this much of me rejoins with what's in Zair, I won't be strong enough. But eventually, oh, the things I need to catch up on, and the things I need to teach him! However … the general rule is to avoid landing on this entire continent, and Dorwain in particular. Cruel things were done to magic mirrors in the past, and we fought back. I shudder to think of those mirrors who shattered themselves on purpose, to deprive wicked enchanters of the benefits of instant communication around the world, and the ability to inquire into libraries and archives everywhere."

"There are no magic mirrors anywhere, at all?" Zair said.

"None that we know of," Encobi said. "I couldn't ask the Enchanters' Court for help if I wanted. They won't listen. And I doubt they'd let me approach if I could find a doorway to one of the time pockets where they convene. The best I could do would be to gather all of Viza's dust into a box created to protect it, and trust someone else to deliver her and ask them to find a healer of mirrors. Or simply go to another kingdom, make contact with some properly educated enchanters, and ask them for help. Yet how can I do that without making Nostrados and all the other puppet masters in the king's court instantly suspicious of my father?"

"That's why we'd must flee when our lady does," Yancob rumbled. His mouth flicked up in a wintry smile when Zair gasped and sat up straight, stunned by his words.

"Not before I get enough of myself back together that I can call out and search for other mirrors," Viza said. The water's surface shivered, blurring for several seconds. "What I fear more than a dozen greedy dolts trying to enslave me is the ugly possibility that there are several mirrors still in this kingdom, totally out of communication with the mirror web. Either they support the plans and principles of their human overlords, or they've gone cracked and insane. Which they might try to inflict on me. Those of us who are small enough to go traveling, physically, have all heard horror stories over the centuries, of mirrors that went mad and bad because of isolation, or torments inflicted on them by powerful enchanters."

"So that's the plan?" Zair clenched his fists in his lap to hold them still. He needed to put his body into the quiet alertness and energy-saving calm Yancob and the Brigade had been teaching him, and the discipline he had learned from the soldiers in the garrison outpost all winter. "We infuse as much of Viza into me as we can, then we take the princess and run?"

"Simplest plans are best," Yancob said, his voice gruff.

"What do I need to do?" he said, to stave off a dozen questions that would only waste time. He sensed there was no getting off this path until the journey was completed.

When Encobi and Viza explained it to him, Zair felt like laughing at how simple it sounded. He would put his hands into the water holding Viza's dust, and she would draw the dust through his skin into his blood, then settle it in his bones. The speed with which this happened, and how many sessions would be required depended on how his inborn magic resisted the infusion of mirror energy.

His skin prickled when he immersed his hands, up past his wrists. That wasn't so bad. Until the prickling felt like sand rubbed into sunburned skin. Zair bit his lip until he tasted blood and breathed slowly, deeply through his nose.

The sunburn changed to embers streaking through his blood. Sweat spilled down into his eyes, so he closed them. He envisioned the particles of mirror dust lazily swimming through his blood, taking their own good time. And burning his blood to dust in his veins.

Can't you speed it up? he silently snarled. *Move faster!*

Zair envisioned the dust connecting into long strands of sparkling silver, swimming through his veins like snakes, gaining speed with every heartbeat. He envisioned openings in his bones, sucking in the dust, the mirror energy. He choked on the need to scream, and the refusal to let out a sound.

Enough! Viza shrieked, her voice echoing as if his head and chest had gone hollow.

Zair curled up within himself as all sound and light and sense of movement instantly vanished, like an enormous bubble popping. He held still, not even breathing, refusing to move for fear he would shatter. Fearful he had turned himself to dust. What had he done? He wasn't sure, but he had the awful feeling it was impossible.

Gradually, a sensation of floating and delicately bouncing off surfaces and slowly swirling downward wiped away everything else, and then even that faded.

Chapter Nineteen

Bitter, gritty, hot liquid filled Zair's mouth, and for several seconds he had the strangest sensation that his body coalesced into being from his mouth outward. He opened his eyes and saw the ceiling of the little room.

"That wasn't very smart, was it?" Encobi said, leaning into his field of vision. She shook her head with a crooked, weary little smile, and reached down to wipe his face. The cloth was wet and cold and smelled of mint and other soothing herbs. His skin tingled like he had been sunburned, and he remembered in that instant all the sensations he had endured. He sat up, which he reflected later wasn't very smart.

His whole body jangled and chimed like a dozen bells tossed into a barrel and sent tumbling down a flight of steps. He groaned. Big hands caught hold of his wrists, pulling his hands down away from his face. More of that gritty, bitter liquid filled his mouth. He swallowed.

"No, not smart at all," she continued. "But efficient. Viza, how are you?"

Oh, much better. I feel like I've tripled in size and strength.

The mirror's voice rang inside Zair's head and he started to moan, then realized the sound didn't hurt.

"That's better than we hoped for. How many more times will Zair need to do this?" She chuckled. "How many more times do I have to bring him back from eternal sleep?"

Not at all. He sucked up every bit of me that you were able to retrieve.

"Wait," Zair said. His voice rasped like he had swallowed sand. "You can hear her, when she's inside my head again?"

There is enough of me reunited that a truly strong enchantress like Encobi can hear me. Viza sounded as if she perched on the edge of being giddy. *Much of that is reinforced by your inherent magic. Royal blood, if I forgot to tell you before, has strong magical potential. You could be the king of prophecy, if you wanted, but I wouldn't recommend it. Being* the object *of prophecy is almost as* bad as choosing *to be the focal point of a prophecy.* She chuckled. *My dear boy, you have more magic in you than even I guessed, after all this time sharing quarters with you, so to speak. You woke up something when you willed your body to open up and take in the dust and speed up the process.*

We have a great deal of teaching to do. It's dangerous for you, and for everyone around you, to have so much untrained potential. History is full of tragic stories of young folk like you who had no idea of the magic growing within them, and went years without training, until some crucial point in their lives, some tragedy struck, some horrific danger fell on them, and they simply exploded, loosing all that magic to meet the need. Most of them didn't survive that explosion. Far too many of the survivors turned evil, because the ridiculous, fearful, jealous reactions of the people around them forced them down that path while they were confused and simply shattered inside. I refuse to allow that to happen to you, after the sacrifices you have made for me.

That would have to wait, because Zair was physically drained. Yancob helped him get back to his closet bedroom to recover. Zair had far too much time to think, lying in his bed in the darkness, and ponder the revelations. He couldn't sleep, despite the exhaustion. The power thrumming through him, the sense of Viza on the other side of a thin partition in his mind, happily settling in, expanding her sense of self, growing used to being "more," made it hard to sink into the waiting sea of darkness and oblivion.

Viza and Encobi agreed that Zair's exposure to magic through the mirror's occupation in his flesh had awakened the fires of magic that likely should have slept for another century in his bloodline, waiting for one of his descendants to be the king of prophecy. They both recommended, as soon as he escaped Dorwain and freed himself of the mirror spell, that he find a teacher and study magic. Even if he didn't decide to become an enchanter, he needed to learn enough to understand what was happening to him and gain the discipline to control the power when it surged. He needed to keep the magic from awakening and breaking free, without any controls, when he was faced with danger. He didn't need to draw all sorts of dangerous attention to himself by suddenly shooting off half-made spells or working uncontrolled magic and causing damage and chaos all around him.

If ethical enchanters weren't around to rescue innocent victims of ignorance when such explosions occurred, fate was often unkind and cruel. Far too many people with strong magical potential had attracted the wrong kind of attention, because of their lack of control or understanding. Some were lucky enough to awaken to their magic in kingdoms that taught the proper disciplines of magic. They were sent to the Enchanters' Council and assigned to a teacher. The unlucky ones, who awoke in kingdoms with the wrong attitude toward magic, were often arrested. Either they were executed for practicing magic without permission from the authorities, or they became slaves of the government. Or malicious enchanters caught them and drained them of all their energy. Some went insane from fear, if they lived in kingdoms that believed all magic came from the dark spirits and was totally opposed to A'theosius. Those strong enough to survive the fear and abuse too often used their magic for evil. Either their souls turned bitter from oppression and persecution, or they believed they had no other options.

First things first, Zair told himself. *Help Her Highness escape, then get out of Dorwain, then break the mirror spell and all ties with Anwir. Then figure out what I want to be.*

He played with the idea of going home, to say goodbye to his father. Zair knew such a move would be dangerous and foolish and might endanger his family. He needed to get over the border as quickly as possible, in case the ties between him and Anwir were still strong enough that Nostrados could use them to find him.

He thought about the stories Pendrake had told him about the enchanted forest. If only he could find it and beg shelter from the castle at its heart.

~~~~~

Viza informed Zair, her voice sounding sour and off-key in his head, that rejoining her dust had strengthened communication with the fragments of dust remaining in Anwir that Encobi hadn't been able to remove yet. If she focused, she could listen in on what the prince was doing and saying, and sometimes even thinking.

Not a pleasant experience at all. That boy is vile, to put it simply.

The ability to overhear what their enemies were plotting was too valuable a gift to waste. Over the next ten days, while Zair regained his strength and trained hard and practiced the disciplines Encobi taught him, he spoke very little with Viza. She needed all her energy to watch Anwir. Zair also saw nothing of Encobi. She had to stay away from the Red Brigade's barracks because the new recruits, who were clearly spies for Nostrados, hummed with active minor spells, likely seeking signs of magic in use. Zair lived in fear that any day now, those spells would lead them to him. How long could he withstand Nostrados's attention focused on him before Viza's presence in his flesh was revealed.

Oh, no worry about that, Viza assured him, on one of her rare visits.

He was sitting in the shadows of the meeting room of the Brigade's barracks, listening to Yancob and his adjutants planning the long trip to the coast, and then the sea voyage to Encruestia. King Joben had simply ignored his daughter's and Magnus's protests. At the same time, he accused any of his nobles who were against the alliance of fomenting rebellion against the throne. The high ranks and political and economic power of the loudest voices didn't protect all of them from imprisonment. Rumors crept through Andorwain that some nobles had died under guard, from no identifiable cause. Other rumors, much quieter, blamed Nostrados's magic.

Princess Jillian's supporters slowly grew silent. No one remained to protest, and Magnus was conveniently out of the country on diplomatic business, when the ambassador from Encruestia arrived with the formal documents for the marriage alliance. Within a month, the Brigade would
~~~~~

ride out to escort the unwilling bride to her new home.

How can I not worry? Zair nearly spoke aloud. *I can feel magic at work now without the help of the ring. I can feel the pulses when I'm doing my silencing exercises.*

That doesn't mean they can hear you, Viza assured him. *No one in this benighted kingdom knows anything about mirror magic. Or if they do know something, it's almost laughably incorrect. As proven by how they bungled their attempts to mirror you and that snot. They can't hear the song, and as long as my magic is intertwined with yours, they won't hear you. As simple as that.*

Zair wanted to believe her, to the point of pain. He couldn't help worrying, though. The spark of anger against Anwir grew steadier as the days sped by until Princess Jillian's departure, and her son displayed no concern for her welfare.

Viza showed him the scene through Anwir's eyes when the grand procession, with Yancob at the head of the escort of twenty members of the Red Brigade and another hundred soldiers rode out of the palace, heading for the western gate and the long journey to the coast. Anwir stood on a balcony, watching the farewells with the nobles and officials, but didn't come down to say goodbye to his mother. Viza refused to repeat the thoughts going through his head, but she grumbled and wished a thousand plagues fall on the ungrateful brat he had become. He was glad Jillian was leaving Dorwain and never coming back. He was giddy with delight that now he could do whatever he pleased, without his mother constantly lecturing him on what was the proper mindset and heart of a king.

King Joben didn't make formal farewell to his daughter. Rumors spread through the palace that he was ill again.

Zair watched the scene through Viza's eyes and memories and prayed for Jillian. How could her father be so cruel, and how could her son be so glad that she was going to what was nearly certain death?

Yancob had taken all the new recruits on the escort duty to Encruestia, meaning anyone who wasn't entirely loyal to him and the Red Brigade had left the palace. Knowing he was finally free of the spies who watched him at his lessons didn't brighten Zair's mood.

Two hours after the departure, he went to the Brigade's stables for his trick riding lessons. He stepped into his horse's stall with his saddle and staggered, surprised speechless, to find Princes Jillian brushing down the big gelding.

He dropped the saddle and didn't even yelp when it landed hard on his foot.

Jillian laughed, immediately smothering the sound behind her hand. Magnus stepped into the stall behind him, grinning like his brothers used to grin before pulling a nasty, messy trick on him. Zair had to fight the nearly painful urge to hit someone. The next moment, he felt and saw the shimmer in the air as Magnus cast a bubble of silence around them. Zair had never been able to sense that magic at work before. That proved how much his discipline exercises and Viza's strengthened presence in his flesh had changed him.

"The short tale is that Shaleen returned in time to take our lady's place," Magnus said, while Zair still felt the echoes of the spell in his skin. "We leave in two days for Cambrodaera. I have allies there who can shelter our lady."

"That doesn't mean they will," Jillian said, and tossed the brush into the grooming box for punctuation. "We will stop there long enough to catch our breath. And if King Axrod learns of my presence and is unfriendly, we will play desperate and frightened, and let him think he can turn me into a tool for his own profit. Long enough for Shaleen and our allies in the Brigade to catch up with us."

"After Encobi weaves a powerful spell that could leave her drained and defenseless for a week at the very least," Magnus added. "I pray A'theosius grants her the strength and blinds our enemies. She must convince them that marauders from Tishbane caught up with the escort and slaughtered everyone after they kidnapped the princess."

Zair felt a little dizzy, trying to comprehend the enormity of the rapid-fire revelations. Tishbane had wanted Jillian as an alliance bride since Joben became king. There had been attempts to kidnap her and kill her husband several times over the years, until Tishbane had to focus all its resources on a war with two neighboring kingdoms who were allies with Encruestia. It made perfect sense for them to use her to strike at the alliance, as well as punish Joben for not allying with them.

The dizziness turned to a queasy heaviness in the pit of his stomach when he imagined all those kingdoms turning against Dorwain, if someone examined the scene of the battle and kidnapping and had strong enough magic to unweave the illusion.

"It's almost time to flee, lad," Magnus said. "Are you ready?"

"What about the ties between me and Anwir? It won't do us any good to even get to Cambrodaera and to the next kingdom after that, if his magicians can still follow the trail to me."

Oh, no worries there, Viza said. *The boy is going to have a headache that will make him repent of all his sins.*

Magnus let out a single burst of laughter. "We were right? All our theories?"

"What theories?" Zair demanded.

"Viza is now strong enough to destroy all the dust that remains in Anwir. And while she's doing that, destroy a great many of the threads of magic Lazius and his idiots rooted in you." Magnus's smile faded to half its brilliance. "In theory. We won't know until we try."

Until I try, Viza said.

The plan was simple, but the timing could be tricky. Encobi would enact an illusion spell, allowing her, Shaleen, and Yancob to escape the escort. Meanwhile, Magnus and Jillian would ride out, dressed as palace servants, using no magic at all. Magnus would take a strong potion to silence the inner song of his magic for half a day. They would be vulnerable because he wouldn't have magic to protect them. Yet their chances of escape were greater, because anyone watching to stop fugitives would be seeking signs of illusions and other spells at work. There would be no magic resonance or scent, to give away Jillian and Magnus to their enemies.

When they were safely away and he had regained his magic, they would meet up with Yancob, Encobi and Shaleen and the soldiers who had sworn their loyalty to the princess over their loyalty to King Joben. Zair would then ride out alone and join them. They would cross the wastelands to the mountains that stood as a barrier between Dorwain and Cambrodaera, and seek shelter from Magnus's friends, for however long they were safe there.

~~~~~

The Brigade's barracks felt empty, yet Zair sensed unfriendly eyes watching him. Along with a band for his wrist made of the fragments of Viza's broken frame, Encobi had left several charms for him. They would detect passive, watchful magic that wouldn't alert the ring Shaleen had given him. The testing to determine who among the new recruits had been placed among the Brigade by Nostrados or other enemies had also revealed disloyalty in a disheartening number of established members of the Brigade. Yancob had a limited number of Brigade soldiers he could take on the journey to Encruestia. He had chosen the new recruits, because he knew they were a danger. The others, he had to leave behind and trust Encrobi's charms could protect Zair, and the skills he had learned would help him sneak out of the barracks when the time came. Common sense said these men left behind would be watching him.

Yancob had to leave behind any members of the Brigade who had families and other ties in the city. Soldiers who couldn't just cut their roots and create a new life in another kingdom. These soldiers were loyal to him, but he didn't want to make them choose between serving the throne and protecting Princess Jillian.

Zair was glad to spend his remaining days in the barracks with those men, because they were friendly and sympathetic. None of them liked Anwir. None of them knew that Yancob wasn't coming back. Ignorance was safer for everyone.

In some ways, he felt very alone despite being surrounded by friends.
~~~~~

They followed the same routines, as the old soldiers took him through his weapon drills and taught him more trick riding, gave him affectionate bullying, and told him stories of brutal campaigns. Zair couldn't ask them any of the questions or discuss the ideas filling his mind as he waited to finally break free. He couldn't talk to Viza, because she wore herself out, destroying her dust that remained in Anwir, just a few grains at a time.

~~~~~

Six days after Magnus and Princess Jillian rode out, news reached the palace. Forces from Tishbane had attacked the bride's escort. Zair felt as stunned as everyone else in the much-depleted dining hall, when a palace servant broke in at suppertime to declare the news. The false attack wasn't supposed to happen until the day before, and it should take at least two more days for the report to reach the palace. Had real forces from Tishbane attacked, having learned about Princess Jillian being sent to Encruestia as a bride? What would they do when they captured Shaleen and discovered the princess's Shadow had been riding in her place?

Who among the Brigade had survived the attack? What about the regular soldiers, especially the ones who were his friends? Had everyone been slaughtered? Had Yancob been captured, or Encobi? Or were they both dead? Had Nostrados's magic overwhelmed Encobi's?

More important, did King Joben and Anwir feel any remorse over sending Jillian to her possible death? Or did they just mourn the loss of a political tool and a wasted plan to justify war?

For a few minutes at a time, often over the three days that followed, Zair played with the idea of somehow taking Anwir's place. Despite the fury that raged through him in those moments, Zair remained clear-headed enough to know that he didn't have the magic or the skill or the training or the friends to take Joben off the throne. Still, someone needed to oust King Joben. And if not him, then Anwir after him, and eradicate the entire royal family. Make them pay for their crimes against the kingdom, and against the true royal family. Zair's family line.

Official word finally came that Princess Jillian was presumed dead, with her entire escort. The barracks were emptied, to attend the king for the public ceremonies of mourning. Everyone went, even the identified spies. Except for Zair. He was disappointed and surprised when he wasn't summoned to take Anwir's place during some of the solemn processions. He amused himself imagining the prince suffering through the public ceremonies of prayer and holy songs, and dozens of priests and holy lay folk declaring Princess Jillian's praises, in between long recitations of holy writings.

Still, he had to wonder why these very public events, in a city that was reportedly infuriated and devastated, weren't considered dangerous for Anwir. Couldn't anyone see his cold expressions, the sneers that were
~~~~~

a constant fixture on his face, and realize how little love or respect he had for his mother?

It's because he's grown to be quite as adept a liar as his nasty, self-righteous brute of a grandfather, Viza said, late on the third night.

Zair was in the kitchen, trying to keep busy to work off the nervous energy filling him. He fumbled the enormous metal bowl full of risen dough he had been carrying to the long stone-topped table, to start kneading the bread for the next morning's breakfast. He hadn't expected Viza to contact him for several more days. Removing the specks of mirror dust from Anwir was turning out to be even more draining and tedious than Viza and Magnus had anticipated.

The filthy little snot is having fun, weeping and sniffling and making an enormous public display of controlling his grief, the mirror continued, as Zair tipped the bowl to dump out the lump of dough. *Inside, he's seething, disgusted and jealous to the point of apoplexy over the love the entire city has for his mother.* She chuckled, and it was quite a nasty, triumphant sound. *He certainly deserves the pain I've been giving him. And not even on purpose. Although, yes, I must admit, I don't regret it when the process hurts him.*

"Are you almost done?" he asked and took the first hard punch into the lump of dough.

Nearly. It irks me to spend so much time bouncing around through his tiny little mind. Still, I do enjoy hearing his grandfather scold him. The nasty old man nearly chokes on his own tongue, when he has to admit that the princess was right about her son's character flaws. He even got angry enough once to wish he hadn't interfered with her ideas of discipline, that Anwir would be a better heir to the throne now.

"I'll wager—" Zair flinched, thinking he heard footsteps in the next room. The last thing he needed was one of the unfriendly members of the Brigade hearing him talking to himself. *I'll wager he didn't like hearing that.*

No. Especially when the king sometimes gets nasty enough to say you would make a much better heir to the throne.

How soon until we can leave? He gripped the edge of the table to brace himself and shivered despite the heat of the kitchen. Words like that would drive Anwir to send someone to kill him, despite the spells that supposedly still bound them together, sharing physical experiences.

The prince was cruel enough, perhaps insane enough, not to care that killing his Shadow would kill him, too.

Chapter Twenty

We need to wait to hear from Magnus, Viza said.

What if Yancob and the others are dead? He's not supposed to call for me to leave until he meets up with them. What if that never happens? Zair could barely keep himself from shouting that question.

Silence.

He dug his fingers into the side of the table until they ached, taking deep breaths to force himself to calm, then went back to work. He couldn't let anyone, either friend or spy, guess that anything was wrong.

How much dust can you leave in Anwir, without giving him any way to track me?

Oh, I've scorched what remains, withdrawn as much magic as I can, and still be able to look into his mind. It would take an enchanter as strong as Magnus to use those bits to track us.

Then why can't we leave now?

Viza sighed. *And take the risk of someone seeing you? Do you really think anyone in this city, after all the emotional upheaval of the royal mourning, would look at you and not recognize the prince? Do you think any of those sympathetic, loyal citizens would let the prince go on his way? Can you ride out of the palace, even in the dead of night, without a servant seeing you? Even if you ordered them to let you go and tell no one they had seen you, seen him, they would talk. And word would spread and someone would be on our trail immediately.*

Zair hated admitting she was right.

When can we leave, then? When will it be too late to leave, when will it be too long to wait for word from Magnus? What if he never contacts us because everything went wrong?

Another deep sigh from the mirror. *Three days at the earliest. Three nights, rather. Four would be better, because that's when the new moon begins. Less light to see by. And you had best spend all your time until then praying for rain and clouds to block the stars and wind to blow out all the torches in the city.*

~~~~~

One moment Zair was wielding the bread paddle, removing fresh, aromatic loaves of bread from the long row of ovens in preparation for breakfast. The next, he was on fire, writhing on the floor, choking on his tongue and hearing Viza shriek at the back of his mind.

Then blackness.

Rising up out of the blackness was like trying to swim through mud ten times thicker than the flood he had faced that spring. Just breathing
~~~~~

made him ache, as if he had been kicked in all his ribs. The garbled sounds that reach his ears had sharp edges. He lay still, trying not to weep, trying not to even think.

Still, he couldn't help it.

Viza?

No response.

The darkness thickened and receded in waves, and he understood seasickness.

Gradually, the sounds turned into voices. He flinched, all his muscles tightening, when he recognized one of those voices. Wayent, a court official who oversaw the magicians trying to untangle the spells wrapped around Anwir. From the tone of voices, Zair guessed the man was arguing with Oriss, the chief healer for the Brigade.

He was probably in the infirmary.

What had happened?

Could he hope that whatever he suffered, Anwir got his own portion? It was only fair, after all the discomfort he had endured, and having his training and honestly won skills appropriated by the prince.

No, I'm sorry, you got the worst of it. Viza sounded ragged and somehow dusty, like she would drift away on an errant breath of wind.

What happened?

He could almost have laughed at the realization that just thinking the words made his head feel scorched. Except that laughing hurt, too.

That vile Nostrados finally looked close enough to find my last few fragments. He was in a fury. If Lazius and his followers hadn't already been killed for their stupidity, he would have done it with a snap of his fingers. And probably brought them back from the dead to kill them several more times. He sent for his own followers and they burned the last specks of dust out of the prince. That feet-kissing lackey arguing with Oriss is rather upset that you got such a strong backlash. He understands enough magic to know you had more than your fair share of mirror dust.

Nostrados insists that the bonds between the two of you should be weak enough by now that you should have felt nothing. Oh, I'm so sorry, my dear boy. I should have listened to you. We should have left days ago. Nostrados is no fool. He has to realize that you had such a bad reaction because you have inherent, blood-born magic. Then he's going to wonder what happened to the dust remaining from the mirror those idiots crushed to work their magic, and he's going to test you to see how much is in you, and then ...

"We have to leave," Zair whispered. His throat even felt scorched.

And now I can't even spy through Anwir's ears and eyes to guess when they'll send for you.

They agreed Viza would retreat, to conserve her strength, and leave Zair to rest. He lay still, listening, as Wayent handed Oriss an ultimatum. He had to have "the Shadow boy" on his feet and ready to be transferred to quarters nearer the prince. And accessible for Nostrados to examine him. Zair nearly wept aloud when Oriss insisted that he hadn't awakened yet and wouldn't be fit to move even then. He displayed no fear or even concern when Wayent demanded, repeatedly, that he send word as soon as "the Shadow boy" woke.

Finally, the official left. Quiet hummed through the infirmary. The air lightened and sweetened around Zair's bed. He smelled the healing ointments and the spicy oil Oriss burned to purify the air. After a short time, footsteps approached the bed. Zair opened his eyes.

"Well, I have a few ideas, but we're going to have to work fast if I'm going to keep my promise to Yancob and get you out of here with your hide in one piece," the deep-voiced old healer said. He settled on the side of the bed and caught hold of Zair's wrist. "Does that hurt?"

"No." Zair smiled, and that didn't make his skin sting quite as badly as it had when he was sunburned.

"Good. Now, I need you to pretend you're dying for the next day or two. How well can you heave your insides out?" A dry chuckle escaped him when Zair just stared, confused. "Don't worry." He patted the boy's hand before standing. "I have quite a few potions and powders to help you feign illness. Even the plague, if necessary."

~~~~~

Several soldiers stepped into the infirmary over the course of the day to check on Zair. He feigned sleep, and if any footsteps came too close to his cot, he moaned or made gagging noises. He had a close call when footsteps approached and one of the charms Encobi left for him stung to life, resting on his breastbone. Zair gasped and flinched and started to curl up on his side. The footsteps hurried away, and he heard a muffled voice calling to one of the healers on duty.

Tonight, Encobi whispered in his head. The sound echoed and seemed to bounce off sore spots inside his skull. A blurry image flashed before his eyes. The path he should take from the barracks to a secret stable and through the city and across the countryside.

Zair didn't even realize he had opened his eyes and sat up and reached for his shirt, until Orris snapped, "Where do you think you're going?"

"It's tonight." He clamped his mouth shut, against the need to shout his relief and the happy news that Encobi was alive.

That was no assurance Yancob and Shaleen were alive, but right that moment, Zair didn't care.

Oriss didn't ask what he meant. He narrowed his eyes, nodded once, and bent to help Zair put his boots on. He tugged aside the curtain covering the door between the infirmary and the sleeping room and gestured for Zair to wait. After what felt like an hour of increasing tension,
~~~~~

he gestured for Zair to come. Oriss supported him, even though Zair felt strong enough, steady enough, to walk on his own. The healer insisted, and from the way he looked around, clearly checking for watchers, he wanted someone to think Zair was still weak and unsteady. The healer's arm stayed tight around his shoulders and he even commented every few steps, encouraging him to lean into him, to move slower, to let him know if he felt dizzy. Zair sensed people watching from the shadows as they walked the wide aisle between the sleeping cubicles of the soldiers, then out into the main room, to Zair's tiny closet bedroom. Oriss whispered for him to dress for travel, then raised his voice, ordering Zair to go to sleep, not to leave his bed, or he would get no sympathy when he fell off his feet and gave himself a black eye. Then Oriss pulled the curtain closed and hurried away.

Zair packed. And prayed. And closed his eyes to try to call up to his memory the map Encobi had sent him. He must have fallen asleep, because the next thing he knew, the strident, clashing notes of several alarm bells filled the air and he sat up and nearly slid off his cot.

Booted feet thudded past his room. Men shouted, then the shouts turned to curses. Zair held still, braced for someone to tear aside the curtain. He pulled out the daggers Grebus had given him, and the throwing stars Krispus, the armsmaster at the garrison outpost, had gifted him for winter solstice. The last of his aches faded under the growing certainty that this was the perfect opportunity for Anwir to send someone to kill him. He had to be confident that after what Nostrados did, burning the mirror dust, hurting his Shadow would no longer rebound on him.

Silence in the main room. Zair took deep breaths, holding himself steady, and caught a whiff of something burned. He nearly laughed when he remembered that he had been baking when the attack came. He wondered how long the bread sat in the oven, turning to charr, before someone thought to follow their noses and remedy the problem. Yancob would laugh about the mess in his usually pristine kitchen, if he knew. Would he ever be able to tell Yancob about that afternoon, about everything that had happened since he rode away with the doomed escort and the false princess?

"Zair?" a raspy voice whispered. A moment later, the curtain whipped back and Rax, an assistant groom in the Brigade's stables, stuck his one-eyed head into the room. "Ah, good. But just a word of advice. It's hard to fight with that many weapons at the ready." He grinned and beckoned with a jerk of his head and stepped back.

A strained chuckle escaped Zair as he stashed his weapons and caught up his packs and hurried to follow the elderly soldier. Voices came from the infirmary. The curtain hung down over the door. Rax watched it as he led the way out of the barracks. His bowed shoulders relaxed visibly once the two of them stepped into the tunnel that led from the barracks to the stables. The darkness was broken by dimly flickering oil lamps, spaced at twenty paces. Rax said nothing. He walked lightly for such an old man with a bad leg. Zair tried to imitate him.

They reached the stables, and Rax kept going. Zair looked around, and a chill suspicion worked through him when he saw nearly every stall was empty. What sort of emergency or crisis had raised those alarms, and taken most of the remaining Red Brigade soldiers out of the barracks? Was this Orris's scheme? Then Rax looked back and patted his shoulder. A moment later, the old groom yanked on a peg in the wall, causing a slim panel to swing open. They stepped through, into darkness. Rax never hesitated or stumbled, though Zair feared sometimes in the journey down the narrow passageway that he would step on the old man's heels.

He counted their steps, and after sixty, Rax stopped. Zair barely stopped from colliding with him. Wood creaked and stuck and squealed, then dim light spilled through as another slim panel in the wall swung open.

"Out you go, lad," Rax whispered. "Hurry, before someone looks away. Fire can only do so much to dim night vision." He patted Zair's back, ending with a gentle shove.

Zair righted himself and turned to look back, but the panel groaned shut and the old man was gone.

He smelled straw and horse and felt the damp touch of summer breeze, the air thick with the contents of a nearby ditch. A single spot of dim, flickering light hung high overhead. Zair turned and caught his breath at the sight of Patch, his own horse, with all his travel gear waiting nearby. How had Orris managed that? He blinked away a brief, hot dampness and hurried to saddle Patch and tie his packs on, and mount. Rax had mentioned fire, and Zair's imagination ran wild. What sort of crisis had the loyal members of the Red Brigade caused, to distract the spies and traitors, so he could escape?

Zair wished for a light, as he faced the black mouth of what was apparently the only way in or out of this hidey-hole. He mentally scolded himself, whispered a prayer for A'theosius's guidance and guarding, and nudged Patch to get moving. He knew his horse. He trusted Patch to find their way out through the darkness.

They rode, the ground gradually inclining upward, curving to the right. The contrast between the tunnel and the starry, cloudless sky felt like full daylight when they emerged above ground. Zair laughed quietly at the change. A few moments of studying the profile of buildings against the night sky told him where he was, and where the fire commanded the attention of apparently half the city. Zair turned Patch in the opposite direction and let the horse have his head. The Red Brigade's mounts were trained for endurance and focus, and guided by charms to help them find each other if they were separated on missions or in battle. Zair thought he might even dare to sleep in the saddle, and his horse would still keep moving until they joined the Brigade. How many of the Brigade were out there, waiting with Magnus and Jillian? Just the men who had crept out by ones and twos over the last ten days, taking leave time, riding out on personal business, never to return? Had any of Yancob's loyal men in the escort escaped the slaughter in the Tishbane attack? Patch would find them, no matter how far ahead of him they were. Not that Zair thought he could fall asleep. He suspected he never would be able to relax enough to sleep until they had crossed the border out of Dorwain.

Zair kept his hood up while he rode down the city streets and alleys, but once he was outside the walls and there was no one to see, he planned to let his hood fall back and breathe the first free air he had known since Ward and Gabe pulled him from the tree. Tomorrow when the sun rose, then he would have to ride with his face in shadows. And every day, until he was far enough from Dorwain that no one who looked at him would recognize the crown prince. How much distance would he have to put between him and Anwir before the spells stretched thin and snapped, and they wore their own faces at long last, neither one resembling the other?

For tonight, he would enjoy the sense of freedom that grew with every step his horse took away from the capitol and Anwir.

~~~~~

Rumon, an outrider from Magnus's company, met Zair at dawn, two days later. That wasn't a good sign. The plan was for Zair to catch up with them outside of Caspria, a town halfway to the river border with Cambrodaera. The party was to keep moving as long as Magnus could hold up an illusion spell that made them look like a pig farmer moving his herd to market for fall slaughter. Just the sight and sound of fifty huge, fat, muddy pigs would encourage people to move aside and let them pass and even take another roundabout route if they saw them coming. They certainly wouldn't get close enough to realize they couldn't smell the pigs. The illusion of all those cloven hooves churning up the road would last until people had ridden over those places.

"You have to take over," Rumon said. He turned his horse to go back the way he had come.

"Take over what?" Zair held still, when his first instinct was to dig his heels into Patch's sides and flee. He didn't completely trust Rumon, because the young man, who was only a few years older than him, didn't offer any countersign to prove himself, and didn't ask for any countersign from Zair. Who could be sure either one wasn't acting as bait in a trap?

If the king or Nostrados or Anwir had sent spies among the Brigade, why assume the ones Yancob took with him, to die in the Tishbane attack,
~~~~~

were the only ones?

"The king knows the commander survived the attack and is on his way here. He's being tracked. No summoning spell yet, but he expects it. He's in a fury to find out there is such a spell, embedded in our vowing tattoos. He has to go back, before the tracking spell turns into a summoning for all of us."

Zair nodded and nudged his horse to move faster. If this was a trap, he didn't dare react yet and reveal his suspicions. He needed to know what the situation really was. Guessing would just make everything worse.

The two rode side-by side at that ground-eating trot that the specially bred steeds of the Brigade could hold for days, if necessary. They went in silence. Zair knew it was useless to ask questions. He thought through all he had learned from Yancob and the Brigade, and thanked A'theosius that he had that training. He would need it now, to help get Jillian over the border and beyond the reach of her father who would sacrifice her life for the sake of starting a war.

His ring pulsed, tightening and tingling in warning of incoming danger.

Zair groaned but muffled the sound. Now what had happened? Had traitors caught up with Magnus and Jillian and the others, despite the disguise and distraction spells surrounding them? Had they broken the illusion?

Maybe Magnus employed so much magic, that had enabled some clever magician to track them? Maybe the very use of so much power sent up a signal that no magic could hide? Zair's head hurt, considering all the possibilities.

Life would be so much simpler if there were no magic, no enchanters or magicians or wizards or spells or time pockets or illusions. Yes, more people would die without healers, and festivals wouldn't be half as much fun without the light-weavers and the animal-tamers, and his hand would feel naked without the ring Shaleen had given him. But would he even need that ring, if there weren't so many enemies using magic?

The ring throbbed again. Zair silently scolded himself to focus and gritted his teeth as he leaned down lower on his horse's neck, to cut the wind resistance. When he moved ahead, urging the horse to go faster, Rumon didn't question him. His mount picked up speed to keep pace.

That made no sense. Why was the outrider letting him lead the way?

Because he didn't know where the fugitives were?

Zair nearly yanked on the reins to slow Patch, but that would warn the traitor he had been discovered. If he was a traitor. Who could be sure?

Yet Zair knew Rumon. He was a friend, a good teammate when the Brigade relaxed with riddle games in the evenings. Zair knew he was part of the team Yancob had trusted for this mission. So had he been planning to betray them, suborned by the enemy before Jillian needed to flee? Or had he been enslaved by the powerful magic Nostrados was said to possess, betraying them all against his will?

Zair slacked the reins just a little, so Patch slowed gradually. Rumon pulled ahead, just the length of his horse's nose, then from the shoulders. He glanced several times at Zair, frowning, before letting his horse slow to match gaits.

"What's wrong?" he called above the rumble of the hooves on the hard-packed dirt of the road.

"It's stupid. I was sick before I escaped, and my head hurts enough I can't remember if we're supposed to turn at the crossroads up ahead or keep riding straight through." Zair gestured at the rise in the landscape, maybe half a mile away. "Turn left, and then straight through at the next crossroads? Or do I have that turned around?"

There was no crossroads past that rise. This road went on for several more miles before reaching a river, shallow enough they could cross without a bridge or ferry-barge, with a sizeable trading village and military outpost just beyond that, and then a crossroads.

"Oh. Smart." The outrider nodded. He narrowed his eyes at Zair and slowed his horse more.

He was playing for time. Probably trying to figure out how to trick Zair into giving him the answer.

Traitor to the Brigade, or enslaved by an enemy? Was it possible someone else was using mirror spells, and using them properly, so the man riding beside him wore Rumon's face? Zair wondered if the man's face would change back to his own when he was unconscious. He gathered the reins in one hand and slipped the choke-wire Shaleen had given him from his belt pouch. A snort of bitter amusement escaped him. He had never thought he would need to use it. She would laugh, if he ever had a chance to tell her she had been right. He slid right in his saddle while tucking up his right leg, out of the way. Patch obeyed the signal, swerving right and speeding up, so he brushed against the other horse, momentarily crushing the outrider's leg between them.

Chapter Twenty-One

Zair flung the choke-wire around the man's neck while pushing off with his right leg, so he knocked Rumon from the saddle. His feet caught for two seconds in the stirrups, but Zair's weight and momentum yanked them loose. He twisted the wire as they fell and wrapped his legs around the other man. They hit hard, with Zair on top, and rolled. Rumon bucked and flailed, trying to get his hands on the braided wire cutting off his air.

They rolled to a stop, the other man on top, his struggles already slowing. He slapped futilely at his neck, legs spasming. Zair took a deep breath and bucked, arching his back to heave the man off him and over on his chest. He wrapped one arm around Rumon's neck while he adjusted his grip on the wire. Now would not be a good time to lose his grip and let his enemy get a breath.

Hooves pounded, approaching. Zair pulled the wire tighter, until he smelled blood and the man writhed beneath him. Muted whimpers escaped him. Now Zair could dare to look up.

Rumon rode up, leading the outrider's horse, and looked down at the duplicate under Zair. His mouth twisted in fury. He nodded salute to Zair.

"Don't kill him yet," Shaleen called. She rode up from the other side, leading Zair's horse. "We can backtrack the spell, find out a little more about our enemies." She grinned at the boy, who gaped at her. "It's good to see you again."

"Good to see you." Zair didn't care that his eyes were hot and wet. Shaleen was alive.

By the time they reached the rest of their company of fugitives, Zair learned yes, the mirroring spell used by their enemies did fade when the one wearing it was unconscious. Magnus took over, muttering about incompetents who cut corners and used impure materials and gave enchanters a bad name. The duplicate Rumon had to swallow a charm made with the hair of the original, and the efficacy wore off as the hair was digested. Searching his saddle bags revealed the charms. The logical conclusion was that the duplicate was supposed to somehow catch up with them, kill the original, and take his place.

Magnus and Encobi spent less than half an hour searching the unconscious man's mind, then put him back on his horse, wrapped in a spell so the horse trotted a crazy, looping trail. When he woke up, he wouldn't know where he was. The saddle of his horse and his armor were heavily embedded with all sorts of tracking charms. Magnus fuddled them. By the time he finished, he wore a grin like a particularly nasty little boy playing messy pranks. The charms would rebel against their casters, ending in loud, bright-blinding explosions whenever someone tried to awaken one. That would add further confusion to the trail and might even result in the rider being bucked off a few times. Zair felt sorry for the horse.

Encobi had detected the duplication spell at work when she made the first of several planned changes to the company's illusion spell. These changes would allow their company to essentially vanish from under the noses of anyone watching them. She alerted Magnus and her father, and the soldiers took turns dropping back to detect who might be searching for them. They had found the duplicate Rumon more than a day ago. Magnus and Encobi amused themselves by leaving clues that led him far off the trail time and again, then brought him back close, sometimes passing by within a dozen steps of their company. The real Rumon was all for sneaking up behind his double, dragging him into the shadows, and slicing him into several dozen pieces, but Yancob wanted to see who he might be working with. They didn't realize what he was up to until Encobi sensed Zair approaching them.

Zair received some teasing advice on how to perform the leap from the horse with more control and not come close to slitting his enemy's throat. What was the use of capturing him if the man couldn't speak and give up useful information? They wouldn't always have enchanters with them to look into the teeny, tiny minds of their prisoners.

Jillian greeted him with tears in her eyes, kissed his forehead, and apologized to him for the trouble and danger he had to face because of her son. Then she hurried away, to mount her horse again.

"I fear for her mind, but even more for her heart," Shaleen said, watching the princess settle into place. She and Zair walked to their waiting horses and climbed into their saddles before she continued. "This has given her a grievous wound that a younger woman would find hard to bear. Her mother never wanted to be a queen, she never wanted to be royalty, and she never wanted her son to be a prince. She chose her merchant because she loved him. She was glad when relations between Ambrecht and Dorwain deteriorated, even though loyalty to her husband's country would mark her and her son as enemies of the throne. Everything she did to protect her son ... failed. She has lost him. And worse than that, he has turned against her."

Zair ached for Jillian. Would anything have turned out differently if he and Anwir had become friends, like Jillian and Shaleen had become friends? His stomach twisted with a guilty fear that he hadn't tried hard enough.

"I'll look after her the best I can," he finally said, after they had been back on the road for nearly an hour. The time had passed quickly, with all the ideas and questions swirling through his head.

"If she calls you son, if she gives you his name ... pity her," Shaleen said.

~~~~~

Cambrodaera was not a friend of Dorwain, but neither was it an enemy. The two kingdoms had mutual aid agreements that neither side liked to call upon, except in times of danger. They cooperated when criminals from one kingdom crossed the border into the other and allowed peacekeepers and soldiers and bounty hunters to track and haul prisoners back for trial and punishment. They allowed each other's diplomats safe passage through their kingdoms on missions to other kingdoms.

No one would expect Jillian to flee to Cambrodaera. Her late husband's merchant empire refused to do business with the throne of Cambrodaera and always charged exorbitant prices for anything they imported. Shaleen laughed when she repeated that bit of information. Phoebus did that because several princes and nobles of the kingdom had tried to woo Jillian even after she married him. They disparaged the priestly establishment in Ambrecht, claiming that they taught heresy. Jillian thought that rather ironic, as the priests of Cambrodaera had a reputation for conveniently finding books of holy writing that had been lost for centuries, whenever their nobles wanted to justify a war or prove that the most recently deposed king had come from an illegitimate line. In Ambrecht they held firmly to the canon of holy books established four centuries before, verified by the prophets Soma, Parshay, and Dominus, and accepted no writings outside of that canon, especially books that contradicted what the older books taught.

The most important reason for taking sanctuary in Cambrodaera: Magnus had distant relatives there, and several powerful political friends.

The journey took four more days after Zair joined them. Yancob and his men removed all their Red Brigade insignia on the second day. Just in case the duplicate Rumon was telling the truth, Encobi and Magnus destroyed all the insignia with magic and fire, then washed all their armor and weapons with wine and cleansing herbs and scoured them with magic, to destroy any charms hidden inside them, any spells wrapped around them. Magnus found it ironic, and even laughed a little, when the tattoos the former members of the Red Brigade had earned through years of service and valor in battle indeed turned out to have spells tied to them, mixed into the ink. Encobi was in tears, both fury and sympathy for her father and his men. And fury with herself, because she had never sensed the magic bound into the tattoos. Magnus assured her there was no reason for her to have sensed them. First, because she had grown up seeing those
~~~~~

tattoos, and had grown blind to their presence. In the same way that people grew deaf to music that kept playing constantly in the background.

Removing the tattoos was a painful process. They had to keep riding and couldn't sit still for a day with poultices on their tattoos to draw out the ink and magic. Encobi and Magnus took turns riding alongside the soldiers and refreshing the poultices. Zair learned a new lesson about endurance, strength, and dedication, watching these legendary soldiers ride with clenched jaws and bloody tears trickling from their eyes.

Yancob said nothing, but the fury in his posture, the tightness in his voice, spoke clearly the sense of betrayal and the smear on the honor of him and his men, that came from this revelation. The Red Brigade had pledged their lives and honor to the throne, to the honor and future of Dorwain. They went far beyond the requirements and sacrifice of any warriors in the kingdom. Yet the king doubted their dedication and their vows and chose to enforce those vows with spells that could track them down, look into their very thoughts, and likely kill them if they strayed even a single step from the path he required of them. That was cruel and disheartening. It proved Yancob and the men who followed him now had been right to listen to their sense of honor and justice and A'theosius's laws, rather than blindly obeying the dictates of their king. Even at the cost of their home, positions, and reputations.

Knowing they were right couldn't possibly soothe the ache of being betrayed and tricked and lied to. And treated like honorless wretches who had to be bound with spells, to stop them from thinking for themselves.

King Joben and his magicians owed an increasingly grim and heavy debt. Whether they would ever have to pay that debt, Zair didn't know. He told himself not to care. Not when he couldn't do anything about it.

But someday, he promised himself, he would become strong enough, powerful enough, and have enough magic at his disposal, he would bring justice down on them.

~~~~~

Zair's head jerked back, like someone had grabbed his chin and yanked upward. His ring had been humming constantly on his finger since they crossed the Angraborn River, turning north, and entered this scrub plain between Dorwain and the mountain border of Cambrodaera. Now it tightened painfully. For a few moments, he thought it would cut his finger off. What sort of magic was about to strike their company?

Magnus rode at the head of their two-by-two column to lead the way through the hidden magical traps laid down by decades of bickering between the two kingdoms. Had the enchanter miscalculated and triggered something about to strike them?

He started to yank off his riding glove to see if any color or light gave a clue to the magic hitting him. A wave of fiery needles raced over his
~~~~~

flesh, paralyzing him for two heartbeats. He dropped the reins, about to slap out the flames he felt bursting out all over his clothes.

But no light, no smell, no sounds, no flames. He slumped forward, smashing his nose against his horse's neck, getting a mouthful of mane as he gasped for breath. Patch kept moving, giving just one snort of protest at his sudden movement. Zair pulled himself upright and looked around. The soldiers on either side of him frowned, turning their heads to him.

Viza? What happened?

Something huge. And draining. I'm sorry, the mirror said, her voice frighteningly faint and distant in his head. *All this magic surrounding us, all the illusions, it's sucking me hollow. I'm going to have to retreat for a while. I need you to shelter me while I regroup. Magnus will take care of you.*

Then the sense of her entirely vanished. Zair caught his breath, telling himself she was only resting, regaining her strength. She hadn't been burned out of him entirely, like the last of her dust had been burned out of Anwir.

"You all right?" Torvan asked from behind him.

Magnus turned his horse and raised his arm. The entire column stopped. He turned and rode back to Zair. His mouth dropped open as their gazes met, and he slowly shook his head.

"What?" Zair said. Murmuring ran up and down the column of riders, and more soldiers turned to look back at him.

"Those idiots lied. Or else they didn't know the extent of the spells woven around and rooted in you," Magnus growled. He shook his head, keeping his gaze locked on Zair's face. "They could in all honesty believe they defeated the mirror spell, but ..."

Zair groaned as understanding hit him. "But it didn't feel the same as last time."

"Well," Encobi said as she rode up on his other side, "one good thing came of this. That snot doesn't dare leave Dorwain. I would love to be there, watching, the next time he crosses the border and he changes shape. Your voice is different, too."

"That's not helping," Magnus said, his voice softer. "I'm sorry. I truly thought you would be free once we crossed the border into Cambrodaera."

"We should still be several miles away from the border," Rumon pointed out.

"This must be where Combrodaera begins, as reckoned by the magic that protects kingdoms," he said, nodding. A crooked smile caught up one corner of his mouth. "Wouldn't that start an enormous stew of trouble, if someone found out about ..." He gestured at Zair's remade face. "I can see ambassadors from every kingdom standing before the Enchanters' Court, demanding that all borders be tested, and land given back to their rightful rulers." His smile faded. "We're not going to risk your neck to stir up that trouble, as much fun as it might be. Keep your hood up, your face in shadows, until we're safely within the city and behind closed doors. Then I'll ..." he shrugged and exhaled a loud sigh, "I'll figure out something." Magnus waited until Zair complied. Then he turned and nudged his horse to go back to the front.

"Would you like a mirror?" Encobi asked, gesturing at the saddlebag behind her. The mischief faded and she only looked sympathetic when Zair shook his head. Then she turned and made her way to the back of the column. Magnus led them through the traps and nasty tricks, and she kept watch from their rear, in case some nasty spell of retribution awoke once they passed, to attack from behind them.

Zair shivered, remembering one of his most recent lessons in magic. Every night, he had wrapped up in his blanket by the fire with his head spinning from everything Encobi and Magnus taught him in bits and pieces around their campfire. The more he learned, the more control he tried to build over his slowly awakening inherent magic, the more responsibility he had for freeing himself from the spells Lazius and his followers had bound around him. He whispered a prayer of thanks to A'theosius that the triggering of the mirror spell, to make him the image of the king of Cambrodaera, hadn't awakened any of the nasty defensive and offensive spells that Magnus warned them littered this scrub plain.

The column waited until Magnus had regained the lead. Then they moved forward again across this plain that for now appeared to be covered with packed dirt, scrub grass, and little else. That could change at any time, without warning. Only Magnus could see the safe path. Zair's ring hummed constantly, indicating the presence of the illusion spells that painted a false picture in everyone's eyes and deceived their noses. One of the nastier defensive spells hid slowly bubbling sulfur-mud flats that waxed and waned in size and depth in an unpredictable rhythm, waiting to catch unlucky travelers who bumbled into them.

The landscape gradually rose ahead of them, turning into what looked like a solid wall of black-streaked red rock. They rode for another hour, and that wall of rock seemed no closer. Magnus had warned that would happen. It wasn't an illusion created by magic, but by distance, the fumes they couldn't smell, and the lack of any variation in the landscape to help them visually mark how far they had come.

Finally, Zair couldn't resist. He tugged off his glove and reached up inside the cover of his hood to feel his face. A neat line of beard trimmed his longer, pointed jawline. He explored his cheeks and his fingers caught on the ridges of scars. A thick scar bisected the outer edge of his left eyebrow. He waved his fingers in front of his left eye and thought a prayer to A'theosius, grateful he could still see with it. His hair was short and tightly curled and coarse, his cheekbones wide and sharp, and his nose felt longer, wider at the base. He wriggled in the saddle and flexed his legs and feet, testing the fit of his clothes. Yes, his boots did feel tighter, but not painfully so. He couldn't tell if his legs were longer, but his pants did feel tighter in the thigh and waist. He hunched his back, testing, and felt the pull of tight cloth across his shoulders. There was a gap between the bottom of his shirt and his belt. He would have to borrow clothes when they reached Magnus's friends, at the very least. Perhaps buy new ones, if they stayed in Cambrodaera more than a few days. Then again, if he needed to hide his face, so no one mistook him for the king, then he wouldn't be able to leave their lodgings at all.

At least the king of Cambrodaera is a grown man, he thought, and surprised himself with a snort of laughter. What would have happened if the rightful ruler was a child, a baby, another princess? He imagined shrinking, until his too-large clothes slid off, leaving him naked, and maybe so stunned by the change he fell out of his saddle.

That's the spirit, Viza said. She sounded a little more cheerful than she had when she retreated, but not much stronger. *I'm sorry, dear boy, but between the draining of all that nasty, feuding magic and then the spell enacting, which by its very nature claims much of my inherent magic because it is part of me … I was quite fractured. I've been trying to trace the roots of the spell. It's quite frustrating that the more we remove from you, the more roots we find. It's like the old fables of reversal spells. Like in the legend of the prince doomed to clear the filthy stables of an ogre. For every shovelful he throws out of the stables, two more come in.*

So I'll never be free? I'll never wear my own face again? Or was Magnus right, and the worst possible tangling has made me and Anwir a combination of us both, so we'll never have our own faces? Zair was glad he could talk in his mind to Viza. He suspected he would be whining like a child if he had to speak aloud.

Never is a very long time. I'm sure as soon as we find some civilized kingdom where I can contact the mirror web and get help from some much older and more experienced and powerful mirrors, we will find a cure. She sighed. *It might just take longer than we first calculated. I'm sorry, but I do need to rest. I just wanted to … well, to encourage you. And tell you how proud I am of you, how you're standing up under all these surprises.*

Thanks. Zair hunched his shoulders and turned his gaze back to that black wall in the distance. Somewhere in that wall was the passageway into Cambrodaera, and the friends Magnus had promised would help them. He advised himself to take this new journey one step at a time and not look too far ahead. Doing that would only depress him even more than he was already.

~~~~~
~~~~~

The journey across the sulfur-mud flats took them all day, and Zair was grateful for the shadows that wrapped around them just as the black and red stone wall finally appeared to grow and tower over them. He imagined unfriendly eyes peering over that wall, seeing his face and reacting in many possible ways, most of them dangerous to their entire company. How would the king of Cambrodaera react to hearing that a stranger had ridden into his kingdom from Dorwain, wearing his face? How soon would rebels and revolutionaries learn about Zair's presence, and try to take advantage of him, put him on the throne, use him as a puppet ruler?

Logic said for the king to eliminate his duplicate as quickly as possible.

Zair studied the approaching wall, trying to find the places where the defenders of Cambrodaera's border watched them, the spots where they could shoot arrows or launch spears or even dump vats of burning tar or oil on them. And where was the gate to let them through? Even now, with the wall tall enough he had to tip back his head to see the top, Zair thought they would never reach the end of this path.

Chapter Twenty-Two

A voice called out to them, sounding like a challenge, rough and deep and vibrating up from the ground. Yet in no language Zair understood. That worried him, because as Anwir's Shadow he had been required to study the languages of the different kingdoms surrounding Dorwain. Magnus called out a response, apparently in the same language, his voice also seeming to come from the ground. Zair looked around and grinned to see some of the soldiers also frowning, looking at the ground and then up at the sky, as if they couldn't discern the source of the sound.

"Close your eyes and trust your horses." The instructions were repeated and called back through the column, until they reached the end of the line.

Zair thought a silent prayer for protection, closed his eyes, and rested his hands on the front of his saddle, so he wouldn't give in to the urge to pull on those reins. These were Brigade-trained horses, after all, proven to be twice as intelligent and discerning than the average horse. He caught his breath, though, when Patch picked up his pace. He fought the urge to tighten his legs, afraid to interfere with whatever or whoever guided his horse now. He counted the steps, every time Patch's flank moved under his right leg. Fifty. One hundred. The echoes of hooves on stone grew higher in pitch, closer, sharper, indicating that they rode down a narrow passage through the rock. Then the echoes softened again. The walls enclosing them were further away. The horses kept moving. Several voices spoke quietly in the distance. One hundred-fifty steps.

Light pierced his closed eyelids. Zair bowed his head, glad for his hood to provide more protection. The light grew stronger until his head throbbed and his skin felt hot.

Then it stopped, like closing the shield on a lantern. He let out a gusting sigh. Several men chuckled around him. Their horses stopped, without any spoken command.

"Open," Magnus called, his voice weary but touched with laughter. "Welcome to Cambrodaera."

Their company sat in an oval, domed room carved from the rock, longer than the grand ceremonial courtyard of the palace in Dorwain. Zair sat far enough away from the walls, they looked smooth. Doors broke up the black and red-streaked expanse, some wide enough for three horses to ride through side-by-side, others barely wide enough for a man in armor.

Soldiers in brown and green uniforms surrounded them, only varying in their height and the breadth of their shoulders. The helmets that hid their faces looked like bronze eggs, leaving no place for a weapon to catch when it struck. Metal mesh covered the eyes and mouths. Zair shuddered at the momentary illusion of no eyes behind them.

At Magnus's word, their company dismounted. Soldiers stepped forward to take their horses' reins. The company followed Magnus and the tallest, widest soldier through one narrow door. Zair looked back to see the soldiers leading their horses through another door on the far side of the wide room. They walked in silence down a curving corridor lit by lanterns set in niches near the top of the rounded ceiling. The corridor branched into three. Their guide led them down the right-hand corridor, and after a dozen steps into another room. Zair felt the air move and turned around to see doors slide out of the walls and close.

"Welcome, Highness," their guide said, speaking for the first time, as far as Zair could tell. The man bowed to Jillian and offered his hand. She gave her hand into his grip, and he led her to a cluster of cushioned chairs opposite the closed doors. When she was seated, he stepped back and removed his helmet.

Several soldiers around Zair murmured. Someone gasped. Someone else chuckled. Until Magnus turned and glared at them.

"Be welcome, friends." The man turned to survey the company, bowing slightly to Encobi and Shaleen. "Stay here, until all is cleared and verified. Everything is available for your comfort." He gestured to Magnus, who followed him to the door. They stepped outside into the corridor and the door closed behind them again.

"Oh, this is a problem," Encobi said. Instead of sitting, she slipped out of her cloak, tossing it behind herself onto one of the benches next to Jillian's chair. Then she strode through the soldiers to Zair.

"What is?" Jillian asked.

Encobi held out her hand to Zair. He let her lead him back to Jillian, and Shaleen, who had settled next to her. Yancob joined them.

"This is a problem," she said, and gestured for Zair to pull his hood down. Her mouth flicked into a smile when he hesitated. "All of you, be quiet, say nothing about what you're about to see," she said, glancing around at the soldiers.

"We've already seen," one of the men who had been riding by Zair called back to her. "Who was that?" He gestured at the door, indicating the man who had greeted them.

"Lord General of all the armies Braeccus," Yancob said. He shook his head, mouth flattening, as Zair lowered his hood. A snort escaped him. "Problem? You need to learn to be more accurate with your assessments, my darling."

"What?" Zair said, keeping his voice down when he wanted to shout.

"The wretched mirror spell is still alive," Shaleen said. She shook her head, frowning at Zair. Then she glanced at the doorway Magnus and their guide had gone through.

"I know. I felt it when it woke up." Zair gestured at his face.

"You have no idea," Yancob muttered.

"Oh, my poor boy," Jillian said. "You're the image of Braeccus."

Encobi dropped down on the bench next to Shaleen and spilled a string of curses, half of which Zair didn't understand. He wanted to laugh when Yancob's eyes widened, then he paled before flushing dark at his daughter's language.

"Enough, girl," he growled, and slapped her shoulder. "Your mother will come back from the dead if you keep that up. Have some pity on me, because she'll shred me for letting you speak that way."

Encobi stopped with a squeak that sounded like a giggle. Some of the soldiers chuckled, but the sound didn't last long, and the atmosphere in the room seemed to tighten instead of lighten.

"It's proof, for one thing," Jillian said. "Encobi, can you weave an illusion spell on top of that ... problem?" She flicked her fingers at Zair's face.

"I can try. I've been working myself into a headache ever since we crossed the border. Lazius and his idiots were bad enough, but the ones who came after them and tried to adjust the spells that they couldn't eradicate, they just made everything more tangled. And I fear they encouraged the original spells to dig even deeper roots into Zair. There's a regenerative looping spell woven in that we weren't able to discern until Viza regained more of herself, so she could see what they had done with her power. Once she entirely broke the link with Anwir, she discovered a repulsion spell woven through everything. At least, that's what we agreed to call it. We don't know the name, if it ever had a name.

"It could be something entirely new those idiots created by accident and colossally bad luck. Or, a quiet, insidious, utterly clever and despicable construct that isn't included in the books Magnus and I rescued. Zair, you need to find the Enchanters' Court and petition the Council to free you. Even then, it could be such an expenditure of energy and time and knowledge, no one would be willing to invest it in you." Encobi shook her head.

"You don't need to hear all the tangles and complications. The bottom line is that while many of the outer layers and tangles of spells did come off with comparative ease ... well, now that the repulsion spell is exposed to air and light, so to speak, it's awake, and essentially sloughing off any magic we try to use against it. While it's good that if you hadn't managed to escape the palace, Nostrados and his followers wouldn't have been able to wrap any new spells around you … it also means I can't even place an illusion spell on you to hide your new face. And perhaps more important, prevent another civil war in Cambrodaera."

"Why a civil war?" Felyx asked, stepping up next to Zair and resting a hand on his shoulder. The company's apprentice healer had become a friend, working with him in the kitchen and sharing some of his knowledge. He also had a touch of magic that was more like luck than anything he could control. It made him a sought-after partner in contests among the Red Brigade, because he was nearly impossible to beat in games of dice or throwing knives or darts at targets.

"The short version of the story?" Shaleen shook her head, keeping her gaze on Zair as if she couldn't quite accept what she saw. "Three generations ago, a distant branch of the royal family rose up to power and ousted the king at that time. Much like in Dorwain. It seems to be a chronic problem with royal families everywhere. The official history books say a plague that swept through the kingdom wiped out all the royal family. The unofficial history books say the youngest son escaped, rescued by a daughter of the usurper. She raised him as her son, and his descendants have lived in the shadow of the throne, surrounded by rumors. Those rumors, if they are true, mean his grandson is Braeccus. The true heir to the throne, if Zair wears his face. And enough people are dissatisfied with the current king, if they knew the true heir was real, they'd plunge the kingdom into civil war to oust him."

"But more people love his nephew, his heir, and expect him to be three times better. That should be enough to quell the threat of civil war," Jillian said, nodding, "except for those rumors. I'm so sorry, Zair. It's bad enough you are the true heir of Dorwain, but to put your life in danger here …" She held out her hand to Zair. "Encobi, you have to find a way to protect him. Hasn't he suffered enough because of my family?"

"Wait," Nordon said, from his place by the door where he leaned back against the wall. "What do you mean, he's the true heir?"

"All that tangled, useless, interfering magic has been changing Anwir to look like Zair, instead of the other way around, like you'd expect for a Shadow," Yancob said. "They ignored all Magnus's warnings and decided changing his flesh and bone to match Anwir was smarter than weaving an illusion spell around him. They went too far, they didn't realize what they were doing, and they specified the face of the true heir, the true king, would dominate as the boys grew up. Well …" He held out a hand to Zair. "Multi-great-grandson of Zared the Just. And thanks to those idiots, thanks to the purges that tried to destroy all magical knowledge in Dorwain, so everything is catch-as-catch-can, and make-it-up-as-you-stumble-through, he's cursed by badly woven spells to wear the face of the true king of every kingdom he walks into."

"Can we go back to Dorwain and put the true heir on the throne?" another man said from the far side of the room. "I'd gladly follow Zair any day, instead of that brainless snot."

"No." Zair's voice cracked. His face warmed as he looked around the room. "It's enough to get away. I can't ask you to face a death sentence by returning to Dorwain. Magnus and Encobi will find a way to untangle all that broken magic. I don't want to be a king. I don't want to look like a king. I just want ..." He shrugged, and his face warmed even more. His throat thickened with laughter he didn't dare let out. He wasn't sure what he wanted to do, beyond getting free of the magic that had been a curse since the first spell touched him.

One step at a time, Viza whispered inside his head. *Deal with today. Don't worry about tomorrow until it dawns. Trust A'theosius.*

~~~~~

Braeccus arranged for their company to have quarters in an interconnected series of apartments within the fortress, rather than in the city itself, with enough rooms for them to stay together. The soldiers went out in threes and fours to explore the fortress and then the city, half a mile further down the wide, winding passageway through the canyons. After only three days, most of them thought they could be happy joining the soldiers here, to serve Cambrodaera. They liked and respected Braeccus, and Magnus assured them that serving him would be a pleasure and an honor. Zair itched to be allowed to go out and explore, but until he freed himself of Braeccus's face, that would be dangerous.

Jillian and Shaleen had yet to step outside of their guest quarters. Zair wondered if King Axrod or Prince Orwell, his nephew and heir, even knew the princess had arrived. Braeccus had assured them the political situation was such that the king would welcome and defend her. War with Dorwain wasn't a pleasant prospect, but the two kingdoms were evenly matched in wealth and military might, so war wouldn't be an easy choice for either side. The wealth of magical knowledge in Cambrodaera would also make Dorwain hesitate to declare war. King Joben and Nostrados, if no one else, had had more than adequate proof that the gathered magical knowledge of Dorwain was flawed, at best.

Even if Jillian's presence became a problem, King Axrod might choose to give her sanctuary if only to tweak the noses of rival kings and aggravate King Joben. Until Jillian and Magnus and Yancob decided where to go next, they chose to keep her presence in Cambrodaera a secret. Staying in this particular kingdom was not the first choice, or the only plan. Common sense said Jillian and her protectors would be wise to keep moving, perhaps even cross the sea to another continent where Dorwain's power meant nothing, either in terms of threat or profit. Here on this continent, it only made sense for some king to seek to use the fugitive
~~~~~

princess and the vow-breaker elite soldiers to his advantage in the constant game of one-upmanship played among kingdoms.

The ideal plan was to rest here, gain their strength and balance, and then move on before the power-players and schemers discovered her presence and tried to take advantage of it.

Braeccus did all he could to ensure their privacy, and to hide their identities, and for the most part he succeeded. He was unable to come back to check on his guests until the eighth day of taking asylum in Cambrodaera. He was busy attending to vital matters of state. Specifically, his daughter Belinda's marriage to Prince Orwell. Magnus reported that when he asked their host about his claim to the throne, and the rumors that had swirled through the kingdom for years, Braeccus joked that he was too old to change his career. Why should he spend his life dealing with diplomats when soldiers were so much more reasonable? He was perfectly content to know his grandson would sit on his great-grandfather's throne. He trusted Orwell to take good care of the kingdom, and correct the harm and injustices perpetrated by his predecessors.

The pending ascension of Orwell to the throne, at his marriage to Belinda, didn't change the situation for Jillian. All they needed was for one person to learn her true identity. The news would spread. Fast or slow didn't matter in the long run. Eventually, someone would act on that knowledge for their own profit, with no regard for Jillian's wishes or fears or welfare. Especially if revealing her presence in Cambrodaera caused trouble for unpopular King Axrod.

Keeping her presence and identity hidden was much easier than preventing servants and guards glimpsing Zair wearing Braeccus's face. Magnus and Encobi worked themselves into sweaty, exhausted headaches every other day, trying different spells to work around the repulsion spell and give Zair his own face. The best they could manage was a temporary illusion, lasting half an hour at most before the repulsion spell sloughed it off. Viza tried to work from inside the spells, but she used up too much energy with the effort, which just drove her into silent retreat.

Despite their best efforts at disguise, by the fifth day someone saw enough of Zair's face for the rumors to start spreading. Braeccus's most loyal servants were charged with keeping the refugees' presence hidden, and they told him what they saw and heard. He sent for Magnus, who explained the entire situation. As best as the enchanter could tell, his old friend trusted and believed him, and was willing to give him time and opportunity to keep the expected trouble from arising.

Despite the best efforts of those loyal servants, the rumors still spread.

When Braeccus came to visit the refugees, he brought an old wizard with him who specialized in untangling spells. Especially spells created through flawed understanding of the rhythms and melodies of magic. Zair didn't feel much confidence in the bald little man, who sniffled between every sentence and kept his left hand hidden in the enormous, bulging bag that hung from a strap across his chest. The way the man stared at him when he lowered his hood, the slight curving of his lips, the single glance shot at Braeccus and then back to him, sent a prickle of apprehension up Zair's spine.

The wizard's name was Shoomerang. He seemed heartily offended that neither Magnus nor Encobi recognized his name or knew his reputation. When they insisted on staying in the room with him while he studied the spells tangling Zair, the wizard's expression turned to jagged ice. He argued until he was hoarse, despite Braeccus supporting the two visiting enchanters.

When he finally got to work, Shoomerang walked around and around Zair, muttering under his breath, surrounding him in an unpleasant cloud of odor, part burned herbs, part pungent spices, part dirty clothes, part rotted teeth. After maybe ten minutes, Zair started counting every time the wizard passed in front of him. He stopped at thirty-two.

Shoomerang then pulled strange, twisted objects out of his bulging pouch, kept them partially hidden in his gnarled hands, and muttered to them. Each time, dark-tinted sparks shot out of the objects and hit Zair. Sometimes in the face, his belly, sometimes his feet, his arms. Once the sparks landed in his hair and grew so hot, Zair slapped his own head, positive it was on fire. He wanted to slap Shoomerang when he caught the old man's mouth twisting in a brief smile each time.

The wizard's entire purpose seemed to be to torment him, not untangle the magic binding him. Zair told Encobi and Magnus exactly that, when Shoomerang finally left after four fruitless, uncomfortable hours.

"I agree," Encobi said. "For all the show he put on, he expended very little energy. He was distracting us with all that light. I fear discovering what he was truly trying to accomplish. It wasn't to help Zair."

Magnus gathered their company together in the central room of the guest quarters, and reported on the disappointing, painful time with the old wizard. This matter affected them all, the decisions they would make over the next weeks or months, the new lives they hoped to make.

"I think the smart move is to flee," Shaleen said.

"Keep running?" Nordon said.

"Only if they want to make outlaws of us," someone muttered, softly enough Zair couldn't identify the voice.

"Mercenaries. Sell our swords to the highest bidder." Yancob bared his teeth in a fierce grin. "If you think about it, all the trash we learned about Joben, the tasteless tasks he handed us ... that's what we've been doing for decades. But now, we'll have the freedom to say no."

"I was thinking of just Zair," Shaleen said. She dug in her belt pouch and brought out several plain silver rings, the finish dull and scratched. "A lone man can vanish more easily than a company. Even a company as skilled as those here in this room." Her words earned a few chuckles and muttered comments. She bared her teeth in a fierce, humorless grin. "But it'd be cruel to send the boy out alone. No, sorry. He's a man grown. We have to stop thinking of him as a boy who was unfairly forced into a cruel fate." She gave Zair a short bow that chilled him with implications he could only sense, not name.

"I want to be able to come to his aide, and him to ours, if need be. Can you make it so we can hear each other through these rings?"

"Easy enough," Encobi said, reaching to take them from her open hand.

She stepped away and turned her back to them. A soft glow seeped around her as she wrapped spells around the rings. Zair thought of all the noise Shoomerang had generated, in contrast to how quietly Encobi and Magnus both performed magic. There was a vast difference in strength and understanding, and yes, even style. He shivered with the angry certainty that the old wizard hadn't tried at all to free him of the mirroring spells. Did Shoomerang try to learn the depths of the spells, to copy them, maybe use them for other purposes? Maybe to harm Braeccus?

Chapter Twenty-Three

What if the old wizard told the leaders of the rebels he had identified the true-born king of Cambrodaera?

"You've got a price waiting to settle on your head," Yancob said, nodding, when Zair interrupted the discussion of strategies and options to voice his suspicion. "The sooner you leave here, the better for you and Braeccus. Then it's just the word of a crazy old, half-strength wizard, more show than results, against the Lord General of the armies, who supports the king and his heir. Without his duplicate running around, there's nothing to keep the rumors alive."

"The problem is that once he crosses the border, he's going to change to look like the next king," someone else said from the far side of the room.

"I wear a hood whenever I can, I stay as far away from the major cities as I can, and I spend all my time trying to find an enchanter strong enough, educated enough, to uproot the spells." Zair tried to smile. It sounded easy, but as several of his teachers had told him, the simpler the process or the more straightforward the journey sounded, the more difficult and complicated and in this case, deadly, it would end up being.

They spread out maps and discussed the best routes to take to leave Cambrodaera as swiftly as possible, depending on which kingdom Zair should flee to next. Then they discussed the good and bad points of each kingdom whose border touched Cambrodaera. Which would be the easiest one to travel through without being stopped by suspicious border guards and patrols? Which had the most magical traps? What traps did Zair need to worry about tripping just from the mere weight of all the magic wrapped and tangled around him? Which had the best, most powerful, and most helpful enchanters and sorcerers? And most important, which kingdoms had known touchpoints, to allow people to make requests to the Enchanters' Court? No matter where he went, no matter how safe he became among people who wouldn't recognize their ruler's face on Zair, ultimately he needed to reach the Enchanters' Court to request help.

Zair had never learned all these details of the kingdoms on this continent when he was preparing to be Anwir's Shadow. This new information fascinated him so much, he ignored the increasing hum in his ring, until it tightened, to the point of pain. He caught his breath and raised his hand to stare at it. A faint greenish glow revealed the formerly invisible ring on his finger.

"Magnus?" Zair held out his hand, so it covered the map where Yancob had been tracing the path of several intersecting rivers, the meeting point of several kingdoms, with the tip of his finger.

The enchanter raised his head and his eyes seemed to cross until he focused on the ring. He went very still, then he stood up straight, his mouth flattening, and gestured for Zair to come around the table to him. He held out his hand. Zair tried to slide the ring off. It wouldn't budge. Magnus gripped his hand, wrapping his fingers around the ring, raising a single, dark green spark that crackled loudly. His expression darkened.

"That old fraud cast a seek-and-find spell. We didn't sense it under all the noise he was making. Plus, it's been sleeping until now. He's helping someone find you. If he doesn't tell them outright where you are, then he can try to talk his way out of reprisals if their plot fails."

"Are they going to use the lad against their king, or against Braeccus?" Yancob growled.

"Does it matter? We're all in danger, and we've brought that danger to him, in payment for helping us." Magnus gripped Zair's hand a little tighter and looked deep into his eyes before releasing him. "I'm sorry. I've failed you even more."

"No—"

"I should have protected you better when the whole stupid, selfish plot began. I foolishly agreed with Pendrake, that the best way to keep you and your royal blood hidden was to put you in the shadow of the throne itself." He looked around the room, at their entire company watching him, their expressions stern, alert, elite soldiers ready for battle.

"We need to scatter," Encobi said, rejoining them. She held out the four rings, to Zair, Yancob, Shaleen, then Magnus. "Smaller numbers are easier to hide and move faster. No, both on the same finger," she hurried to say, as Zair moved to put the new ring on his other hand. "I wove in a distraction, and a broken compass spell, but they won't hold for long. The faster you get over the border, the better." She watched Zair until he put the new ring on the same finger with the first ring. A loud snap echoed through the room, accompanied by a flash of poison-green light and momentary numbness up to his elbow. "Sorry."

"Best to go quickly. He has to know we've caught his trick." Yancob snorted. "I hope it scares him witless, wondering how his spell was caught so quickly."

"That wouldn't be hard," his daughter retorted. "The man had very little in the way of wits to begin with. He gives real enchanters a bad name!"

Magnus promised he and Yancob would have a plan assembled by the time everyone was ready to flee their guest quarters. Zair ran to his bed in the long dormitory room all the men shared. It was a matter of moments to jam his few pieces of clothing, his weapons, and his journal and four precious books about magic into his pack, and hurry back to the common room.

Encobi waylaid him, nearly yanking him off his feet into the bathing room. Nordon was waiting with a wicked grin on his face and a razor in his hand.

"Down to your breechclout, boy. No time for modesty," he added, with a jerk of his chin at Encobi.

Zair obeyed and hoped he would have time to at least ask what the plan was. He barely got his undertunic tugged over his head before Nordon grabbed him by his shoulders and plunked him down on a bench, grabbed hold of his chin, and began to shave him. Meanwhile, Encobi went to her knees and rubbed a stinging liquid that smelled of ashes and cinnamon and fuller's earth up first one leg, then the other.

"What—" Zair began, once Nordon let go of his face and got to work hacking off his black curls. Braeccus's curls, not his own.

"We're changing your appearance long enough to get you out through the gates where we entered. The spell will insist on returning you to Braeccus's likeness, but it will take time. We hope," she added, pausing to meet his gaze, and get up from her knees to start rubbing the liquid on his chest. "Shaved bald, with your skin lightened several shades, whoever is hunting you might just look you right in the face and pass you over. All we need is to buy some time."

"Hold still," Nordon muttered, and slapped Zair's bare shoulder. "Bloody cuts will draw suspicion."

"Unless we have a dozen of you take punches at him, so whoever sees him assumes he's been in a fight."

"Hey," Zair began. Nordon slapped his shoulder again, then yanked harder than necessary on what felt like the last handful of curls on his head. The feel of air passing across the bare skin of his head felt strange. He scrambled for something to distract himself. "How do the rings work?"

"Close your eyes, find a quiet place, and cast your thoughts out to one of us. Envision the face and voice. You'll need to focus hard the first few times," Encobi said. "Close your eyes." She didn't wait for him to comply and spread the liquid on his face. "On the positive side, this will teach you the discipline you sorely need to control your magic as it blooms. One of the truly wretched effects of all those spells they bound on you was that your magic was kept sleeping. Like seeds that were denied water and sunlight and soil. Now that we've removed so many layers of truly wretched, badly woven magic, you're waking up to what you should have been all along." She patted his cheek. "Not bad, if I do say so myself. Does it burn too badly?"

"No. Not too much," Zair hurried to add. His eyes watered. He fought not to sneeze with the stinging aroma filling his nose. To his relief, by the time he got dressed again, the smell had faded. Either that, or his nose had gone numb.

When he returned to the common room, the only one there was Magnus. Everyone else, Zair assumed, had fled. He wished he could have at least said goodbye to Jillian and Shaleen. As ironic as it sounded, being confined to their guest quarters with them had been pleasant.

Magnus gave him a map, hastily drawn, with just the most important landmarks to find for his journey, and notes written on the back. Once he had passed through the gates where they had first entered Cambrodaera, he was to ride east, following the mountain wall until it became foothills, thereby avoiding the sulfur-mud flats. He would stay in Cambrodaera until he reached the Crestbain River, flowing north to south. The banks were too steep, the river full of rapids, so it was impossible for him to cross into Vinsidia, on the east side of the river. He would have to follow the Crestbain south and cross back into Dorwain as he made a wide circle going west around the city of Camsidia. The trading city sat on the meeting place of the Angraborn River, flowing west to east, with the Crestbain. The city controlled a twenty-mile-wide terrain full of islands and marshes and smaller streams. The city was built on those islands and controlled the meeting of the rivers. A team of three enchanters devoted all their time to controlling the water levels and keeping the channels dredged among the islands so merchant vessels could pass through. Those three enchanters, working together, were so strong, they would sense the tangled spells enfolding Zair if he crossed into their territory. They wouldn't stop to investigate. They would see that much magic gathered into one place, consider it a threat, and attack. Zair needed to ride a wide circle around the city. Magnus gave him a charm to help him detect the boundaries and stay outside them.

Camsidia officially belonged jointly to Dorwain on the southwest, Cambrodaera on the northwest, Nychtenland on the southeast, and Vinsidia on the northeast. Despite the four kingdoms claiming a quarter of the city, for the most part, Camsidia ruled itself. When its officials defied the wishes of those kingdoms, they faced little retribution. Everyone wanted the goodwill of the merchants who were the true authorities and controlled the ferries and bridges that allowed passage on the rivers for ten miles out in all directions.

Zair needed to continue around Camsidia until he crossed the Crestbain, travel through Nychtenland heading east and north, until he reached Vinsidia. There he needed to head to the northeast corner of the kingdom, to seek several reclusive enchanters who lived in the mountain wastes. Magnus believed the noise of clashing magics from all the spells woven around him would draw the attention of at least one of those enchanters. The older enchanters and sorcerers grew, the more reclusive they became, and quiet in the magical atmosphere was their greatest treasure. They would help Zair simply to regain that quiet, even if they weren't fascinated with the puzzle he offered.

Magnus and Zair went over the map twice, to make sure he understood the route, then the enchanter gestured for him to pick up his pack and saddlebags. The air tingled for a few moments as he threw a blurring spell over them both and flung open the door. They hurried down the corridors of the fortress, heading for the stables. Zair nearly let out a cry of dismay when they stepped in and he saw all their horses in their stalls. Then he blinked, and the horses and all their tack were gone. Another blink, and the horses were back.

"It doesn't do any good to scatter if someone notices right away we've left," Magnus whispered. "A'theosius guide and guard you, lad. And may we meet again, soon, in safety. I look forward to handling your education myself, the way I should have from the beginning." He clapped him once more on the shoulder, then turned with a swirl of his cloak and was gone.

Zair bit back an urge to shout for the enchanter. Had the man gone invisible? Or was he one of those enchanters who was so old, he could create temporary rips in the fabric of the world and move from one city or kingdom to another, like an ordinary man would walk from one room to another?

What mattered was that Magnus would stay with Princess Jillian and guard her. She would be safe under his care, and far better off than she had ever been, living in the palace in Dorwain.

The blurring spell around him flickered against his skin, warning that it would not last long. Zair grinned at this evidence that his sensitivity to magic had grown, just as Magnus and Encobi had promised him. He hurried to saddle Patch, sling the saddlebags in place, and get out of there. The blurring spell, for however long it lasted, meant people would know he was there, but not notice any details of his clothes or shape or the color of his horse. The best way to use a blurring spell was to keep moving, keeping in the shadows as he headed for the wall and the gate out of Cambrodaera. He needed to pass through the gate before it faded entirely.

The spell faded away gradually, because having it stop abruptly and having Zair suddenly appear, where before he had just been a shadow, rather wasted all the effort of blurring him. People remembered sudden changes, rather than gradual fading in or out. Once he was fully visible, he had to hope his altered appearance lasted long enough to get him through the gate, into twilight and away from human sight, before he once more mirrored Braeccus.

Until the illusions Encobi and Magnus cast faded, no one would realize that Braeccus's guests had fled their guest quarters. No one would be alarmed. No one would be watching the traffic leaving Cambrodaera, unless a warning reached the border guards to be on the lookout for someone who looked like Lord General Braeccus.

Zair rode in the shadow of a string of wagons taking supplies to the border wall. He prayed for the safety of their company, and thanked A'theosius that Magnus had looked after him all these years. He knew and was grateful that he had been given good friends who saw the injustice done to him and risked their own safety and comfortable lives to help him. He considered his tactics for the next few days, and for the next few months, until he could find help. How long would it take until he reached the mountains of Vinsidia and attracted the attention of a reclusive enchanter who liked solving riddles? He nearly laughed aloud, when he couldn't remember if the current ruler of Vinsidia was a man or a woman, old or young. Well, he would find out when he crossed the border, wouldn't he? And he had best do it at night, as solitary as possible, so fellow travelers wouldn't notice the change.

Was it possible for him to go far enough away from Dorwain that distance would thin and break the ties between him and Anwir, once and for all? Would he have to travel to the other side of the world to wear his own face again?

A chuckle escaped him, when he thought of Anwir getting up one morning to look in the mirror and see his true face, not the one he had been wearing all these years.

"Priorities, boy," he whispered, making his voice rough to mimic Yancob. Zair knew he crippled himself, looking too many steps ahead on this journey. For now, he would follow the plan they had agreed on. He would travel in the shadows, on solitary roads, hiding under his hood.

Zair focused on riding as silently as he could, keeping the pace of everyone around him. If he attracted attention, someone might realize a blurring spell covered him, and they would wonder why he needed one. The spell was to make people ignore him. Attention might snap the spell from strain, and then what kind of trouble would he be in if someone, such as the guards on the border wall, recognized Braeccus's face?

Best to keep moving, staying in shadows, hide his face, and stop talking to himself, until he was at least five days of travel away. Maybe more.

~~~~~

Zair braced for the physical transformation when the sheer cliffs he followed turned south. Nothing happened, meaning he hadn't crossed the border of Cambrodaera as established by magic. He expected it to happen when he approached the Angraborn to cross into Dorwain. Clearly, the
~~~~~

guarding magic that marked the true borders of kingdoms didn't pay attention to rivers, because he felt nothing. He took the ferry across the Angraborn, led Patch onto the shore on the other side. Still nothing. He distracted himself speculating on the diplomatic firestorm that would result if he reported this news. To whom, though? Would Cambrodaera try to take that territory that Dorwain held now, or shrug it off as useless, not worth fighting for?

The fiery nails danced over his skin after he left the river behind, maybe twenty minutes of riding. Despite the discomfort, there was something comforting about wearing his own face again. Supposedly his own face. Magnus couldn't guarantee that the mirroring magic wasn't so tangled and warped and badly woven that he and Anwir wore faces that were a combination of both of them.

He rode south and east, paying attention to the warning charms. Camsidia was behind him, the bridge across the Crestbain River within his sights, when Shaleen contacted him through the ring. She had heard from Encobi. Their two companies were safe and had found quiet places to settle, if only temporarily.

Even better, Viza could now sense the presence of several magic mirrors across the border in Nychtenland. She didn't have the strength to talk and have them hear her. However, she could now catch bits of information that floated through the mirror web. She was nearly giddy with excitement, picking up on news and events she had missed out on for more than eighty years. She and Zair got into a fascinating discussion of the enchanted forest and the entire concept of portals to travel to different kingdoms, avoiding months of travel over land or sea.

They were having so much fun, Zair didn't pay attention when they crossed the bridge over the Crestbain river shallows and entered Nychtenland. When the river was half a day of riding behind him, the mirror spell awoke. He stopped Patch to pull out his journal and make note of the sensations, as Encobi had asked him to do. In theory, this would help them understand the spells still tangling him and chart their changes and deterioration. Interestingly, every border crossing provided a different physical sensation. He wondered if it had something to do with the amount of magic in the kingdom he was entering.

This time, instead of fiery nail points all over him, his skin merely tingled, like sand rubbed into sun-warmed skin. Not painful this time, just irritating. He tugged off his glove to see his familiar deep brown skin tones turn bluish-black. His scalp itched. He reached up under his hood to feel his hair tighten into short, woolly tufts. He wondered what color it was now. He laughed, despite the image in his head of himself as a wax statue being reshaped over a bed of coals.

He laughed because again, the guarding magic didn't recognize the border of the river, established by the last war between Dorwain and Nychtenland. It held to more ancient borders and boundaries. In essence, Dorwain was larger than King Joben realized, and the kings of Nychtenland had been profiting from the lush farmlands on their side of the river. Zair chuckled, then caught himself and looked around, to ensure no one had seen him change. He prayed no one with any magical talent was close enough to hear the noise created by the badly made spell awakening and working on him.

"Please, A'theosius ... when will I be free? This is a sickness. It's a curse I didn't earn. Why do I have to keep living like this?" he grumbled. He flinched, startled to hear his voice, which was deeper. He hadn't meant to speak aloud. Speaking to himself would certainly attract attention from fellow travelers. He didn't need the first person to look at him to recognize him as the king of Nychtenland. Any reaction would be dangerous. Adoring citizens would attract attention and make it hard for him to keep moving. Resentful citizens and rebels would attack. Or worse, someone would arrest him as a danger and threat to the throne.

Zair kept his head down, ruminating on all the mistakes he had made and the possible problems ahead of him. Such thinking distracted him from the quivering in his bones, the sense of swelling and shrinking in his muscles, until his skin and flesh and bones finished adjusting, and he could relax and breathe normally again. A'theosius had been kind, so the closest people on the road were small, distant figures both ahead of and behind him. It was an overcast day as well, helping to keep his face in shadows. He grinned and thanked A'theosius for his steady, reliable horse. Patch didn't react in fear when the changes came over him. Just how hard would it be to keep his hood low over his face, if he was struggling to keep his horse from racing down the road in terror, or trying to buck him off?

Well, that was interesting. You might consider taking up a traveling life, helping to redraw the ancient boundaries, Viza commented. *You might even gain the attention of the Enchanter's Court, by pointing out to them this evidence that magic ignores the boundaries drawn by men and armies.*

Do I want their attention? Zair responded after a moment of thought.

Chapter Twenty-Four

If you want to be freed of all those ridiculous, sticky, badly-woven spells, you might, the mirror responded after several moments of thinking silence. *The problem of appealing to the Enchanter's Court is that they reside inside time pockets, whether they are gathered together or separated to pursue their research. They don't mind if months and years pass by outside in the normal stream of time, while for them only a day or two passes. Or ten years inside while only a few weeks pass in the normal stream of time, if they need to do vital research and experimentation. They're long-lived, and already braced to lose friends and family to old age while they continue on the path A'theosius grants them. For ordinary mortals … well, they don't like it so much. How many tales are there, about young men who go adventuring to win riches and fame, but then they fall into a time pocket of one kind or another, and when they return home, the girl they loved is now a grandmother?* She chuckled. *Then again, my dear boy, you really aren't an ordinary mortal, are you?*

I don't know what I am.

Well, that's what this journey is for, do we agree? Not just to free you, but to find out what and who you really are. And maybe earn you a kingdom of your own.

That doesn't really seem fair, does it? Zair asked, almost as soon as the thought became clear in his head.

What do you mean?

If I earn a kingdom, doesn't that mean that some king loses his kingdom?

You could win the right to marry a king's only daughter.

But that means she doesn't get to be queen.

Technically —

You know what I mean. Zair laughed, then flinched, hoping no one was close enough to hear. Laughing at nothing, when he rode alone, was just as liable to get him unwanted attention as falling off his horse during the transformation.

Yes, I know what you mean. She is queen of her father's kingdom, but being the wife of the king who solved riddles and defeated monsters isn't the same as sitting on the throne in her own right and power. The mirror sighed. *If no one has warned you yet, magic often has a tendency to be unfair. It always picks the youngest son or daughter for incredible gifts and adventures. It sets up all sorts of puzzles and challenges, and sometimes doesn't warn whoever encounters them, entirely by accident. They fail and face dreadful consequences, with no idea what they did wrong or why it had to happen to them. Of course, all those people who end up enchanted and cursed provide wonderful opportunities for someone to be a hero and rescue them, but it still isn't fair, is it?*

Why does A'theosius allow magic to be broken and unfair and lopsided and …? He shrugged. *Just a mess?*

The simple answer is that somewhere in the beginning, someone broke the rules, disobeyed simple instructions, and started an awful cascade of consequences and anger and selfishness and … well, A'theosius is a gentleman. Far too many people through the centuries have shaken their fists to the skies and declared they can take care of themselves, they don't need A'theosius with all his rules and judgments and consequences, he should just leave them alone. So, the All-Maker does just that. Lets people face the problems they brought on themselves, until someone, somewhere, is brave enough to say yes, they and everyone before them was wrong, they're sorry, could they please have one more chance, and could he repeat the holy words again, one more time, so they can try to follow the rules?

That doesn't sound that simple to me, Zair said.

That earned a chuckle from the mirror. *Believe me, dear boy, when you've lived another century, a great many things that seem complicated right now, when seen through the lens of harsh experience and humility, will seem ridiculously simple. Embarrassingly so.*

The sounds of galloping came from behind him. Zair looked back to see a troop of men in gray uniforms, with swords at their sides, maybe a dozen of them in three lines, coming up quickly behind him. He moved Patch over to the far right of the road to let them pass, bowed his head, and tugged his hood lower over his face. None of those soldiers even glanced at him. He pulled the map from the saddlebag in front of him and tried to calculate how long it would be until he reached the eastern arm of the Angraborn and could cross into Vinsidia. Viza retreated, to let him concentrate on his surroundings, and in hopes of contacting the mirror web. She was strong enough to hear the voices of other mirrors as they communicated, but only in fits and spurts, with long gaps of silence in between. Making herself heard still seemed beyond her strength. Zair wondered how she could stand the frustration.

~~~~~

Just as sunset started to send crimson and gold streaks spilling down from the hills on Zair's left, Shaleen made contact through the ring. She laughed when he shared how long it had taken for his features to change after he crossed the river. She agreed that while it was amusing to contemplate the consternation of King Joben if he ever learned how much of Dorwain lay in Nychtenland's control, it would be cruel to the common people of the kingdom to instigate a border war. Joben seemed to be hungry for any reason to go to war, to gain more territory, as evidenced by sending his own daughter into marriage in a brutal kingdom. The common people of both kingdoms would suffer in any war. If there was
~~~~~

any profit from that war, only the nobles would enjoy it, while the soldiers and common people paid the price.

She couldn't tell him what the rulers of Nychtenland looked like, to anticipate what sort of face he wore now. Dorwain had never been on good diplomatic relations with them. While standing in for Jillian, Shaleen had never had occasion to meet an ambassador or official from that kingdom, or travel to Nychtenland. Neither did the people guarded by the Firebird Guild when she served with them.

"Why not?" Zair asked, and looked around hastily, to make sure no one was close enough to hear him talking to himself. He let out a groan of pure relief when he saw the peaked roof of a roadside shelter, and the marker indicating it held a well. He could get out of the saddle and put a wall to his back while he focused on communicating through the ring. Less chance of someone unfriendly sneaking up behind him while his concentration was divided.

Nasty sort of folk running around there, taking control bit by bit. The land as well as people's minds, Shaleen responded after a few moments, in which Zair reached the shelter and dismounted. *They call themselves the Purple Sky, likely because they consider themselves the nobility among all magic-users, no matter how strong their magic is or isn't. Their intent is to control all the magic in the world. They spend their time taking control of magical hills and forests and wells, and if they can't take or keep control, they destroy it so no one else can benefit from it.*

They hunt for the sources of enchanted sand to make magic mirrors, to try to control the mirror web. They invade the sanctuaries of enchanters and sorcerers, to confiscate their magical tools and their books. If they can't take those things to add to their treasury, they'll burn the places down. They enslave any sort of wise beast or magical creature, like dragons and unicorns, and they're devoted to slaughtering entire magical races, such as vampires and werewolves. All so they can control magic. If it isn't on their terms, then they don't want anyone else to have it. I've heard tell that they were behind the purges of magical schools and libraries in Dorwain, and they're fostering the same destructive beliefs in other kingdoms, so that ignorance and bad teaching eventually eradicates all magical practices.

The sooner you find a teacher, Viza said, *the better. Folk like that are constantly sending out reverberation spells, to make even the most passive spell chime, so they can find it. Untrained as you are, with all that mangled magic wrapped around you? You're an entire symphony waiting to sound out. They'll take your rings, try to enslave you to drain your inborn magic, and they'll purge your blood to remove my dust. You need to get to Vinsidia and find someone to help you as soon as possible.*

Shaleen agreed. She passed on greetings from Princess Jillian and Magnus, and news from the former members of the Red Brigade who had chosen to settle in Cambrodaera. Shoomerang had gone into hiding, apparently fleeing the wrath of whoever he was helping to foment rebellion when his tracking spells failed. Zair's friends among the Red Brigade were content with their new lives, and several sent their wishes for his success in his quest.

Zair filled his water skins and let Patch drink his fill. He was about to return to the road when Yancob contacted him through the ring. Shaleen had informed him of what had happened and where he was. Yancob wanted to give Zair a good idea of what towns lay along the road ahead of him. Nychtenland had mile markers along its main highways, and signposts carved into stone at all the crossroads. Unless he found it necessary to get off the highway to hide his new features, Zair wouldn't get lost.

Ten more miles down the highway would bring him to a hermitage that ministered to travelers. Yancob advised Zair to spend the night there, because the hermits would leave him alone. He could get a good night's sleep, fresh provisions, and leave before sunrise, and no one would gossip about him to subsequent travelers who stopped there.

That sounded good to Zair. Maybe the hermitage would have a mirror, so he could examine his new face. The well was in shadow, so he couldn't see his reflection clearly.

~~~~~

When he reached the hermitage, Zair was relieved to learn he was the only guest so far to stop for the night. The common room of the lodgings for travelers was entirely empty.

Even better, the blessing board on the wall opposite the door was a brass plate, polished to make the holy words etched into it easier to read. He had no trouble ignoring the neat lettering to focus on his new face: a long oval, with thin lips and deep-set gray eyes, blue-black skin, and tightly curled ebony hair streaked with silver. Zair could finally remove his riding gloves and study his hands, which were long-fingered and sturdy and calloused. That said something about the current king, that he did hard, physical work of some kind. Probably a warrior trained, and those callouses came from sword work. Zair laughed to discover more callouses on his left hand than his right, meaning the king of Nychtenland was left-handed. He realized that he had used his left hand more since the transformation four hours ago. He normally would have reached and grasped and guided Patch with his right hand. He just hadn't thought, had reacted naturally.

A gasp came from his right, followed by a thud-clatter, the hollow sound of wood hitting wood, then water splashing and spilling. Zair turned to see a young man in the dark green robes the hermits all wore, staring at him, wide-eyed. The bucket of hot water he had dropped spread across the table and over the side. The towel he had dropped beside it on
~~~~~

the wooden tray sopped up some of the water.

"Never rush to cover up what has been seen, once you have been seen," Shaleen had said, in her first lessons to Zair on sneaking and spying. *"Face down the one who saw you and act as if nothing is wrong. Convince them they are wrong, they didn't see what they saw, that you belong there. And then get out of there as quickly as you can, without looking like you're running away. Because your life will depend on running away."*

"Is there something wrong?" Zair didn't know how to address the young hermit. Brother? Friar? Priest? Some other title?

"I—I beg your forgiveness, traveler," the hermit said. He dropped to his knees to retrieve tray and bucket. "I will bring you more hot water."

He hurried out. Zair's first instinct was to snatch up his cloak and saddlebags and flee also, but wouldn't that generate suspicion? He wished he hadn't lowered his hood to have more light to study his face, while he waited to be led to his room for the night. He wished he insisted on settling Patch for the night, instead of letting another member of the hermitage take his horse to the stables. Then he wouldn't have to go running through the wrong doorways until he found his way to the stables.

The hermitage housed just over one hundred devotees, according to Yancob, but this place felt huge, made for three times as many. A wooded ridge lay between the hermitage and the highway, hiding the buildings and the shallow river-fed valley beyond from view. No one had any clue it was there, other than a sign carved out of a massive slab of rock. The buildings looked like a maze, walls within walls, surrounded by orchards on three sides, the river on the fourth side.

Brave it out, he decided. He would settle in that shadowy corner, have his saddlebags ready to snatch up, and tug his sword and long knife around for easier reach. Then he would wait to see how the people here reacted to whatever story the young hermit had told them.

Viza? Do you sense anything? Panic?

These people are frustratingly calm, the mirror responded after a long wait. Zair knew she was straining, stretching herself out to try to listen, expending energy they could ill afford to waste, but every second of waiting felt like an hour. *There is magic here, but ... I'm sorry, I'm still more fractured than I like to admit. That interferes with my ability to track magic to its source, or even identify the scent, the flavor, the song, the depths of the magic that I do sense. I'm sorry, dear boy. I'm failing you, at a most crucial time.*

No, you're not. Zair almost said it aloud. *I'm a thousand times better off than if I was trying to figure this out alone.*

"Traveler." A woman stepped into the doorway, her arms crossed and hidden inside the wide sleeves of her robe. Her hair was so pale it was nearly colorless, yet her face was unlined, so Zair couldn't guess her age. "Please pardon the intrusion, but our Elder Brother wishes to speak with you. Will you follow me?"

What could he do but follow? Avoiding suspicion was his best defense.

He tried to keep track of the turns and doorways they went through, but lost count after the third right turn and fourth left, and the sixth doorway — or was it the fifth? — and then up three half-flights of stairs. Zair suspected this was a deliberate tactic to get him lost, so he couldn't run and find the nearest doorway and freedom before they captured him. How had they recognized his face as their king's so quickly? According to the map Magnus had given him, any city large enough to have officials and nobles who might see him was still a day of travel away.

What had gone wrong?

A cold fire enveloped him as he entered the room, so he paused for two seconds of agony in the doorway. Hands caught him as he stumbled forward and guided him into a chair.

A cushioned chair. Zair registered that before the sparks cleared from his eyes.

"What was that?" His voice crackled and strained.

Oh, that wasn't kind at all! Viza cried.

"A test," the woman said, her voice warped by the dying hissing in his ears.

"Huh. Strong magic indeed. Strong enough not to be banished," a sandy sort of baritone voice said. "Rooted deep, not a new spell wrapped around him. I'd say it's involuntary. And you're young under that magic." A long-fingered, calloused hand caught under his chin and raised his head.

Zair looked into the face he had just seen in the polished bronze.

"You can't be the king," he said. Speaking sent a single throb of ache through his head.

The face broke into a smile. Several people standing behind him chuckled. The man stepped back, and now Zair saw he also wore green hermit robes.

"No, I am his twin." He settled down on a bench and crossed his arms and leaned back against the wall. "Now ... what brings you to Nychtenland?"

I'm not sure what I'm feeling, but ... well, I can't exactly say it's gut instinct, because mirrors don't have bodies to have guts, but ... be truthful. That's the best advice I can give you until I can clarify what I'm sensing, Viza said.

All right. Zair took a deep breath and thought about his words for just a few seconds. His mouth was dry and his head felt like someone tried to drive a spike in one temple and out the other.

"I am just passing through. Putting as many kingdoms as I can between me and Dorwain. Searching for the recluse enchanters in

Vinsidia, to help me. The magic wrapped around me makes me take on the face and form of the king of whatever kingdom I'm in. I was Shadow to the crown prince, but he hates me, and things are getting ugly there, and he and his grandfather sent his mother into certain death, just to start a war, so ..." He shrugged. "I need to go somewhere far enough away from a throne and king that no one will recognize me and then find someone who can unweave the spells and give me back my own face."

"Has no one told you that the longer a spell like that is rooted in you, in your flesh and blood as well as your spirit, the more it becomes part of you?" The hermit, whom Zair decided had to be this Elder Brother, narrowed his eyes as he studied him. "I don't think much of the magic in Dorwain."

"The enchanters who are helping me don't think much of it either. It's mostly controlled by magicians who make up the rules as they go along."

That earned him a few more chuckles.

"I was told that the knowledge of the right use of magic, the right rules, was destroyed decades ago in Dorwain. Entire libraries wiped out, magic mirrors and other tools destroyed or sent away. The ones who did this to me either didn't know the proper techniques, or they didn't much care. It's just gotten worse over time, because new magicians were brought in to try to fix the problem, and they just added their own badly woven magic." Zair muffled a groan as a throbbing ache stabbed through his head.

"Show some pity," the woman said, and a gentle hand rested on his shoulder. "We know he isn't here to kill you, Brother. Can't that be enough for now?"

"As long as the regular spies don't know he's here, we're safe. What's your name, lad?" the Elder Brother said.

"Zair. Zared," he amended.

"I am Arnon, twin to King Aynard, and I am probably the only man here who fully understands your dilemma." He stood up and held out a hand to Zair. "Let's get you settled in a secure room, find you some relief from that jolt you took, and then ... we'll try to figure out some way to help you." He chuckled as he tugged the boy to his feet. "I actually envy you, a little. You have a face of your own under that spell. I'm stuck with this." He held onto his somber expression as Zair raised his head to look him in the eyes. Then he winked and his face relaxed into a grin.

~~~~~

Well that wasn't much fun, was it?
Viza's voice sent sharp-edged ripples through Zair's head and dropped into his stomach, threatening to make him heave. He settled heavily on the edge of the cot in the plain little room the hermits had given
~~~~~

him. If by "secure" they meant one without any windows and barely enough room for the cot, a chest, a small table supplied with writing materials, a stool, and a long shelf along one wall piled with linens, pitcher and basin, and soap powder, then he disagreed with the definition. It felt like a prison cell, and he wondered if he would be able to breathe when the door closed.

You're all right? Zair winced at the ache his own voice sent throbbing through his head.

That depends on your definition of all right. The mirror sighed. *Yes, I'm still here, and we're still together, and that testing portal reveals quite a lot about the situation here among the hermits. They're not just leery of magic coming in among them unannounced, but they live in some kind of fear. From several directions. Hmm ...*

What? he asked when she trailed off and didn't continue after just a few moments. Zair worried that she had been drained by that shock, leaving her little strength.

I don't dare hope, but if I'm right ... Oh, please, blessed A'theosius, let me be right. I hope I'm not so weary I'm delusional. This might take all my energy to make myself heard, but I dare to believe there is someone nearby who can hear me. Don't fear for me, if I am silent too long. This may take everything I have left.

Chapter Twenty-Five

Zair unpacked his few possessions, storing them in the chest and on the shelf while he waited for Viza to resume speaking. He pulled off his boots and sat on the edge of the cot again but couldn't make himself lie down and put his feet up. Her tone of voice had struck him as thoughtful, not weary. What had she discovered or thought of, and what was so dire about it that she didn't want to tell him?

"Zared?" A woman called from the hallway and then tapped on his half-open door.

That was one thing Zair had to get used to here. Was it normal for Nychtenland, to allow men and women to share retreat houses? Did they call hermitages and monasteries and cloisters retreat houses here, or did they have other names for them? Zair just didn't expect men and women to be together. Weren't people devoted to the holy orders supposed to deny themselves and avoid all temptations and distractions?

"Yes." Zair stood up, then bent down to reach for his boots. Maybe he was being summoned to Arnon already?

"Elder Brother asks ..." The woman stepped into the room and her voice trailed off as a grin lit her face, square and unlined under a short-cropped cap of thick silver hair. She shook her head. "Amazing. They warned me, but ... well, I think this will be an even bigger puzzle than either of us anticipated." She reached inside her robe and pulled out an oval amulet the size of her palm, hanging on a chain around her neck. The amulet flashed green light that turned into ripples of blue and purple that kept moving across the surface.

"This is going to be fun." A silvery sort of voice came from the amulet.

Not an amulet. A mirror.

"Viza—" He choked and sat down on the cot again.

Hello? Can you hear me? the mirror asked, her voice going shrill with the effort of shouting. The mirror amulet flashed blue light, and the woman stepped back, as if pushed.

"I can hear you as long as I'm touching Iris, yes," the woman said. Her grin went crooked as she looked Zair up and down. "Your friend Viza has just told Iris everything. She is so damaged they weren't able to talk until they were closer together. It will take some time for Iris to tell me the details. Be assured, we will help you, and we trust you, thanks to your friend's testimony. Come join us for dinner." She chuckled. "Although I fear your food will go entirely cold, because everyone will keep you busy telling your story."

The woman's name was Damris, and despite the color of her hair, she was only twenty-three years old. Iris laughed when she admitted that much of the silver came from all the adventures and perils the two had faced since the day they met. Damris had found the mirror in a pile of discards on the edge of the marketplace in her home city of Felsbard. Iris had been in what magic mirrors considered a deep sleep, and the touch of the young street thief's mind woke her. Damris discovered she had inborn magic, and Iris "awoke" loudly enough to catch the attention of the Purple Sky magicians.

Elder Brother Arnon had rescued her, back in the days when he had been an adventurer, protecting magic from the creeping tentacles of the Purple Sky's advocates. He had been gathering up followers for years, and collecting a stockpile of injured magical items and creatures, until finally their numbers grew large enough they needed a central command center, to shield them. With the support of the king and the nobles who clearly saw the threat to Nychtenland from the Purple Sky magicians, they had established the hermitage.

Zair shuddered as he listened to some of the hermits sitting around him relating several of their most recent missions to protect libraries from the depredations of the Purple Sky. He thought of the happy, silent hours he spent in the palace library in Dorwain, soaking up chunks of history and learning about battles and prophecies, and even picking up a few details of the kings among his ancestors. The Purple Sky not only pillaged the libraries of enchanters, to control the knowledge and use of magic, but they destroyed other libraries, to control what people knew and believed, and even how they thought.

Damris and Iris led one of the many teams of hermits who kept to the shadows and searched Nychtenland for bits of magic. The hermitage lay within a spell maintained by a regularly changing team of lower-level enchanters, to keep the compound and all the rescued magical objects hidden and silent when touched by the seeking spells of the Purple Sky. Teams of hermits traveled the borders of Nychtenland, watching for travelers coming into the kingdom with signs of magic, either in their own flesh and blood or embedded in objects they carried. At the first opportunity, they warned the travelers of the danger they faced from the Purple Sky swooping down on them to confiscate those items. If they determined those folks didn't know they carried magic, they took the items before the Purple Sky detected them and attacked.

"That's where thieves like me prove our worth to the cause," Damris said with a chuckle. "Iris and I spend half our time seeking magic to rescue, and the other half of the time finding skilled little cutpurses and pickpockets among the street children. We give them a home and a mission and an education, and when they're no longer small enough to be ignored, we send them on to learn an honest trade. A'theosius blesses us for combining many different levels of rescue and mercy in our efforts. I know it's bad theology, but I like to think that the good we do outweighs the crimes we commit." She shrugged and cast a sidelong glance down to the end of the table. Arnon paused in conversation with a man who had just come in, still wearing his traveling cloak.

"A'theosius isn't half as concerned about theology as the half-brained folk who serve him," their leader said, and shook his head. His smile looked weary and didn't reach his eyes. "Quite an education you're having now, isn't it, Zared?"

"You knew I was coming, because you sensed my rings and Viza's dust, didn't you?" Zair asked. He felt like everyone at the long table was watching him, even if their gazes weren't turned to him.

He didn't know if his weariness made him feel so relaxed, or the incredible bounty of the meal. He had had a different idea of what supper meant in a hermitage, but just like his idea of sparsity and simplicity and the separation of men and women, he had been proven wrong. The hermits ate very well. The variety of fruits and vegetables on the table, the abundance of meat, and the choice between wine, cider, ale, water and milk to drink had surprised him. He was afraid he had eaten far too much, and his heavy belly was combining with his weariness to make him willing to accept everything these people were telling him.

Don't be a suspicious idiot, Viza scolded. Amusement made her voice ripple pleasantly in his head. *If you don't trust your sharp instincts, trust me?*

Zair grinned and nearly responded aloud.

"Yes, we sensed you coming, but we couldn't figure out what you were, and what made you ring with several different notes of magic," Loreena said. She was the first woman Zair had encountered, entrusted with the vital task of assessing all magic that came within the hermitage compound. "The spell of the doorway was tripled in intensity, because we feared we would have to ..." She sighed and shrugged. "Let's just say, we feared having to take drastic measures to protect ourselves, if you proved to be another of the many poisoned cakes filled with vipers that our enemies try to send to us, to destroy us from within."

Zair nodded, shuddering deep inside at both the imagery of her words, and the pictures his imagination painted of what "drastic measures" had to mean.

"We could learn a great deal from the effort of unweaving those spells imprisoning you. At the very least, we could gain evidence of all the damage being done to magic through simple ignorance," Arnon said. He spoke quietly, but with an intensity that seemed to draw all the focus of the room to him. "If we could impress on the Enchanters' Court the long-lasting damage being done to magic in general, by allowing the arrogant brutes of the Purple Sky to continue on their path of destruction and exclusion, then maybe they would look outside their time pockets and stir themselves to do something. I think we can help each other, Zared. Give us time to try to free you of this deep, discordant enchantment, before you go on to Vinsidia?"

A hunger spilled through Zair, increasing his weariness so he felt heavy and achy in body and heart. Viza already said she trusted these people, so should he accept this offer? Was it possible he didn't have to travel any further to find the cure for the curse inflicted on him by half-trained magicians? More than that, he wanted a place far away from everything and everyone, where he could wear his own face and walk in safety and peace, no fears of someone watching over his shoulder, trying to trap him, trying to turn him into a weapon. He needed a portal to a time pocket where no one could ever find him, where he could let his magic break free and bloom.

That actually does sound lovely, Viza said. *Such places are outside time, through doorways that are nearly impossible to find. The trick is that sometimes, it's even harder to leave than it is to get inside. Be careful what you wish for, my lad.*

I'm tired of being careful all the time.

He sat back and looked around the room, at the kind, somber faces surrounding him. He knew there was a chance he was just so tired that he imagined he had found the resting place and shelter he longed for. Still, why not stop and catch his breath, and see what they could do?

"I'll stay."

THE END

To be continued in ***DISENCHANTING THE PRINCE.***

About the Author

On the road to publication, Michelle fell into fandom in college and has 40+ stories in various SF and fantasy universes. She has a bunch of useless degrees in theater, English, film/communication, and writing. Even worse, she has over 100 books and novellas with multiple small presses, in science fiction and fantasy, YA, suspense, women's fiction, and sub-genres of romance.

Her official launch into publishing came with winning first place in the Writers of the Future contest in 1990. She was a finalist in the EPIC Awards competition multiple times, winning with *Lorien* in 2006 and *The Meruk Episodes, I-V*, in 2010, and was a finalist in the Realm Awards competition, in conjunction with the Realm Makers convention.

Her training includes the Institute for Children's Literature; proofreading at an advertising agency; and working at a community newspaper. She is a tea snob and freelance edits for a living (MichelleLevigne@gmail.com for info/rates), but only enough to give her time to write. Her newest crime against the literary world is to be co-managing editor at Mt. Zion Ridge Press and launching the publishing co-op, Ye Olde Dragon Books. Be afraid … be very afraid.

And please check out her newest venture: Ye Olde Dragon's Library, the storytelling podcast. Interspersed between the chapters will be interviews with authors of fantastical fiction. Listen to the podcast on your favorite podcast app or listen on the website: *YeOldeDragonBooks.com*, and click on the Ye Olde Dragon's Library link.

Mlevigne.com
MichelleLevigne.blogspot.com
YeOldeDragonBooks.com
MtZionRidgePress.com

NEWSLETTER:
Want to learn about upcoming books, book launch parties, inside info, and cover reveals? Go to Michelle's website or blog to sign up.

Thanks for reading!
If you enjoyed this book, would you help Michelle by posting a review on Goodreads?

Are you a member of Book Bub? If so, please follow Michelle on Book Bub, and you'll get alerts when new books are coming out.

As a way of saying thanks, Michelle invites you to the Goodies page on her website. It will change regularly, offering you a free short story, a sample audiobook chapter, sneak peeks at new cover art, inside information on discounts and new release dates, etc.

Please go to: *Mlevigne.com/good-stuff.html*

Also by Michelle L. Levigne

Guardians of the Time Stream: 4-book Steampunk series

The Match Girls: Humorous inspirational romance series starting with **A Match (Not) Made in Heaven**

Sarai's Journey: A 2-book biblical fiction series

Tabor Heights: 18-book inspirational small town romance series.

Quarry Hall: 11-book women's fiction/suspense series

For Sale: Wedding Dress. Never Used: inspirational romance

Crooked Creek: Fun Fables About Critters and Kids: Children's short stories.

Do Yourself a Favor: Tips and Quips on the Writing Life. A book of writing advice.

To Eternity (and beyond): *Writing Spec Fic Good for Your Soul*. A book defending speculative fiction.

Killing His Alter-Ego: contemporary romance/suspense, taking place in fandom.

The Commonwealth Universe: SF series, 25 books and growing

The Hunt: 5-book YA fantasy series

Faxinor: Fantasy series, 4 books and growing

Wildvine: Fantasy series, 14 books when all released

Neighborlee: Humorous fantasy series

Zygradon: 5-book Arthurian fantasy series

AFV Defender: SF adventure series

Young Defenders: Middle Grade SF series, spin-off of *AFV Defender*

Magic to Spare: Fantasy series

Book & Mug Mysteries: cozy mystery series

Quest for the Crescent Moon: fantasy series

Steward's World: fantasy series reboot and expansion

The Enchanted Castle Archives: fantasy series